Fall 2005   Vol. XXV, no. 3
ISSN: 0276-0045   ISBN: 1-56478-441-X

THE REVIEW OF CONTEMPORARY FICTION

T0198472

Editor

JOHN O'BRIEN
Illinois State University

Senior Editor

ROBERT L. MCLAUGHLIN
Illinois State University

Associate Editor

IRVING MALIN

Book Review Editor

JEREMY M. DAVIES

Production & Design

N. J. FURL

The *Review of Contemporary Fiction* is published three times a year
(January, June, September) by the Center for Book Culture at
Illinois State University (ISU Campus Box 8905, Normal, IL 61790-8905).
ISSN 0276-0045. Subscription prices are as follows:

Single volume (three issues):
Individuals: $17.00; foreign, add $3.50;
Institutions: $26.00; foreign, add $3.50.

DISTRIBUTION. Bookstores should send orders to:

Review of Contemporary Fiction, ISU Campus Box 8905,
Normal, IL 61790-8905. Phone 309-438-7555; fax 309-438-7422.

This issue is partially supported by a grant from
the Illinois Arts Council, a state agency.

Indexed in *American Humanities Index*, *International Bibliography of
Periodical Literature*, *International Bibliography of Book
Reviews*, *MLA Bibliography*, and *Book Review Index*. Abstracted
in *Abstracts of English Studies*.

The *Review of Contemporary Fiction* is also available on 16mm
microfilm, 35mm microfilm, and 105mm microfiche from
University Microfilms International, 300 North Zeeb Road,
Ann Arbor, MI 48106-1346.

www.centerforbookculture.org

THE REVIEW OF CONTEMPORARY FICTION

BACK ISSUES AVAILABLE

Back issues are still available for the following numbers of the *Review of Contemporary Fiction* ($8 each unless otherwise noted):

NOVELIST AS CRITIC: Essays by Garrett, Barth, Sorrentino, Wallace, Ollier, Brooke-Rose, Creeley, Mathews, Kelly, Abbott, West, McCourt, McGonigle, and McCarthy

NEW FINNISH FICTION: Fiction by Eskelinen, Jäntti, Kontio, Krohn, Paltto, Sairanen, Selo, Siekkinen, Sund, and Valkeapää

NEW ITALIAN FICTION: Interviews and fiction by Malerba, Tabucchi, Zanotto, Ferrucci, Busi, Corti, Rasy, Cherchi, Balduino, Ceresa, Capriolo, Carrera, Valesio, and Gramigna

GROVE PRESS NUMBER: Contributions by Allen, Beckett, Corso, Ferlinghetti, Jordan, McClure, Rechy, Rosset, Selby, Sorrentino, and others

NEW DANISH FICTION: Fiction by Brøgger, Høeg, Andersen, Grøndahl, Holst, Jensen, Thorup, Michael, Sibast, Ryum, Lynggaard, Grønfeldt, Willumsen, and Holm

NEW LATVIAN FICTION: Fiction by Ikstena, Bankovskis, Berelis, Kolmanis, Neiburga, Ziedonis, and others

THE FUTURE OF FICTION: Essays by Birkerts, Caponegro, Franzen, Galloway, Maso, Morrow, Vollmann, White, and others ($15)

NEW JAPANESE FICTION: Interviews and fiction by Ohara, Shimada, Shono, Takahashi, Tsutsui, McCaffery, Gregory, Kotani, Tatsumi, Koshikawa, and others

Individuals receive a 10% discount on orders of one issue and a 20% discount on orders of two or more issues. To place an order, use the form on the last page of this issue.

RCF Call for Contributors

www.centerforbookculture.org/review

The *Review of Contemporary Fiction* is seeking contributors to write overview essays on the following writers:

Felipe Alfau, Chandler Brossard, Gabrielle Burton, Jerome Charyn, Stanley Crawford, Eva Figes, Karen Elizabeth Gordon, Carol De Chellis Hill, Violette Leduc, Julián Ríos, Esther Tusquets.

The essays must:

- be fifty double-spaced pages;
- cover the subject's biography;
- summarize the critical reception of the subject's works;
- discuss the course of the subject's career, including each major work;
- provide interpretive strategies for new readers to apply to the subject's work;
- provide a bibliographic checklist of each of the subject's works (initial and latest printings) and the most important (no more than five) critical pieces about the subject;
- be written for a general, intelligent reader, who does not know the subject's work;
- avoid jargon, theoretical digressions, and excessive endnotes;
- be intelligent, interesting, and readable;
- be documented in MLA style.

Authors will be paid $250.00 when the essay is published. All essays will be subject to editorial review, and the editors reserve the right to request revisions and to reject unacceptable essays.

Applicants should send a CV and a brief writing sample. In your cover letter, be sure to address your qualifications.

Send applications to:

Jeremy M. Davies
Review of Contemporary Fiction, ISU Campus Box 8905, Normal, IL 61790-8905

Inquiries: jeremy@centerforbookculture.org

Contents

Flann O'Brien

Neil Murphy

"There is no answer at all to a very good question."
—The Good Fairy, *At Swim-Two-Birds*

Beginnings

The difficulty with writing about Flann O'Brien's work emerges as soon as one pens the name of the author, itself a most slippery signifier in a fictional universe of evasive signification. Born Brian O'Nolan, the author was variously known as Brian Nolan, Brian Hackett, Brother Barnabas, Samuel Hall, Myles na Gopaleen, and Flann O'Brien. Appropriately enough, for an author who was possessed with a persistent desire to challenge fixed systems, names appear to have been provisional, a potential source of amusement rather than significant identity-markers. In addition, the publication dates of the novels pose a minor difficulty because the work that represents O'Brien's greatest lasting achievement, *The Third Policeman*, having failed to secure a publisher during his life, was published posthumously, but it was the second novel he wrote, immediately after *At Swim-Two-Birds*. Moreover, one of his five novels, *The Poor Mouth* (*An Béal Bocht*), was written in Gaelic and was not available to an English-speaking audience until 1973, thirty-three years after it was initially published. The consequence of this, for O'Brien, was that of his three most accomplished novels (*At Swim-Two-Birds*, *The Poor Mouth*, *The Third Policeman*), only *At Swim-Two-Birds* was known to English readers during his lifetime, a personal tragedy that is likely, in Anthony Cronin's view, particularly with respect to the nonpublication of *The Third Policeman*, to have contributed to the destruction of O'Brien's creative self-esteem (Cronin 212). Following the sequence in which they were written, this essay will focus only on Brian O'Nolan's five completed novels, four of which were written in English under the name Flann O'Brien, and one, *An Béal Bocht* (*The Poor Mouth: A Bad Story about the Hard Life*), which was written under the name Myles na Gopaleen. In the interests of consistency and clarity, I will use the name Flann O'Brien throughout. Although there is one final unfinished novel, *Slattery's Sago Saga* (or *From under the Ground to the Top of the Trees*), it is hardly more than a fragment and it does not lend itself to useful critical analysis. Flann O'Brien also produced an enormous amount of journalistic commentary in his *Cruiskeen Lawn* columns for the *Irish Times*, for which he was more famous during much of his life, but the nonfiction lies outside the perimeter of the present essay.

While the critical reception to Flann O'Brien's fiction has grown steadily over the past few decades, what has generally emerged resembles a diffusion of perspectives rather than any sustained theoretical framing of his work. That this is partly a result of the inherent diversity in O'Brien's fiction is undoubted, at least on the surface level of plot and characterization, if one can write of such factors with any solid conviction in O'Brien's fiction. More significant is that his work does not lend itself to recent critical trends that seek to locate social and political implications in literary texts, despite the efforts of McKibben to emphasize the postcolonial elements in *The Poor Mouth* or Davison's consideration of the "male construction of 'the female grotesque' " in *The Hard Life* (Davison 55). Ideologically inclined readers have tended to avoid *At Swim-Two-Birds* and *The Third Policeman* primarily because no amount of deliberation on gender or nation could possibly yield a plausible critical model in texts that are so clearly focused on breaking down narrative centers rather than allowing them utterance. Nevertheless, some extremely coherent critical observations on O'Brien's fiction have been penned over the past decade or so, most notably, Keith Hopper's *A Portrait of the Artist as a Young Postmodernist* and M. Keith Booker's *Flann O'Brien, Bakhtin, and Menippean Satire.* While Booker uses the term *postmodern* to describe O'Brien's work only once, and Hopper to some degree uses postmodernism as his critical frame, their views coincide in terms of how they ultimately view O'Brien's work. For example, Booker believes that O'Brien's work conforms to a Bakhtinian interpretation of Menippean satire, which he describes as "a diverse collection of competing styles and voices, that . . . tends to interrogate and satirize various philosophical ideas (usually in a highly irreverent way), and that . . . is centrally informed by the energies that Bakhtin refers to as 'carnivalesque' . . . a celebration during which normal rules and hierarchies were inverted or suspended and in which representatives of various social groups intermixed far more freely than in normal life" (Booker 1-2), and Hopper too uses Bakhtin as one of his critical frames, when writing of *The Third Policeman* (Hopper 198-99). Booker draws our attention to the dark aspect of Bakhtin and suggests that "O'Brien's central theme would seem to be the futility of almost all human endeavors in the modern world" (Booker 6), while Hopper comments on O'Brien's fascination with "the limits of consciousness" (Hopper 152) in the context of his postmodern fascination with the fictionality of all modes of knowledge. So while Booker utilizes a primary model of Bakhtinian Mennipean satire to explore Flann O'Brien's fictional universes and Hopper offers a frame composed of McHale,

Hassan, and other critical commentators on literary postmodernism, both arrive at what appears to be the most fruitful way to consider O'Brien's work: as a perpetual assault against all forms of human knowledge, usually by using various parodic modes within polyphonic texts that repeatedly draw attention to the obvious fact of their own construction and, by inference, to the fact of the construction of all texts, all knowledge.

The author engenders a deep, consistent spirit of resistance to all forms of knowledge in the five texts, despite the fact that each novel is significantly different in style, tone, genre, structure, and mode of characterization. Furthermore, despite the varying levels of artistic achievement that each individual novel represents, the author repeatedly seeks to register new ways to discredit the vanity of human epistemological systems. In this, O'Brien participates in what might be described as a tradition of radical doubt stretching forward from Menippean satire to Nietzsche, Swift, Joyce, and Beckett, to metafiction, postmodernism, and poststructuralism. In these five short novels the narrators, and there are many, manage to parody and discredit science and mathematics, sequential time, spatiality, empirical thought, Gaelic "culture," Gaelic autobiographical fiction, old Irish *Immram*, or voyages in consciousness tales, cosmopolitanism, Irish Catholicism, the novel genre, Joycean "aestheticism," and the possibility of meaningful dialogue. Comically masked behind this desire to unmake, discredit, and parody there lies a despairing image of human existence. Try as they will, O'Brien's characters achieve nothing except, in many of the novels, to reveal an essentially repetitive, meaningless place of habitation, in which the major figures, often hilariously, set about constructing ever more unlikely fictions to explain their worlds and dignify their lives. From the mad scientist de Selby to the bogus intellectual Sergeant Fottrell to the tortured quasi-detective Mick Shaughnessy, O'Brien's characters repeatedly reveal the inadequacy of their intellectual systems, systems that are almost always rooted in Cartesian empiricism, and thus the mode of thought by which these characters slavishly live proves also to be the primary source of their absurdity and the emptiness of their lives. Thus, despite the oft-quoted description of O'Brien's novels as comic, and indeed they are frequently wildly so, the comedy is always extremely hollow, primarily born in the prison of the characters' helpless, repetitive lives.

At Swim-Two-Birds (1939)

That *At Swim-Two-Birds* still receives more critical attention than any of O'Brien's other works would surely have maddened its author, who long professed that it represented "mere juvenilia" (Cronin 211).

Aidan Higgins claims that O'Brien actually "detested the novel," and its success continued to vex him throughout his life (Higgins 6). Whatever the reasons for his response, *At Swim-Two-Birds* certainly represents a key moment in the development of twentieth-century fiction, and despite the fact that Sterne, Gide, Huxley, and, less famously, James Branch Cabell had employed the *mise-en-abyme* and/or self-reflexive narration in their works before O'Brien, he pushed these devices to hitherto unseen limits, to the point of the extinction of the narrator and perhaps even the text itself. One of the first people to review *At Swim-Two-Birds*, Jorge Luis Borges, cited Schopenhauer's view that dreaming and wakefulness are the pages of a single book that we read in order to live and suggested that books that branch into other books, like O'Brien's first novel, "help us sense this oneness" (Borges 162) between dreaming and wakefulness, a testimony of the highest order from the author who wrote his masterpiece, "The Garden of the Forking Paths," just two years later.

The title of *At Swim-Two-Birds* is an instant indication of the spirit of unmaking that presides over the novel. The term is a literal Anglicization of the Gaelic Snámh Dá Ean, a place name whose sense is confused when translated into O'Brien's literal English version. Snámh Dá Ean was one of the mythical Sweeney's resting places, as Anthony Cronin points out (Cronin 88), but the title also alludes to the historic ford at Cluain Mhic Nois, near the location of the legend of Estiu (warrior and bird goddess), the wife of Nar, who had a lover who took the shape of a bird in order to hide their illicit secret from her husband. Furthermore, Sweeney, one should remember, lived in trees and thus had more than a hint of flight about him. The shape-shifting challenge to logic thus already exists on an intertextual level, prior to O'Brien's second layer of mutation, offering a quite significant indicator of the persistent assaults on encyclopedic reality, conventional narrative structure, authorial control, and the capacity to assert anything with conviction. There is also a distinctly Gaelic, parodic echo of the plethora of Greek and Christian wings and images of flight in Joyce's *A Portrait of the Artist as a Young Man.*

The Chinese box, or *mise-en-abyme*, structure of the novel can be briefly summarized as follows: the student narrator pens a novel about a writer called Trellis, who in turn writes about a group of characters assembled in the Red Swan Hotel with whom he interacts to such a degree that he sexually assaults one of them, Sheila Lamont, who subsequently gives birth to a son, Orlick. Inheriting his father's literary skill, Orlick then proceeds to pen a story about his father Trellis, who by now sleeps almost continuously as a result of the drug his characters have administered to him. In Orlick's

tale, embedded four layers down, the "fictional" Trellis is tried in
a kangaroo court and brutalized by his own characters, until, in
a random act, a servant at the Red Swan, Teresa, feeds the fire
by burning several sheets of writing, which effectively erases some
of Trellis's characters, in turn releasing him from the embedded
nightmare's torturous existence. That Trellis and the student narrator both spend an inordinate amount of time in their respective
bedrooms implies an implicit connection between them. If Trellis is
drugged and brutalized by his characters while he sleeps, then so too
may the student narrator suffer while *he* sleeps and so too, in turn,
may the author of the "real" book with the somewhat unreal title.

On its most obvious level *At Swim-Two-Birds* parodies conventional fiction or fiction that assumes any level of seriousness in
regard to its own enterprise, a point repeatedly registered in the
novel, in the most literal of fashions: "a satisfactory novel should be
a self-evident sham to which the reader could regulate at will the
degree of his credulity. It was undemocratic to compel characters
to be uniformly good or bad or poor or rich. Each should be allowed
a private life, self-determination and a decent standard of living.
This would make for self-respect, contentment and better service"
(19). This "autocritique," as Lowenkron has it, or "tendency of the
metanovelist to criticize his own novel within that very novel"
(Lowenkron 354), allows the text to comment on its own making to
such a degree that the possibility of fictional illusion is punctured,
and the process of illusion-making and illusion-breaking becomes
the primary focus of the text. This focus is essentially a critique of
knowledge or the means with which we construct knowledge. The
extensive use of self-reflexive commentary in metafictional texts
like *At Swim-Two-Birds* serves to undermine the legitimacy of the
meaning expressed in the text; everything is rendered provisional
and all illusions are exploded. The novel employs an enormous variety of literary devices that further such an end. In addition to the
Chinese box mechanism, there are many other embedded texts and
textual digressions: letters, extracts from a variety of texts including an *Extract from Literary Reader, the Higher Class, by the Irish
Christian Brothers*, and the narrator frames the story of his own
"reality" within a series of "biographical reminiscences." O'Brien
also frequently uses the device of peppering the plot, particularly
that of the student, with a series of revelatory headings, like *The
two senses referred to*, and *Description of my friend*, and *Nature of
chuckles* (17-18), all of which offer information that would normally
be simply built into descriptive passages. The effect of this is to
continually remind the reader of the constructed nature of the
narrator's existence. The intention, again, is to perpetually force
meaning into an incomplete space.

Dermot Trellis's "aestho-autogamy" theory, or the "elimination of conception and pregnancy" in fiction whereby characters are born fully formed, also serves to jeopardize the illusion of authenticity or, as Brian McHale suggests, "the ontological instability and tentativeness of the fictional world is demonstrated," and "the ontological superiority of the author is dramatized" (McHale 211). In both cases, the primary intention is a refusal to allow the text to become a self-contained object and to delegitimize the fiction's capacity to generate secure meaning of any kind. Similarly, O'Brien undermines the principle of meaning and sequential conclusiveness by the extensive use of omissions; for example, the narrator discovers that there is an "inexplicable chasm in the pagination" (59) and offers instead a brief summary of events as follows:

> *Synopsis, being a summary of what has gone before*, FOR THE BEN-EFIT OF NEW READERS: DERMOT TRELLIS, an eccentric author, conceives the project of writing a salutary book on the consequences which follow wrong-doing and creates for the purpose
> THE POOKA FERGUS MACPHELLIMEY, a species of human Irish devil endowed with magical powers. (59-60)

That most readers are likely to appreciate the narrator's ineptitude at mislaying several pages, especially since the synopsis greatly clarifies the increasingly convoluted plot, is a minor issue compared to the intended rupture to sequential narrative that is generated. The narrator is clearly intent on negating any fixed epistemological grounding in the multilayered fictional ontology, reinforced later in the novel with the omission of eleven pages of "undoubted mediocrity," and once more compensated for with a brief synopsis (156).

With *At Swim-Two-Birds*, O'Brien revises the rules of engagement between reader and writer, ceaselessly playing not only with self-reflexive tactics but with the creation of a *bricolage* composed from fragments of a fascinating array of textual predecessors that include cowboys and Indians from the fake novelist William Tracy, James Joyce's *A Portrait of the Artist as a Young Man*, Irish myth (in particular the Finn Cycle and *Buile Suibhne*), Irish superstition and folklore, and various texts with metafictional elements, like Gide's *The Counterfeiters* and Huxley's *Point Counter Point*. The arrangement and rearrangement of the various characters, depending on which embedded narrative level they exist (for example there are two Sweeney/Suibhne characters in the novel, as Foster notes), added to the juxtaposition of the radically different genres, generates fictions in which there are cowboys and steers running through Dublin and Indians fighting with Irish policemen. The mixture of borrowings (imagined or otherwise) results in a fictional

Dublin circa 1940 that is home to ranches, imported slave labor, and Irish mythical figures. These anachronisms, standard fare in metafictional novels, serve to further destabilize the veracity of the fictional world because they do not conform to encyclopedic reality and undermine the capacity of the imagined world to reflect any kind of historical actuality. The text thus becomes essentially ahistorical, antirealist, and primarily textual. The textual, nonrealist tenor of the text is, of course, no surprise considering the student narrator's insistence that the "modern novel should be largely a work of reference" (19), an echo of Eliot's "tradition," although parody rather than pastiche is what O'Brien clearly has in mind. Similarly, Thomas Shea terms *At Swim-Two-Birds* a palimpsest or "a written document, typically on vellum or parchment, that has been written upon several times, often with remnants of earlier, imperfectly erased writing still visible" ("Patrick McGinley's" 275). Thus *At Swim-Two-Birds* for Shea is a site of unmeaning (at least of the referential kind) that self-consciously draws attention to its own construction by compressing unlikely genres together in anachronistic layers, none of which are complete and all of which bear traces of each other.

Most pointed perhaps is O'Brien's parody of Irish myth and superstition and James Joyce's work, especially *A Portrait*. The parody of the Finn Cycle is effected primarily by further exaggerating the notoriously hyperbolic Gaelic tales. In *At Swim-Two-Birds* there is, for example, almost a two-page list of animal noises and sounds of nature that appeal to Finn, a send-up of the much-vaunted affinity supposedly felt by the ancient Celts for nature, while the savage humor that is generated by the exaggeration of the prowess of the Gaelic heroes is obvious in the description of Finn: "Each thigh to him was to the thickness of a horse's belly, narrowing to a green-veined calf to the thickness of a foal. Three fifties of fosterlings could engage with handball against the wideness of his backside, which was wide enough to halt the march of warriors through a mountain-pass" (8). Here O'Brien registers his disdain of a particular brand of self-indulgent heroic Irishry, a narrative frame that had always been entwined with other forms of nationalist rhetoric and with which the author would have been extremely familiar. Furthermore, the deflation of the heroic extends beyond the mockery of Irish myth and can be interpreted as displeasure at all kinds of serious-minded mythmaking, especially since the author saw fit to merge this myth with a variety of other frames in the novel.

Joyce's Dedalus, of *A Portrait*, is very likely the model upon whom the student narrator of *At Swim-Two-Birds* is based, something that actually produces a double layer of irony. Perhaps not having fully grasped the inherent irony in the character of Dedalus in *A Portrait*, O'Brien sets up his own student hero as a distinct parody, largely by mocking the intellectual, or mock-intellectual, conversations that the narrator has with his fellow students on subjects like language usage, figures of speech, aesthetics—although the aesthetics is of a radically different kind from that proffered by Dedalus. Both characters are artist figures, students at University College Dublin, both are engaged in writerly activity, and both novels are quasi-bildungsroman. O'Brien's narrator, of course, is engaged in an altogether more radical endeavor in that he is trying to unmake a novel while Stephen prepares to write one, *Ulysses*, which ironically is also to be one that poses severe problems for the process of novel-writing. In one sense *At Swim-Two-Birds* can be interpreted as an attempt to write back against *A Portrait*, with the narrator offering a perpetual antiheroic alternative to Joyce's part mythic, part hero-artist Stephen. But, as always with O'Brien, the parallels are never as straightforward as they might initially seem. Late in the novel, Trellis is reputed to suffer from "an inverted sow neurosis wherein the farrow eat their dam" (238), which again reverses the logic proffered by Stephen in *A Portrait*. In O'Brien's novel the offspring will eat the sow, the motherland, an implicit comment perhaps on Stephen's overblown departure from Ireland at the close of *A Portrait*. More significantly, the offspring can be cast in the role of the characters who attempt to devour the sow, the author, and while Trellis escapes by virtue of the casual burning of a few pages of fiction, one must remember that he too is a character, and his creator, the student, has disappeared by the close of the novel, to be replaced by some other nameless fictional substitute. The fiction has eaten the author, the text has evaded its origins and broken free.

The parody in *At Swim-Two-Birds* ultimately reflects inward upon itself-as-text. As previous mentioned, Trellis's aestho-autogamy theory undermines the ontological stability of the characters and the text, but it also forms part of a running commentary on the nature of fiction. As well as effecting a mockery of the referential act, it is also a parody of the conception process in literary texts and implicitly reminds us that literary characters are constructed linguistic apparitions rather than pretend people, a point that extends to our consideration of the character-author Trellis, especially since he is disempowered both as character and as author when Furriskey administers sleeping draughts to him. The illusory lives of the characters are further emphasized by the fact that when the invented bastard son Orlick tells his story, Trellis and many of his characters are duplicated, so we now have different versions of the same characters at different ontological levels in the text. The implausibility of this again emphasizes that we are dealing with fiction and only fiction, and this refusal to countenance anything resembling the illusion of realism marks all of O'Brien's first three novels. In this, *At Swim-Two-Birds* is effectively an autotelic text, to use Eliot's term. Like all self-referential metafictional texts, its primary focus is its own telling, its own possibility and the ontological limits of the text are purely textual.

At Swim-Two-Birds is a sophisticated assault on the pretensions of knowledge. In addition to a sustained, essentially dismissive interrogation of the workings of fiction, the assumptions of narrative sequence, and the pretensions of narratives of national heroism, the novel flattens the difference between high and low culture by mixing them at will (popular cowboy stories, James Joyce, and Irish myth). It also offers ironic commentary on the pretensions of science, a theme that is later extended in *The Third Policeman*, by applying mock-scientific precision to everyday life: "*Minutiae*: No. of cigarettes smoked, average 8.3; glasses of stout or other comparable intoxicant, av. 1.2; times to stool, av. 2.65; hours of study, av. 1.4; spare-time or recreative pursuits, 6.63 circulating" (161). Thus from the outset, O'Brien's work uses black humor to register its deep hostility toward the validity of knowledge, the pretensions of science, and the possibility of a coherent telling of human experience. Although he was clearly not the first author to use the embedded narrative, with Gide and Huxley being the most obvious immediate predecessors, or self-reflexive self-parody, à la Sterne's *Tristram Shandy*, the degree to which he pushed such technical devices reveals a spirit of subversion that forces the novel into an essentially negative dialectic or, as Shea contends, the text is "a performance that constructs and breaks the frame of the tale, the novel flaunts its reflexive potentials, reminding us how all inscriptions refer to other words that act as traces of continually deferred meanings" ("Patrick McGinley's" 278). The meaning may be continually deferred in *At Swim-Two-Birds* because there is more than a suggestion that the author doesn't believe in the authority of meaning, of human epistemological systems, and when he moves beyond the narrative play of the first novel into *The Poor Mouth* and *The Third Policeman*, the depth of his disdain toward the ways in which we order our experiences becomes even more evident.

The Third Policeman (1940)

Ostensibly a conventional, sequential narrative at the outset, despite the in medias res plunge into the narrator's grisly past, the erosion of the realist illusion swiftly asserts itself. Initial peculiarities include the vague reference to the narrator's age, "I was born a long time ago" (7); and the casual mention of his parents' deaths in an extremely imprecise way doesn't lend much to the principle of creating a lucid context for the events that will follow: "Then a certain year came about the Christmas-time and when the year was gone my father and mother were gone also" (8). A quality of the indefinite appears to attend many of his memories and with good reason. The revelation that our narrator is dead isn't made until near the end of the text by which time the limits of logic have long since been breached in many ways. The narrator's tale is told from death by a man who appears unaware that he is dead and this poses a number of difficulties for readers in terms of how they assesses the ontological status of the world in which they find themselves. Arguably the frame narrative in *The Third Policeman*, that told by the dead narrator, is the dominant ontological level, but there are moments where worlds overlap, especially at the end when the narrator invades the "real space" of his former home and confronts his likely murderer, Divney, who then "dies," apparently of heart failure, and accompanies the narrator to what appears to be *his* death, which is precisely the same as the journey upon which our narrator had earlier embarked. Thus Divney's journey, like that of the narrator before him, is the beginning of an eternally recurring journey, which resembles life but in which the laws of physics, temporality, and spatiality are repeatedly broken. The narrator assumed he had merely been absent for a few days, but it transpires than he has been "dead" for sixteen years. This fictional device had been widely used in Gaelic legend, as in the tale of Oisin and *Tír na nÓg* (Land of the Young), but its particular use in *The Third Policeman* appears to be yet another way to undermine the legitimacy of the world in which we find ourselves and the tale that we have just been told.

The precise status of the fictional world that we have just encountered is itself a critical conundrum. Unlike the multilayered Chinese box that is *At Swim-Two-Birds*, *The Third Policeman* is built in a singular frame within which there are a series of in-between spaces or zones, like the "Eternity" to which the narrator journeys with Sergeant Pluck or Policeman Fox's tiny police station in the walls of Mathers's house. Of course, the primary challenge to rational comprehension is that the entire tale, even the remembered predeath days, is told from the perspective of a dead man, and the normal regulatory logic of everyday reality no longer applies. This technically offers an enormous amount of authorial freedom, but the convergence of fantasy with a semblance of reality poses an enormous challenge to any author. Most importantly, as O'Brien himself observed, this fictional landscape "where none of the rules and laws (not even the law of gravity) holds good" (*The Third Policeman* 200) offers endless possibilities for the author, particularly one whose primary intention is to parody the presumption of human intellectual systems.

In such a landscape, the use of a narrator whose name we are never told, who subsequently bemoans how he has forgotten his name, despite being warned by Divney not to forget his name, and whose lack of a name subsequently accounts for the ease with which he is "convicted" of the crime of murder makes it more than obvious that this character will be of little use to us in unearthing the significance of the peculiar events. He is already dead from the outset and clearly doesn't understand his context, and it is likely he never did, even when he was alive. In his retelling of the story of his youth, he appears disconnected from his environment and detached from his family, so in life, as in death, our narrator fails to grasp what happens around him. In fact, when he forgets his name, he is unconcerned at the fact and even revels in it: "A thing not easy to account for is the unconcern with which I turned over my various perplexities in my mind. Blank anonymity coming suddenly in the middle of life should be at best alarming, a sharp symptom that the mind is in decay. But the unexplainable exhilaration which I drew from my surroundings seemed to invest this situation merely with the genial interest of a good joke" (40). O'Brien's narrator thus perpetually seems to hover on the very edge of his own identity, where the social signification of a name becomes irrelevant. Of course, on a logical level he is dead, and thus the absence of identity is a perfectly logical fact; but the absence of a fixed persona also registers the author's reluctance to allow his primary voice any real authority. In fact, later in the text the narrator's intellectual, bodily, and spiritual presence almost evaporates:

> Lying quietly and dead-eyed, I reflected on how new the night was, how distinctive and unaccustomed its individuality. Robbing me of the reassurance of my eyesight, it was disintegrating my bodily personality into a flux of colour, smell, recollection, desire—all the strange uncounted essences of terrestrial and spiritual existence. I was deprived of definition, position and magnitude and my significance was considerably diminished. Lying there, I felt the weariness ebbing from me slowly, like a tide retiring over limitless sands. The feeling was so pleasurable and profound that I sighed again a long sound of happiness. (116-17)

In this moment of near extinction, O'Brien approaches a stripping away of definition, of epistemological systems, and allows his character a moment of freedom from the limits of being a human, sensory perception, and psychological longing.

Throughout the novel, there is a persistent assault on various other kinds of systematic thought and a savage parody, particularly of scientific systems. The primary focus of O'Brien's parody of science resides in the construction of the text in a quasi-scholarly fashion, replete with footnotes from and continual summary of the work of de Selby, who makes his first appearance as an epigraph to the text proper. Our narrator is a student of de Selby, and it is ostensibly for de Selby that the narrator ultimately murders old Mathers, because he needs money to publish his book. The barely disguised parody is obvious: a man, blinded by his search for scientific knowledge and scholarly success, loses his soul in the process. The caliber of the scientific knowledge in question is, of course, of a most dubious kind, including de Selby's belief that human existence is a "succession of static experiences each infinitely brief," a view that allows for travel between vast distances by "resting for infinitely brief intervals in innumerable intermediate places" (50), a theory that would seem to be borne out by the ease at which the narrator later travels to and from eternity and seamlessly from death to life and back. So bogus science then supports fictional fantasy, and both are essentially removed from encyclopedic reality. This is echoed by the narrator's take on de Selby: because he held that "the usual processes of living were illusory, it is natural that he did not pay much attention to life's adversities and he does not in fact offer much suggestion as to how they should be met" (92).

Of course, de Selby is simply a device that allows the author to parody scientific knowledge, and the foolish adoration with which the naïve narrator initially approaches the scientist acts as a caustic comment on the legitimacy that is generally bestowed upon scientific thought. But de Selby is just the beginning. The quasi-scientist-Sergeant's hilarious "Atomic Theory" and the outrageous scientific theories of the mad scientist-philosopher de Selby are of equal significance in *The Third Policeman*, again deflating the pretensions of serious branches of knowledge. Pluck's Atomic Theory, we are told, is "between twice and three times as dangerous as it might be" (87) and acts as the scientific logic behind the way in which humans take on the characteristics of bicycles and vice versa, and the same applies to anything made of atoms (i.e., everything). The use of scientific language to explain Pluck's theory effects a biting parody of science, the facade of precision collapses into farce and nonsense, and meaning becomes unmeaning when the desire for exactitude is pushed too far. Precision itself becomes the object of scorn and ridicule, delivered as it is in semicolloquial terms: "Everything is composed of small particles of itself and they are flying around in concentric circles and arcs and segments and innumerable other geometrical figures too numerous to mention collectively, never standing still or resting but spinning away and darting hither and thither and back again, all the time on the go. These diminutive gentlemen are called atoms" (84). The application of atomic theory to objects of everyday use intensifies the parody because the bogus scientific abstraction is imposed on the commonplace with outrageous results, like the Sergeant's great-grandfather spending the last year of his life as a galloping, hay-eating horse because he spent too much time astride a horse during his life.

The critique of scientific endeavor is everywhere in the novel, with repeated challenges to verifiable notions of time, space, and mass in evidence. Rational spatial dimensions are frequently disrupted, as when the narrator initially approaches the police station only to discover that there is a front and back but no sides to the building: "It did not seem to have any depth or breadth and looked as if it would not deceive a child" (52-53). He subsequently claims that the station house is like something "glimpsed under ruffled water" (53) and approaches the building, peers in, and sees a policeman inside, despite the fact that the building has no depth and he can see front and back simultaneously. The disorientating effect that this has on the reader is immense since the fictional frame is now clearly one in which the habitual empirical modes of comprehension with which we are equipped can no longer suffice. What follows includes a magnifying glass that "magnifies to invisibility" (136), a machine that "splits up any smell into its sub- and inter-smells the way you can split up a beam of light with a glass instrument," and a machine that has a similar function when applied to taste (139). This mockery of the empirical practice of comprehending an object on the basis of splitting it into its smallest particles gains much currency when applied to commonplace things because mixing abstractions with sensual aspects of reality inevitably produces farcical results.

The human comprehension and ordering of time is also a focus of O'Brien's barbed humor. The novel is littered with provocative, subversive comments about temporal order, like the Sergeant's clarification to the narrator that "This is not today, this is yesterday" (60) and the narrator's observation that he and the Sergeant "were now going through a country full of fine enduring trees where it was always five o'clock in the afternoon" (80), while the policemen, we are told, have been there for "hundreds of years" (35). The general temporal arrangement is frequently compromised by such playful irregularities, but the central plot is also reordered due to temporal inconsistencies, as for example, when Inspector O'Corky informs the Sergeant that "a man called Mathers was found in the crotch of a ditch up the road two hours ago with his belly opened up with a knife" (96). The time frame is completely disrupted because at this point old Mathers has been dead for years, and he hadn't originally been stabbed, so temporal zones are broken, as are descriptions that were previously presented as factual.

The novel also challenges the way in which we perceive and order time, particularly when the narrator and Gilhaney search on the floor of the police station for the tiniest of MacCruiskeen's chests (so tiny that it is invisible): "How long we remained at our peculiar task, Gilhaney and I, it is not easy to remember. Ten minutes or ten years, perhaps . . ." (113-14). The temporal play is more than just a narratorial hint that a lot of time is actually passing—it also destabilizes the normal understanding of time as measurable and comprehensible, an issue that is repeatedly foregrounded in the novel, especially when one remembers that the main events of the novel take place in a matter of days and yet also take place over sixteen years. There are two temporal zones compressed into one, and the effect is to destabilize the ultimate validity of either. The narrator's few days among the policemen unfold, while on a different ontological level (life) almost two decades pass by. These two zones are superimposed upon one another at the close of the novel, and the disorientation of temporal reality is complete. It is complete but it should hardly be surprising, considering the play on time elsewhere in the text, in particular in the "Eternity" zone where people do not age, grow, or diminish in any physical way, which is not terribly odd considering that the place has no spatial dimensions either, according to MacCruiskeen. So while they appear to be active in "Eternity," they do not age, and the world outside hasn't changed either: "It was two or three hours since the Sergeant and I had started on our journey yet the country and the trees and all the voices of every thing around still wore an air of early morning. There was incommunicable earliness in everything, a sense of waking and beginning. Nothing had yet grown or matured and nothing begun had yet finished. A bird singing had not yet turned finally the last twist of tunefulness" (142-43). The compression and freezing of time in certain zones and the existence of variable temporal ontologies throughout the novel further emphasize that O'Brien sought to construct a fictional world in which the given perimeters that accompany ordered empirical comprehension are continually breached.

Another key device in the text that ultimately serves the same end is the "black box." The novel is built around a few black boxes, emblems of the pursuit of knowledge to both the narrator and the Sergeant. The narrator's "black box" nominally contains the booty from the robbery of old Mathers, but its value to the narrator lies in his access to producing a seminal work on de Selby, and his search for it resembles a distorted search for the Holy Grail, also a symbol of supreme understanding. The "black box" makes another appearance in the police station, this time as a mechanical contraption attached to a mangle whose purpose is to discover scientific truth. This is effected by "Stretching the light" (109) in the mangle until it emits a shriek, variously interpreted as "Don't press so hard," and "Two bananas a penny" (108). The secret to all of this is, as MacCruiskeen informs the narrator, Omnium: "Omnium is the essential inherent interior essence which is hidden inside the root of the kernel of everything and it is always the same. . . . It never changes. But it shows itself in a million ways and it always comes in waves" (110). Later in the novel Policeman Fox tells the narrator that the contents of the "black box" that he stole from old Mathers was four ounces of Omnium, with which he can do anything. Fox laughs at the games he has played on the other policemen with the Omnium, effectively mocking their belief in science, which they thought had been responsible for the miracles in "Eternity."

The general irregularities with time, the unremitting parody of scientific endeavor, and the play with recognizable spatial structures all add to the undermining of any systematic comprehension or analysis of reality, and as the novel progresses, the inability to conceive of any meaningful grasp on his surroundings gradually becomes the only defining aspect of this nameless narrator, as when he struggles to grasp what day it is upon waking near the close of the novel: "When I awoke again two thoughts came into my head so closely together that they seemed to be stuck to one another; I could not be sure which came first and it was hard to separate them and examine them singly. One was a happy thought about the weather, the sudden brightness of the day that had been vexed earlier. The other was suggesting to me that it was not the same day at all but a different one and maybe not even the next day after the angry one. I could not decide that question and did not try to" (151). Again, temporal dislocation is linked to epistemological instability, a condition of mind that gradually envelops the mind of the narrator, a problematic eventuality considering that he is, nominally at least, our guide to the events that are being dictated; so when he tells the reader, midway through the novel that "I don't know. How can I know why I think my thoughts?" (117), the consequences for the status of meaning as a humanly attainable goal are clear. The value of the quest for knowledge is raised several times in the novel, as early as when the one-legged robber advises the narrator that "Is it life? Many a man has spent a hundred years trying to get the dimensions of it and when he understands it at last and entertains the certain pattern of it in his head, by the hokey he takes to his bed and dies!"(44-45). In O'Brien's *The Third Policeman* the possibility of the attainment of secure knowledge beyond the omnipotent Omnium appears to be, quite literally, a fool's game. Whether one is a scientific genius or a mad policeman with aspirations to supreme knowledge, it matters little because empiricism, epistemological systems, our comprehension of time and space, all produce nothing more than ever-increasing layers of farce.

The primary frame narrative of *The Third Policeman* is a hetero-cosmic space that exists in opposition to the "real" world, although it certainly has a relationship with that world. In fact even within the primary frame there are several heterocosmic levels, substrata of imagined spaces within. The primary frame is located after death, and the theoretical oppositional frame is "life." In *The Third Policeman* life appears to be a zone of lesser significance from which both the narrator and Divney retreat, after a brief sojourn there at the close of the novel, to return to the primary frame, death. The implication of the foregrounding of death as a viable fictional zone are many. First, as previously mentioned, the freedom that this allows the nonrealist author is immense, and technically speaking the novel never becomes a fantasy or a horror novel, because all the peculiarities are explained by virtue of the fact that they occur after the narrator has died. There is little doubt however that the author has availed of this freedom to make direct commentary on the vanity of human scientific endeavor in particular, but more generally on all attempts to order and know the human environment on spatial and temporal levels. This direct commentary on life curiously ensures that "death" begins to resemble "life" with its follies and egomania. The more convinced the Sergeant or MacCruiskeen are of their scientific discoveries, the more foolish they become. The more ideas that they have, the more real they seem. O'Brien's technical achievement in this is extraordinary. In consciously evading the limits of the real in his ontological frame, he manages to direct a devastating commentary to such a degree that our comprehension of the real is radically adjusted. By the time he has done with us, we, like the narrator, begin to witness the world of the "real" as "simply irregularly shaped . . . endless variety . . . dimensional dissimilarities" (135). The parodic spirit that underpins the relentless desire to expose human intellectual systems in *The Third Policeman* could be said to define all of O'Brien's work. He had earlier used it to great effect in *At Swim-Two-Birds*, in which the structure and fabric of fictional narratives were spectacularly exposed. In the novel that was written immediately after *The Third Policeman*, *The Poor Mouth* (*An Béal Bocht*, in its original Gaelic), O'Brien appears to radically shift focus because the subject matter is significantly different from the earlier novels, but the same desire to parody, to uncloak fixed presumptions and clichéd thinking, is ever-present.

The Poor Mouth (An Béal Bocht) by Myles na Gopaleen (1941)

The Poor Mouth was originally written in Gaelic under the title *An Béal Bocht* by one Myles na Gopaleen ("Myles of the little horses"), the pen name that was to become Brian O'Nolan's nom de guerre in his "Cruiskeen Lawn" column in the *Irish Times* for the next two decades. The novel is set in the fictional Corkadoragha in the townland of Lisnabrawshkeen, a location that could be any number of Irish parishes on the western seaboard of Ireland circa 1900, and our primary access to this misery-cursed landscape is the distinctly un-Irish sounding Bonaparte O'Coonassa, son of Michaelangelo O'Coonassa.

O'Brien claimed that he wrote *The Poor Mouth* because he was so disturbed by Thomas O'Criomthainn's (Tomás Ó'Crohán) *An t-Oileánach* (Cronin 126), and that his novel is primarily intended as a parody of *An t-Oileánach* (translated by Robin Flowers as *The Islandman*) is clear from the fact that the subtitle to the Gaelic original, *An Béal Bocht*, was *An Milleánach* ("The fault finder"), which rhymes with O'Criomthainn's autobiography. In addition O'Brien perpetually repeats variations of the phrase "Our like will never be there again," an echo, as Jane Farnon points out, of the same phrase used on the title page of *An t-Oileánach*. O'Brien endlessly overuses the phrase in his novel, stripping it of any of its original pathos and transforming it to a repetitive moan.

Bonaparte's opening convoluted remarks are a stark warning of what is to follow: "I cannot truly remember either the day I was born or the first six months I spent here in the world. Doubtless, however, I was alive at that time although I have no memory of it, because I should not exist now if I were not there then and to the human being, as well as to every other living creature, sense comes gradually" (11). This is a direct parody of the opening to *An t-Oileánach* in which the speaker informs us, "I was born on St Thomas's day in the year 1856. I can recall being at my mother's breast, for I was four years old before I was weaned" (O'Criomhthain 1). The author wastes no time in initiating a parody of memory and time and swiftly proceeds to blur any kind of exactitude. For example, he has a special kind of logic to explain the obvious, which is never obvious to him: "I was very young at the time I was born and had not aged even a single day; for half a year I did not perceive anything about me and did not know one person from the other" (14). This parodies various kinds of bildungsroman by overemphasising Bonaparte's surprise at not knowing things from birth. Also, in the first chapter it is revealed that Bonaparte can converse perfectly but cannot yet walk or move. On one level this is simply comedy, but it is also part of a progressive dismantling of the regularized order that one expects from a realist account and as such offers an indication of the deep levels of intellectual subversion that are at work (and play) in the novel.

However, the most overt parody that is evident in *The Poor Mouth* is that of Irishness and all that it entailed to O'Brien.

The primary textual target of his wit is a style of writing more than a specific author or title, and anyone familiar with the work of Máire (the pen name for Séamus Ó Grianna from Donegal) or Thomás O'Criomhthain (Blasket Islands, Kerry) or Peig Sayers (West Kerry) will immediately recognise the blunt parody of certain stylistic and thematic characteristics. Throughout the novel, there is continuous discussion about the incessant rain, culminating in chapter 8, which deals solely with rainfall, effectively a mockery of the Irish predilection to discuss the weather as a mode of initiating and maintaining conversation, especially as it is presented in the aforementioned Irish-language works. O'Brien also makes continual reference to potatoes, misery, hunger, and a perpetual condition of being "destroyed" throughout the text. In fact, throughout, potatoes are deemed necessary to keep both hunger and despair at bay, and a few potatoes usually make life a little better in this place of relentless rain and misery.

The Poor Mouth also mimics the style of the Gaelic texts especially via Bonaparte's occasional use of a semilofty mode of expression when habitually formalizing the most outrageous of events, like describing his mother's incarceration of his newly wed wife, Mabel: "Mabel was in the end of the house at this juncture with my mother on top of her. The poor girl was trying to escape back to her father's house and my mother endeavouring to make her see reason and informing her that it is compulsory to submit to Gaelic fate" (84). Irrespective of the level of peculiarity that is unfolding, a similar tone of mock-seriousness is employed that generally adds to the ironic tone of the text and encourages the reader to reserve any significant responses to the narrator's increasingly unlikely accounts.

Told as the tale is from the perspective of a rural-dwelling Gaelic speaker, to whom English is a very peculiar language, the appearance of English-speaking Irish people who are trying to immerse themselves in "authentic" Irish culture provokes O'Brien's most direct satire. Initially this occurs when we are told a tale about a gentleman from Dublin who comes to experience Gaelic life and folklore, a possible parody of Robin Flowers, O'Criomhthain's translator and associate. He manages to record the snorting of a pig, believing it to be Gaelic, and departs happy the following day, after which, due to his success in recording a Gaelic that was "so good, so poetic and so obscure," he had a fine academic degree bestowed upon him and gave learned talks on continental Europe (45). More pointed, however, is O'Brien's inclusion of a chapter dealing exclusively with the "Gaeligores" (parody of Gaelgoirí, or those who encourage the development of Gaelic-speaking), upon whom he unleashes a torrent of sarcasm and derision. Old-Grey-Fellow arranges a *feis* (Gaelic cultural event that includes music and dance) to swindle money from the culture-hunters. In the novel they embark on a series of exaggerated speeches about being Gaelic: "We are all Gaelic Gaels of Gaelic lineage. He who is Gaelic, will be Gaelic evermore. I myself have spoken not a word except Gaelic since the day I was born—just like you— and every sentence I've ever uttered has been on the subject of Gaelic" (54). In this, O'Brien, himself a fluent Gaelic speaker, appears to target the insincerity of those who used the language and culture as a form of self-aggrandisement, accounting for the fact that many Gaels (authentic ones) die from the burden of listening to the incessant speeches; throughout the overall event, deaths multiply from the building of the stage, an excess of dancing, a scarcity of food, fatigue, drinking, fighting, and general revelry. While the insincerity of the Gaeligores is O'Brien's primary target, it is also very clear that he is playing with the stereotypical emblems of Irishry, like drinking, unrestrained merriment, and famine-induced misery. The ultimate purpose of this kind of unremitting criticism is to demolish the validity of any narrative, clichéd or otherwise, that may be used to define the nation or race, even if on a comic level. Beginning with the title, a common Irish saying that draws attention to a tendency to feign poverty, O'Brien's novel is more an attempt to foreground and undo the rigidified, clichéd images of Irishness by irony and parody than it is a direct critique of the Irish, a fundamentally different enterprise.

The same desire is evident in the way in which O'Brien creates the landscape(s) upon which the events play out. The fictionality of the location is somewhat compromised by the fact that it is frequently punctuated with real references that contribute to the destabilization of geographical space in the novel. For example, from the windows of his house, Bonaparte can see the western coast of Donegal, the peninsula Bloody Foreland, and Tory Island, all of which is just about feasible, if a little fanciful. But he can also see West Galway, Aranmore, and the town of Kilronan, a lot more fanciful and less feasible, but he can also see the Great Blasket and Dingle town on the west coast of Kerry, effectively an impossibility. It is indeed an extraordinary house, and it stretches one's imagination to envisage exactly where Corkadoragha is that Bonaparte can see the length of the west coast of Ireland from his house. That this is a playful reminder of yet another Irish cliché, the tendency to exaggerate, is undoubted, but this is also the author of *The Third Policeman* and *At Swim-Two-Birds*, in which the legitimacy of spatial location is rarely accepted as a given. In fact, throughout *The Poor Mouth*, the reader is exposed to a series of physically impossible scenarios that compromise his or her spatial sense, nowhere more so that when Bonaparte attends school for the first (and last) time and offers some detail about his fellow students: "Some of them were crawling along the road, unable to walk. Many were from Dingle, some from Gweedore, another group floated in from Aran. All of us were strong and hearty on our first school day" (29). The problem with this bizarre scenario is that Bonaparte's schoolmates have crawled, walked, and floated from various places along the west coast of Ireland to get to the same school, in the process diminishing the size of the country (Ireland is approximately 300 miles long). Here the text again takes great liberties with spatial dimensions, further destabilizing its impact as a genuine didactic text, despite the initial illusion that it may be so. There are quite simply too many disruptive elements in the text, and unlike the practical currency gained by an author like Swift in his satirical "A Modest Proposal," the parody here yields no such sustained social criticism.

In fact the parody is so sustained in the text, it is not possible to ascertain if there is any direct sincere comment on Irish life being made. In addition to the mock-heroic portrait of the Old-Fellow, the scornful assault on Gaeligores, the constant ridicule of the narrator's foolishness, and the disparaging of all emblems of Irishness, O'Brien parodies grief-stricken mothers of sons lost at sea ("one poor mother screaming: Who'll save my Mickey?" (67)), common supernatural beliefs, and courtship, marriage, and birth: within four pages Bonaparte is married and has a child, and then both wife and child die from consumption. He accounts for this misfortune in the way that he does with all other events in his life, as just another misfortune in the life of the Irish, like bad weather. In fact, the depiction of Ireland is so bleak that one character, Sitric O'Sanassa, tired of his misery-laden impoverished life, takes up residence in a large spacious room embedded in rock beneath the sea, a kind of underground cave where he can both have the company of and the nutritional value of the seals: "Where he was, he had freedom from the inclement weather, the famine and the abuse of the world. Seals would constitute his company as well as his food" (98). Living in the textual space that is O'Brien's version of inclement Ireland, O'Sanassa chooses to live among the creatures of the sea rather than to live among the half-living on shore, which spurs stories among Bonaparte's neighbours that O'Sanassa has turned into a fish. Furthermore, in Irish legend there are a number of instances of people who live in some realm beyond the "real," the most prominent of whom were the magical *Tuatha de Danaan* who were reputed to live underground or in the ocean or beneath the sea. There is, of course, a vast difference between the existence eked out by O'Sanassa and the illustrious supernatural tales of the *Tuatha de Danaan*, but this is an indication that O'Brien's parodic impulse extends beyond Gaeligores and self-indulgent versions of contemporary misery. All national narratives are appropriate targets of his desire to uncover and rebuke.

O'Sanassa's transformation into a fish, real or rumored, does not exceed the ontological limits (or lack of) elsewhere in the tale, because they are continually stretched. For example, early in the novel a pig returns home wearing breeches containing tobacco, a shilling, and a bottle of spirits, and the events that transpire when Bonaparte locates the mythical Maeldoon O'Poenassa are dictated by the conditions of fantasy rather than realism. Maeldoon O'Poenassa is based on the ancient Gaelic story from the eighth or ninth century, *Immram Curaig Máele Dúin*, which is itself likely to be a hybrid of other sources. O'Brien's version is in part a parody of the Gaelic *Immram*, in this case a voyage-adventure with treasure, magic, and disasters combined, but, as Farnon correctly observes, the novel borrows quite a few emblems and plot elements from the original and reinvents them (Farnon 104). For example, in the *Immram*, Mael Duin is an illegitimate child and his father is a vague, undefined individual. In *The Poor Mouth* there are questions over Bonaparte's origins, and he hardly knows his father. In the chapter that directly mimics *Immram Curaig Máele Dúin*, the deluge that precedes Bonaparte's quest also echoes the great biblical flood and the flood in the *Epic of Gilgamesh*. Bonaparte journeys in search of treasure to the Hunger-Stack mountain (another invention), aboard no ship, and encounters a magic fountain that keeps an eternal flame alight because it emits whiskey. Bonaparte intensifies the lampooning of the original by incorporating the language of high adventure, like "journey to the mountain" and "the mountain of destiny; my ominous unknown objective" (104). In the magic cave the whiskey fuels a fire and also provides sustenance via a spring in the earth, while Maeldoon O'Poenassa, barely alive, has lived on whiskey for centuries, long-withered but capable of speech, appropriately in ancient Gaelic.

The Poor Mouth is an elaborate caricature of a range of influential emblems of Irishness, Gaelic autobiography, Irish legend, and ancient poetry to such an extent that the author effectively strips away the legitimacy of many of the governing narratives that were prevalent in Ireland. This will to unmake is very similar to that which is evident in *At Swim-Two-Birds* and *The Third Policeman*, and it is in this sense that O'Brien exhibits tendencies that came to be termed postmodern by later critics. The legitimacy of all existing interpretive models is undermined, and the landscapes out of which they emerge are continually compromised by the introduction of elements that might even be described as magic realist, as William Spindler's explains, "texts where two contrasting views of the world (one 'rational' and one 'magical') are presented as if they were not contradictory, by resorting to the myths and beliefs of ethno-cultural groups for whom this contradiction does not arise" (Spindler 78). The difficulty, of course, when applying such well-meaning categorical definitions to any of Flann O'Brien's novels is that the comic impulse undermines one's ability to write of earnest labels like "ethno-cultural groups" with any real conviction. Similarly, Sarah McKibben discovers in *The Poor Mouth* a site of declared postcolonial conflict: "In a postcolonial riposte, *The Poor Mouth* lays bare the servitude of the Gael and his language to the ideological demands of the linguistic majority in the new state—something arguably continuing to this day. The text thereby powerfully critiques a repressive and hypocritical nationalist discourse that replicated colonial attitudes and relations well after independence" (McKibben 96). That O'Brien satirizes "Gaeligores," effectively a critique of "hypocritical nationalist discourse," as McKibben has it, is certainly accurate. What is less certain is the suggestion that O'Brien, even inadvertently, is engaging in a critique of postcolonial politics. There is nothing in the novel to suggest that O'Brien has any more faith in a "pure" national culture than the bogus one he so savagely dismisses. In fact, throughout O'Brien's work, the spirit of unravelling various sites of pseudolegitimacy is the dominant artistic mode as opposed to championing any particular ideological cause, and to suggest that the "ideological demands of the linguistic majority" is being seriously attacked is a little peculiar since all of O'Brien's fiction and much of his journalism was written in English thereafter. It is much more plausible to see in O'Brien's satirical impulses an affinity with what was to become the postmodern disaffection with the legitimacy of grand narratives, and his work consequently becomes a multifaceted arena in which he repeatedly sought to reveal the self-indulgence of human ordering systems, whether national cliché in *The Poor Mouth* or artistic construction in *At Swim-Two-Birds*.

The tragedy with O'Brien is that after *The Poor Mouth*, a point at which he was clearly at his comic and artistic peak, he didn't publish another novel for twenty years and wrote almost nothing of literary value during this period. The reasons for this hiatus lie beyond the scope of this essay, but suffice to say that on the point of greatest promise, something was lost and the two novels that were eventually published in the early 1960s, while still indicative of the early powers, had diminished somewhat in the execution. Nevertheless, the same desire to dismantle all kinds of significance remains and in *The Hard Life* had perhaps become even more profoundly nihilistic.

The Hard Life (1961)

The Hard Life initially masquerades as a conventional nineteenth-century realist novel, replete with departed parents, orphans, urban squalor, and an apparently earnest attempt to be honest about the mode of depiction, all set in late nineteenth- and early twentieth-century Dublin. However, this "Oirish" variation of English novels of the previous century also resembles Joyce's *Dubliners*, with more than a passing nod to *A Portrait* and *Ulysses*, unlikely source texts for a realist novel. The time frame is approximately 1890 to 1910, which precedes O'Brien's own birth. The novel is set in a squalid Dublin, has children at its center, explores issues of Dublin life and religion, and pits the cosmopolitan Manus against the essentially parochial Mr. Collopy, alluding to many of the central issues in Joyce's work. In addition, M. Keith Booker points out that the recurring ellipses, or gaps in communication that one encounters so frequently in *Dubliners*, are revisited throughout *The Hard Life*, most obviously in the "consistent refusal to name Collopy's project, a refusal that keeps the nature of this project not only from the reader but also from Finbarr and Manus, who frequently witness the conversations of Collopy and Fahrt on this topic" (Booker 89). Apart from their significance as echoes of Joyce, these empty conversations are of central significance in any discussion of the novel because they contribute so much to the sense that the novel disenfranchises language, a point to which I will presently return.

Despite its initial masquerade as a realist fiction, *The Hard Life* also contains a range of early indicators that will eventually undo any illusion of referentiality. Finbarr, the narrator, concedes at an early stage that "That's merely my recollection of the silly sort of conversation we had. Probably it is all wrong" (5). He confirms his vague apprehension of events soon after when, after describing Mr. Collopy, he swiftly withdraws the validity of the description: "There is something misleading but not dishonest in this portrait of Mr. Collopy. It cannot be truly my impression of him when I first saw him but rather a synthesis of all the thoughts and experiences I had of him over the years, a long look backwards" (9). This admission of his tendency to offer impressionistic commentary effectively registers his intention hereafter to offer his comprehension of events and people rather than pretend to offer true representation. Thus his awareness of the requirements of narrator is often coupled with an admission of failure: "It is seemly, as I have said, to give that explanation but I cannot pretend to have illuminated the situation or made it more reasonable" (14). The implication here is that he will fulfill his obligations as narrator of an ostensibly real set of events, but he refuses to admit to their absolute veracity. Furthermore, at the beginning of chapter 4, the reader discovers that six years have been passed over and, while the sequence is technically maintained, there is a lack of continuity in terms of temporal development: "And still the years kept rolling on, and uneventfully enough, thank God. I was now eleven, the brother sixteen and convinced he was a fully grown man" (22). This, added to the fact that we never really get to know the narrator very well, ensures that while the essential fabric of the sequential realist tale is maintained, there is a curious unsettled quality about the novel.

The use of the realist novel structure is maintained throughout, however, even to include elements of the epistolary form for most of the final third of the novel, involving the narrator's receipt of a series of aimless and increasingly fantastic letters from his brother Manus, who now lives in London. And yet, even within the frame of the letters, a device traditionally used to generate realism and provide crucial pivotal information, there is an endless procession of trivia, far-flung fantasy, and verbiage. For example, after one of Manus's typically overblown rhetorical epistles, the narrator observes, "Well, that was a long and rather turgid letter but I found myself in agreement with the last paragraph [take no action for the present]. In fact I put the whole subject out of my head . . ." (129). Finbarr's response is more than just an indication of fraternal indifference. It also points to a pattern of general disdain for the fruits of language in the text as a whole. The whole of Manus's catalog of bogus books of questionable expertise acts as a constant reminder of the dubious nature of the written word and both the perils and effectiveness of high-flown rhetoric to unsuspecting people. His first book, on tight-rope walking whose title page reads "THE HIGH WIRE—Nature Held at Bay—Spine-chilling Spectacle Splenetizes Sporting Spectators—By Professor H. Q. Latimer Dodds" (47), is composed in jargonized prose whose only function is to generate the illusion of authority, without actually knowing anything. It eventually leads to a young boy almost drowning, suggesting that books can be bad for one both physically and mentally. Later Manus sets up the "Zenith School of Journalism," repeatedly plagiarizes from the National Library, and is ultimately responsible for the death of Collopy as a result of his bogus medicine, "Gravid Water."

The sense that textual items like books and letters are essentially hollow forms of discourse is extended to include other linguistic formations in the novel. Many critics have observed that the conversations between Collopy and the unfortunately named Father Fahrt are excellent examples of empty rhetorical games (Shea, *Flann O'Brien* 142; Booker 93; Cronin 215), a suggestion hinted at by Finbarr in the observation that "As usual, the subject under discussion was never named" (30). Anthony Cronin suggests that these conversations represent the central achievement of the novel, claiming that they are "classics of pointless dialectic" (215), a point echoed by Booker but extended to suggest that almost "all of the language in *The Hard Life* is . . . without the backing of any firm conviction" (93). Despite the almost casual masquerade as a realist novel, O'Brien clearly engendered in his text an extended critique of the value of language, and the prognosis appears to be that language, at least in social modes of discourse, is ultimately empty and incapable of achieving anything beyond the temporary game that is being played out at any given time. *The Hard Life* may actually be the most radically dismissive of all of O'Brien's works in the sense that it allows language to have no significant purpose, and words achieve very little in this nauseating world of recycled conversations and, as Booker observes in the case of Manus, a "commodification of language" whose sale-value is its only significance (94), explaining the somewhat puzzling overemphasis on Manus's endeavors. Far from being simply a comic resource, the bogus texts are powerful indicators of the dissolution of meaningful discourse, and as Thomas Shea contends, the novel becomes an exploration of how "discourses collapse, sounding only a desperately squalid void" (*Flann O'Brien* 142). The novel that initially resembles a Dickensian adventure into social commentary ends up acting as an unsettling and intensely negative text, expressing the author's revulsion at a closed lifestyle on the one hand and disdain at the charade of empty cosmopolitanism, epitomized by Manus on the other.

Throughout the text there is no genuine center of meaning. Much of the substance of the plot revolves around empty conversations and Manus's empty pursuits, language is deflated, and there is no genuine sense of meaning apparent. In this, despite all the appearances, the novel is very much a postmodern text, one that clearly dramatizes, to cite Ihab Hassan, "the disease of verbal systems" (32), but one in which there is also a peculiar sense of not being able to come to grips with anything in particular, something that is suggested by Manus's adjustment of Keats's epitaph ("Here lies one whose name is writ on water") to read "Here lies one whose name is writ in water" (172), that is, invisible. He takes an already precarious scripted image and makes it vanish completely, and the world of the novel becomes less and less tangible, a quality that extends to the narrator himself. It appears at times that he is actually bereft of a recognizable character, incapable of any meaningful intervention in the life of the text, and this accounts for the sense that the novel doesn't have a center, a factor that Tess Hurson blames on the lack of "authorial interference" (120), although I would argue that none of Flann O'Brien's novels exhibits overt levels of authorial intervention of any kind, which conversely explains their success. It seems that what Hurson notices is a hollow center of significance—absent meaning—because the narrator, representing little more than the style of reportage, offers little by way of ambition, intent, or focus. So the fake realist novel fails to fulfill its bogus promise and the reader is left floundering in the aftershock of the dark joke; there is no center because there is no meaning or value. There is no centrally significant character because no action is worthy of centrality or significance. This is the dark, centerless hollow to which O'Brien finally journeyed, and having long ago outgrown the textual metafictional games of *At Swim-Two-Birds*, he retained the sense of indefinability that resides in all three prior novels written two decades before. *The Hard Life* exhibits none of the gripping fantastical elements of *The Third Policeman* or *The Poor Mouth* because the episodes that include the Pope and Collopy's death are more farce than fantasy and consequently fail to achieve the lasting fictional emblematic status as O'Brien's bicycles or dressed up pigs, and it is in this sense, as a writer of fiction, that O'Brien's gift had faded. The satirical impulse remains, may be darker than ever, but the capacity to enshrine his vision in powerful fictional images is diminished.

The Dalkey Archive (1964)

When O'Brien's last novel, *The Dalkey Archive*, appeared in print in 1964, his second novel, *The Third Policeman*, had not yet been published. It appeared only posthumously in 1967. This partly explains some of the weaknesses in *The Dalkey Archive*. O'Brien had clearly dredged up some key elements from the earlier unpublished novel and reconstituted them or, in the case of De Selby, elevated them from footnote status in *The Third Policeman* to a full-blown character, around whom much of the plot lingers. The Mollycule Theory that is expounded by Sergeant Fottrell in *The Dalkey Archive* has clearly been plundered, word for word in places, from its earlier incarnation as Atomic Theory, as expressed by the Sergeant, and so has the explanation of how it operates with recourse to the example of the human tendency to transform into bicycles and vice versa. That the author borrowed heavily is also indicated, as Anthony Cronin points out, by the prevalence of odd anachronisms in *The Dalkey Archive*, a novel that was meant to be a new work focused on contemporary events in Dublin: "Women were not served in the Metropole Lounge; the side roads of Dalkey were empty and silent; trams still ran in the streets of Dublin" (Cronin 228). By the time that O'Brien was supposed to have started writing *The Dalkey Archive*, circa 1962, none of the above was accurate. Whatever the problems with plundering from previously unpublished work, more serious, Cronin argues with some justification, is that the substance of De Selby's theological conversation with Saint Augustine and indeed the various scientific discussions in the novel are quite basic. One could, of course, offer the argument that since neither mode of knowledge actually held much genuine significance as viable epistemological constructs, the author didn't seek to inquire further or include much more detail than was necessary for parodic purposes. Notwithstanding Cronin's concerns, *The Dalkey Archive* certainly does not achieve anything close to the artistic success of its more accomplished predecessor of twenty years earlier.

The spirit of resistance to realism clearly persists from the outset with De Selby holding forth on the vagaries of time in an effort to explain to Mick and Hackett how he has managed to brew whiskey in a week by suspending time and "negative its apparent course" (14). The litany of false assumptions and errors of judgment that litter the novel begin during the first few chapters, for example Teague McGettigan's confusion of De Selby's desired name for his house, Mór Lawn, with "Lawnmower," which he paints on the house gate. Another example of how error leads to farce is the logic behind Mrs. Laverty's naming of her public house "the Colza Hotel," after she misinterprets colza oil to be a holy oil used for miraculous purpose by "Saint Colza" (25), failing to see the implicit contradiction between a bar full of drunks and a saint—real or imaginary. Furthermore, in the latter half of the novel, Mick grows increasingly paranoid about the perils posed by De Selby and meets "James Joyce" in Skerries, who denies having written *Ulysses* and almost everything else too. He misreads his relationship with Mary and almost loses her to Hackett in a most peculiar scene in the Colza Hotel at the end, and De Selby apparently simply "changes his mind" about his plans to destroy the world. In short, the plot contains many misunderstandings, error-prone characters, and curious episodes, like the oddly disturbing closing chapter that doesn't appear to have any significant connection with the novel proper and could just as easily have been a short story, or the question of the fire in De Selby's house, which is never resolved and is as inexplicable as the mad scientist's departure.

Echoes of *The Third Policeman*'s scientific focus are everywhere in *The Dalkey Archive*, most prominently through the development of De Selby who claims that Einstein's work on relativity is "bogus" (14) and proceeds to offer his own observations on time in the following manner: "You confound time with organic evolution. Take your child who has grown to be a man of twenty-one. His total life-span is to be seventy years. He has a horse whose life-span is to be twenty. He goes for a ride on his horse. Do these two creatures subsist simultaneously in dissimilar conditions of time? Is the velocity of time for the horse three and a half times that for the man?" (15). This self-evident nonsense, cloaked in quasi-scientific logical terms, seeks to parody scientific discourse. It is telling that throughout the novel, ultralogical discursive language is utilized to impel the discourse toward self-reflexive parody, as when Fottrell discusses Judas Iscariot with Mick and observes that "O'Scariot was a man of deciduous character inferentially . . ." (66). In all of this, of course, O'Brien is simply revisiting old parodic ground by repeatedly deflating any attempt to construct logical analytical arguments followed by definite assertions about the world. Certain observations about the passage of time also add to a general evasion of any category of systematic measurement. For example, Mick mentions that time, or "a diluted sort of time, drifted past him, and perhaps he dosed" (128). In moments like this O'Brien offers subtle challenges to the idea that the momentum of time is regular and there are breaches in the natural order of things.

Midway through the novel, Mick's paranoia grows ever more acute, and he begins to see himself as a messianic figure who will save the world from the mad genius De Selby, with the assistance of the pseudo-scientist Sergeant Fottrell: "But his present situation was that he was on the point of rescuing everybody from obliteration, somewhat as it was claimed that Jesus had redeemed all mankind. Was he not himself a god-figure of some sort?" (119). The dramatic irony here partly emerges from the fact that he had earlier felt sickened by what he interpreted as De Selby's claim that he was a new Messiah. Mick's account henceforth assumes the tone of a farcical detective novel that includes a robbery plot and the "James Joyce" encounters, both of which are connected to Mick's comprehension of De Selby and Joyce as mad geniuses who might together create some extraordinary new knowledge. The twin plots or journeys that have absorbed him for much of the novel have been provoked by his encounter with Saint Augustine, whose ontological status fascinates Mick much more than the precise meaning of the exchanges between the saint and the scientist, and the peculiar concluding remark by Mary about having a baby may be interpreted, along with the couple's rapprochement, as a return to the tangible universe after the heady nonsense of epistemological pursuit. Mick is no De Selby, or even a "poor man's De Selby" (90), as Mick calls Fottrell, and he is not a James Joyce whose mind, Mick thinks, is "unbalanced" (139).

The parody of James Joyce, frequently part of O'Brien's focus in the previous works, takes full tangible form in *The Dalkey Archive*, as though the ghostly father finally materializes as a fully developed creature. But, predictably, O'Brien's Joyce is a deflated parody. He is very pious, lives in Skerries, works in a bar, names Oliver

Gogarty as the co-author of *Dubliners,* and claims to be unaware of the existence of *Ulysses* but believes that it must be the work of "Various low, dirty-minded ruffians who had been paid to put this material together. Muck-rakers, obscene poets, carnal pimps, sodomous sycophants, pedlars of the coloured lusts of fallen humanity" (176-77). More pointedly, O'Brien mocks what he saw as Joyce's inaccessibility when he has Joyce tell Mick that his thoughts are "ineffable" (135) and describes his writing as "Assembly" (133). O'Brien admitted to his publisher that the "stuff about Joyce is withering in its ineptitude" (qtd. in Cronin 231), and while this self-criticism may be somewhat harsh, there is little doubt that the integration of a parody of Joyce, so effective elsewhere in O'Brien, had simply become too literal and adds little to the novel apart from a juvenile kind of humor. A more accomplished example of Joycean parody is evident later in the novel when Mick meditates on his own increasingly important place in the universe, appropriately during an afternoon in Saint Stephen's Green: "He got up and walked abstractedly about winding pathways. His mood was a formless one of renunciation. What about his mother? That grand lady was old, decayed enough so far as health went. . . . No, separation from his old mother would be no obstacle and the knowledge that he was becoming a priest would shine over her closing years, like a blessed candle" (143). The allusion to Stephen in *A Portrait* is clear and Mick's decision (never followed through) to become a Trappist monk again deflates the apparent sincerity of Joyce's protagonist's intention, if not his creator's.

There is an unsettling blurring of focus evident in *The Dalkey Archive* provoked primarily by the continual vacillation between realism and fantasy and the coupling of science and farce. Mary tells Mick that the whole Saint Augustine scenario is "absolute lunacy" (59) and thus offers us the perspective of relative normalcy, revealing that Mick's and Hackett's initial responses to the underwater meeting with Saint Augustine were inappropriate. While they do express doubts, they are simply too casual about freezing time, supernatural goings-on, and an underwater world, and Mary's presence, however minor, reminds us of the peculiarity of the events. Mick, of course, tries to normalize matters but decides to keep an open mind: "True, there seemed to have been a breach of the natural order in that apparition of Augustine in the grotesque chamber under the wave but several explanations might be forthcoming . . ." (61). The explanations never emerge and De Selby's erratic science is not sufficient to explain anything, all of which means that the reader, like Mick, is never in a position to grasp the true status of the version of reality that is presented. The persistence of bogus science in the novel, both in the shape of De Selby and Fottrell, serves to further confuse matters. The reason that Mary is so secure in her pragmatic dealing with reality (she arranges for Mick to meet Father Cobble) is that she refuses to search like Mick (or De Selby and Fottrell), the implication of which is that intellectual quests generate extraordinary, entertaining fictions that ultimately confuse more than they clarify, and if Mick is to find peace, he will find it in the steady arms of Mary and the absolute promised realism of a child.

Mick's search is driven by a desire for order in the face of a situation that has become "deplorably fluid and formless" and an awareness of a "pervasive ambiguity" (163). The problem for him and many other characters in the novel is that order appears to be dissolving on many levels. The ontological status of the everyday lives of Hackett and Mick has been totally destabilized by the arrival of De Selby, Fottrell's mollycule theory essentially means that the atomic structure of the world is more fluid and formless than hitherto believed, time has ceased to be a constant, James Joyce is alive and well, didn't write *Ulysses*, and wants to be a Jesuit, medicine is discredited by both Dr. Crewitt and medical student Nemo Crabbe, and the final antidenouement sees Mick entering into a promise of marriage during a series of events that "seemed to have been perversely pulled inside out" (203). The very issue of indefinability had already been raised early in the text, during the conversation between De Selby and Saint Augustine, in the following passage (Saint Augustine in italics):

> – The prime things—existence, time, the godhead, death, paradise and the satanic pit, these are abstractions. Your pronouncements on them are meaningless, and within itself the meaninglessness does not cohere.
> – *Discourse must be in words, and it is possible to give a name to that which is not understood nor cognoscible by human reason. It is our duty to strive towards God by thought and word. But it is our final duty to believe, to have and to nourish faith.* (41)

De Selby's view is unsurprising, especially considering his earlier pronouncement that, "Divergences, incompatibilities, irreconcilables are everywhere" (15), indicating his disdain of fixed categorical systems. Saint Augustine's reply, clearly an attempt to register the issue as a central textual concern, is a standard Catholic position, but it also points to the essential incompatibility between the empirical and Christian worldviews. De Selby objects to abstractions, formulations that are fundamentally distinct from reality, while Saint Augustine preaches in favor of faith and language, despite the inadequacy of words. On the basis of the novel as a whole, this dichotomy is not resolved for the author or for Mick.

Saint Augustine's position evaporates as surely as his apparition does and De Selby is clearly discredited both as a scientist and as a comic figure; he was more effective as a series of footnotes in *The Third Policeman*.

As with *The Hard Life* and *The Third Policeman*, O'Brien's final novel ultimately registers a note of bleak hopelessness and eventually peters out, having nowhere else to go and nothing else to say. The central comic inventions, De Selby, Fottrell, and Joyce have simply been erased, and with that, Mick, Mary, Hackett, and the other prosaic characters in the Colza Hotel simply remain. Nothing can be expected but more uncertainty, and in this, despite the uneven nature of the novel, it is clear that the dominant perspective in all of O'Brien's fiction remains: the repetitive lives of people circulate around various bogus branches of knowledge, are always disappointed and confused, and never achieve anything significant, or as Manus from *The Hard Life* observes, "Every day you meet people going around with two heads. They are completely puzzled by life, they understand practically nothing and are certain of only one thing—that they are going to die. I am not going to go so far as to contradict them in that but I believe I can suggest to them a few good ways of filling up the interval" (112). Here, O'Brien resembles Beckett more than Joyce, and despite the relentless Joycean comparisons, there may potentially be a closer relationship between him and Beckett. For example, as Booker indicates, even on the surface level of plot devices there are powerful echoes: "The fictional worlds of both writers are liberally populated with bicycles, pigs, big dumb Irish policemen, cripples, slothful narrators who lie in bed while constructing their fictions, and abject instances of violence and degradation" (10). More significantly, both Beckett and O'Brien's collective energies can be described as radical rejections of existing narratives frames within highly innovative fictional forms. Their respective critiques of language, epistemological centers and literary genres are self-evident, while their embracing of self-reflexivity, *mise-en-abyme*, and polyphonic intertexts all indicate a desire to unmake, or remake, existing narratives.

Although Keith Hopper's arguments about Flann O'Brien are extremely persuasive, I cannot concur with his view that *At Swim-Two-Birds* is "best considered as a late-modernist, transitory text which critiques both realism and modernism in an openly deconstructive manner, and in the process comes to the brink of an exciting new aesthetic" (14), although he does acknowledge that *The Third Policeman* is the first great masterpiece, along with *Finnegans Wake* "of what we generally refer to as post-modernism" (15). Alternatively, I would argue that *At Swim-Two-Birds* is already a postmodern text, and *The Third Policeman* also fits the conditions indicated by such critics as Brian McHale and Patricia Waugh. Waugh views the foremost difference between modernism and postmodernism to be the former's lack of the systematic flaunting of artifice in evidence in the latter (Waugh 22), and O'Brien's highly self-reflexive first novel certainly conforms to the latter. Furthermore, *At Swim-Two-Birds* is dominated by overt metaleptic practices and openly reveals each narrative level to have no more legitimacy than any other and in fact calls into question the validity of artistic activity itself, a point echoed by David Cohen who clams that *At Swim-Two-Birds* is "an anatomy of itself, and stands as the record of its own opposition" (228). Waugh also alludes to the self-anatomizing of metafictional texts in the following manner: "For Sterne, as for contemporary writers, the mind is not a perfect aestheticizing instrument. It is not free, and it is as much constructed out of as constructed with, language. The substitution of a purely metaphysical system (as in the case of Proust) or mythical analogy (as with Joyce and Eliot) cannot be accepted as final structures of authority and meaning. Contemporary reflexivity implies an awareness both of language and metalanguage, of consciousness and writing" (24). Brian McHale's perspective that postmodern fictions tend to be dominated by ontological concerns rather than the epistemological questioning that he associates with modernism also appears to be relevant to the clear fascination with multiple ontological levels in *At Swim-Two-Birds*, while O'Brien's fascination with the breaking of frames and mixing of genres also resembles McHale's prescription for postmodern fiction: "Postmodernist fictions, by contrast [with modernist fiction whose associations gel together, i.e. the snowy arctic] often strive to displace and rupture these automatic associations, parodying the encyclopedia and substituting for 'encyclopedic' knowledge, their own *ad hoc*, arbitrary, unsanctioned associations" (48).

Ultimately, innovative work tends to invent or reinvent the categories in which it is positioned, and O'Brien's work, particularly the first two novels, are repeatedly cited as early examples of fiction that came to be termed metafiction or postmodern. That O'Brien in turn was influenced by predecessors from what might be described as a skeptical tradition is certain, something that the author, who framed all of his best work against a backdrop of multiple integrated textual materials, would have openly acknowledged. In addition, despite the apparent relative conservatism of the final two novels, replete with their unevenness as literary texts, O'Brien's work remains aggressively antiformal and essentially at odds with the primary master narratives that retained authority during his lifetime: Irish Catholicism and empirical thinking. Although both of these texts, in places, resort to juvenile in-jokes, the desire to elevate a negative dialectics to a place of prominence remained and, with the other three novels, made a hugely significant contribution to twentieth-century Irish and international literature. But perhaps the truly astonishing feature of O'Brien's body of work is that he managed to publish three significantly different novels within three years, each of which, in its own unique way, made an enormous impact on what is contemporary innovative fiction.

Works Cited

Booker, M. Keith. *Flann O'Brien, Bakhtin, and Menippean Satire.* Syracuse: Syracuse UP, 1995.

Borges, Jorge Luis. *Selected Non-Fictions.* Ed. Eliot Weinberger. New York: Penguin, 1999.

Cohen, David. "An Atomy of the Novel: Flann O'Brien's *At Swim-Two-Birds.*" *Twentieth Century Literature* 39 (1993): 208-29.

Cronin, Anthony. *No Laughing Matter: The Life and Times of Flann O'Brien.* New York: Fromm International, 1998.

Davison, Neil R. " 'We are not a doctor for the body': Catholicism, the Female Grotesque, and Flann O' Brien's *The Hard Life.*" *Literature and Psychology* 45.4 (1994): 31-57.

Farnon, Jane. "Motifs of Gaelic Lore and Literature in *An Béal Bocht.*" *Conjuring Complexities: Essays on Flann O'Brien.* Ed. Anne Clune and Tess Hurson. Belfast: Queen's University of Belfast, 1997. 89-109.

Foster, Thomas C. "Flann O'Brien's *At Swim-Two-Birds.*" *A Casebook on Flann O'Brien's "At Swim-Two-Birds."* Ed. Thomas C. Foster. Center for Book Culture. <http://www.centerforbookculture.org>.

Hassan, Ihab. *The Postmodern Turn: Essays in Postmodern Theory and Culture.* Columbus: Ohio State UP, 1987.

Hopper, Keith. *A Portrait of the Artist as a Young Postmodernist.* Cork: Cork UP, 1995.

Higgins, Aidan. "The Hidden Narrator." *Asylum Arts Review* 1.1 (1996): 2-7.

Hurson, Tess. "Conspicuous Absences: *The Hard Life.*" *Conjuring Complexities: Essays on Flann O'Brien.* Ed. Anne Clune and Tess Hurson. Belfast: Queen's University of Belfast, 1997. 119-31.

Lowenkron, David Henry. "The Metanovel." *College English* 38 (1976): 343-55.

McHale, Brian. *Postmodernist Fiction.* London: Routledge, 1987.

McKibben, Sarah. "*The Poor Mouth*: A Parody of (Post) Colonial Irish Manhood." *Research in African Literatures* 34.4 (2003): 96-114.

O'Brien, Flann. *At Swim-Two-Birds.* 1939. Normal, IL: Dalkey Archive Press, 2005.

—. *The Dalkey Archive*. 1964. Normal, IL: Dalkey Archive Press, 1993.

—. *The Hard Life*. 1961. Normal, IL: Dalkey Archive Press, 1994.

—. *The Poor Mouth: A Bad Story about the Hard Life*. 1941. Trans. Patrick C. Power. Normal, IL: Dalkey Archive Press, 1996.

—. *The Third Policeman*. 1967. Normal, IL: Dalkey Archive Press, 1999.

Ó'Crohán, Tomás. *The Islandman*. Trans. Robin Flower. Oxford: Oxford UP, 1993.

Shea, Thomas F. *Flann O'Brien's Exorbitant Novels*. Lewisburg: Bucknell UP, 1992.

—. "Patrick McGinley's Impressions of Flann O'Brien: *The Devil's Diary* and *At Swim-Two-Birds*. *Twentieth Century Literature* 40 (1994): 272-81.

Spindler, William. "Magic Realism: A Typology." *Forum for Modern Language Studies* 29.1 (1993): 75-85.

Waugh, Patricia. *Metafiction: The Theory and Practice of Self-Conscious Fiction*. London: Methuen, 1984.

A Flann O'Brien Checklist

Novels

At Swim-Two-Birds. London: Longmans, Green, 1939; Normal, IL: Dalkey Archive Press, 2005.

The Third Policeman. London: MacGibbon & Kee, 1967; Normal, IL: Dalkey Archive Press, 1999.

An Béal Bocht: nó an milleánac: droc-sgéal ar an droc-saogal. Dublin: National Press, 1941; *The Poor Mouth: A Bad Story about the Hard Life.* Trans. Patrick C. Power. London: Hart-Davis, MacGibbon, 1973; Normal, IL: Dalkey Archive Press, 1996.

The Hard Life. London: MacGibbon & Kee, 1961; Normal, IL: Dalkey Archive Press, 1994.

The Dalkey Archive. London: MacGibbon & Kee, 1964; Normal, IL: Dalkey Archive Press, 1993.

Collections

The Best of Myles: A Selection from "Cruiskeen Lawn." Ed. Kevin O'Nolan. London: MacGibbon & Kee, 1968; Normal, IL: Dalkey Archive Press, 1999.

Stories and Plays. London: Hart-Davis, MacGibbon, 1973.

Further Cuttings from "Cruiskeen Lawn." Ed. Kevin O'Nolan. London: Hart-Davis, MacGibbon, 1976; Normal, IL: Dalkey Archive Press, 2000.

The Hair of the Dogma: Further Cuttings from "Cruiskeen Lawn." Ed. Kevin O'Nolan. London: Hart-Davis, MacGibbon, 1977.

A Flann O'Brien Reader. Ed. Stephen Jones. New York: Viking, 1978.

Myles away from Dublin. Ed. Martin Green. London: Granada, 1985.

Myles before Myles. Ed. John Wyse Jackson. London: Grafton, 1988.

At War. Ed. John Wyse Jackson. London: Gerald Duckworth, 1999; Normal, IL: Dalkey Archive Press, 2003.

Guy Davenport

David Cozy

It is no surprise that Guy Davenport admired the work of Henry Darger. Beginning with the landlords who discovered Darger's immense project when they went to clean out his apartment after the artist's death, every discerning viewer who has encountered it has been impressed. What is refreshing, given that Darger usually has the epithet "outsider" hurled at him, even by those who mean to praise his work, is that Davenport recognized Darger's true worth. "Far from being a folk artist doing 'outsider art,'" Davenport wrote, "Darger was an accomplished writer and illustrator who had the integrity to work in peaceful solitude from 1912 until his death in 1973" ("Illuminations" 966). Davenport's sympathetic understanding of Darger had its source, one imagines, in his own life. Davenport, too, chose integrity and peaceful solitude and therefore, like Darger, remained outside the dominant (not to say vulgar) paradigm. Rather than involve himself in literary-artistic fads and fashions, he chose instead, from his Lexington, Kentucky, fastness, to do his bit toward extending what he called "the long duration of a European literature from Homer to Joyce" ("Hunter Gracchus" 8). He did so with his translations from the Greek, Latin, and other languages, with the masterful essays he gave us on topics from Kafka to Jesus to Zukofsky to table-manners, with (somewhat more obliquely) his painting, drawing, and illustration, but perhaps most strikingly he did so with his fiction.

Born in Anderson, South Carolina, in 1927, Davenport studied English and classics at Duke University before a Rhodes scholarship took him to Oxford where he wrote the first thesis ever accepted at that institution on James Joyce. From there, with two years out for a stint in the military during World War II, he moved on to Harvard and completed his dissertation on the first thirty of Ezra Pound's cantos. In 1963, having taught at Washington University, Harvard University, and Haverford College, he accepted a position at the University of Kentucky, where he remained until his retirement from teaching in 1991. He lived in Lexington, Kentucky, for more than forty years.

This sketchy biography is, Davenport would probably have said, irrelevant. "I have no life," he told the *Paris Review* interviewer John Jeremiah Sullivan (50), and in so saying, he affirms that, like Darger, he was uninterested in celebrity and that, like the modernists who were his first scholarly focus and a continuing inspiration, he took the work, not the life, to be the thing. Sullivan reports that in the course of that interview, whenever "some question strayed too close to what Davenport deemed personal, he would interrupt by saying, matter-of-factly, 'I thought we were talking about my work'" (46). And Davenport, of course, was right. It is the work that we should be talking about.

As Wyatt Mason wrote in his review of Davenport's final collection, *The Death of Picasso: New & Selected Writing*, Davenport's first published stories appeared in the 1940s in the Duke University literary magazine. "In tone and language, subject and theme," Mason tells us, "all of Davenport's early stories were Southern Stories" (Mason 88).[1] After leaving Duke, Davenport ceased publishing not just Southern fiction, but all fiction. Though he kept his pen busy with reviews, essays, translations, and scholarly articles, he published no stories between 1949 and 1969. His first collection, *Tatlin!*, named for an obscure Russian constructivist artist and designer, did not appear until 1974, and so different was it from what had come before that one would be excused for believing that the stories collected in this volume had come from a different hand altogether.

Tatlin! (1974)

Tatlin! is the best place to begin a consideration of Guy Davenport's fiction, and that is not only because it comes first. It is ideal because, like many major artists, Davenport had a set of concerns, interests, and methods to which he returned again and again, and though many of these concerns, interests, and methods had first surfaced in the reviews, essays, and scholarly articles Davenport produced in the decades during which he published no stories, they get their first fictional treatment in the tales collected in *Tatlin!* As Davenport explained to a critic who had misunderstood them, these stories "imagine the tragic endurance of a Russian genius within the Soviet tyranny, the psychological temper of a few days in Kafka's life, the discovery of the prehistoric paintings at Lascaux, Herakleitos talking with a disciple, an entertaining lie of Poe's taken at face value, and the life of a modern Dutch philosopher whose studies of Samuel Butler and Charles Fourier constitute a critique of European history" ("Life of the Mind").

We see in these stories Davenport's interest in figures such as Kafka and Tatlin, artists who, like Darger and like Davenport himself, had the integrity to do their work in spite of publics and institutions uninterested, uncomprehending, and sometimes hostile. (Kafka will return as a character in more than one of Davenport's fictions.) In Lascaux and Herakleitos we see the archaic, a past that, as both a classicist and a student of modernism, Davenport finds again, still vital, in the work of artists such as Picasso. And in Davenport's life of the Dutch philosopher Adriaan Floris van Hovendaal we find a critique not only of European history but of the European and American present as well, a present in which adults police their own sexuality as vigorously as they deny that children have sexuality. Modernism and modernists; the archaic in the modern in the archaic; the imagining of a society in which relationships, including sexual relationships, of adults and children and between adults and children, are conducted in a manner more humane than they are at present: all of these return again and again in Davenport's work.

Likewise, the methods Davenport employs in *Tatlin!* include many to which he will return: the use of drawings, pictures, and collages as components of his stories; prose, ranging from the severely classical to the exquisitely ornate, beautiful in either mode thanks to the care that Davenport—also a poet—lavished upon it; the avoidance of simple first-this-happened-then-that-happened narratives; and the use of quotations and allusions drawn from a mind at home with the Western tradition (and not only the Western tradition) from Homer through the modernists and beyond. These qualities and concerns occur throughout the collection, and indeed most are present in its first story, the tale from which the collection takes its title: "Tatlin!"

Learning that "Tatlin!" recounts the story of an artist of that name who actually existed, a contemporary of Khlebnikov, Mandelstam, Chagall, and Picasso, one may expect—or dread—a conventional historical fiction festooned, as such fictions so often are, with fustian. Davenport, however, has written a different sort of tale, and perhaps one factor that prompted him to do so is that Tatlin, like many of the characters and historical events that Davenport chooses to consider, is "in the position of being, as fact, almost not there" ("Ernst Machs Max Ernst" 376). Thus Davenport was able to build his portrait of Tatlin out of imagination informed by scholarship and an eye for what would produce the most compelling pattern rather than the scattering of cherry-picked details a lesser writer would flaunt in the interest of creating atmosphere. Davenport explains, "Verisimilitude of the kind invented by Scott and Flaubert, which achieved its apotheosis in D. W. Griffith's and Cecil B. De Mille's movie sets, I sidestepped at the outset, trying instead for Kafka's description of America (skyscrapers symmetrically placed in wheatfields, the Statue of Liberty with a sword in her hand)" ("Ernst Machs Max Ernst" 376-77). For a character as elusive as Vladimir Tatlin, this approach is appropriate. It is not too much to say that Davenport pioneered a new sort of historical fiction, one as rich in imagination and formal integrity as in period detail, and he had the skill to bring it off.

We might, looking at the first page of the story, believe that we are in for a straightforward account. There is the title, "Tatlin!," and then a section heading, "Moscow 1932." This is conventional enough. The second page of the story, however, is not text at all, but a picture, a rendering of the artist Tatlin before a constructivist work of art. What used to be called comic books and are now called graphic novels have thrived for years (and the illustrated book has been around for centuries), but back when *Tatlin!* appeared, with rare exceptions, picture books were not to be confused with literature. Thus early readers of this tale might well have found the illustrations jarring, and one guesses that even readers in our own image-saturated age may have difficulty knowing what to make of them. Realizing this, Davenport in later years came to believe that the pictures he included with some of his texts were "a great flop. A bomb that never detonated." "People reading the stories," he lamented, "do not look at the pictures" (qtd. in Sullivan 61).

The failure to do so is a great mistake.[2] James Joyce famously said of *Ulysses*, "I can justify every line" (Ellmann 715), and in this respect (as in others) Davenport is the most Joycean of writers. Attention must be paid not only to every line of a Davenport story but also to every picture, and one must notice not only what the pictures contain but also how the images are distributed in the narrative. Studying their placement in "Tatlin!," we note that, though they do not correspond in any simple way with the text around them, they do provide a neat synopsis of the life of Tatlin and also of the life of Russian futurism: initial exuberance ultimately crushed by a state with which Tatlin and his fellow constructivists had—or so they believed—fleetingly been allied.

Carefully positioned throughout the account, the illustrations occur in this order: a picture of Tatlin posing before a constructivist artwork (2); portraits of Lenin posing before the Soviet flag (4, 15); renderings of artwork by Tatlin (20, 22, 24, 26, 28); the portrait of Lenin again (32); and then, ominously, Stalin in a military uniform looking off into the future, stern (38, 44, 49). Fleshing out the narrative these pictures suggest is not difficult. We begin with Tatlin as a young dandy—he sports striped trousers and cradles a straw boater in the portrait on page two—proud of the work he is doing; next, the five examples of Tatlin's art that are presented between portraits of Lenin suggest that Tatlin thrived during those years in spite of the clouds already gathering. Finally, when Stalin appears, Tatlin and his art disappear: lucky though he was not to have been murdered, the artist has been marginalized, removed—in the best Soviet style—from the picture.

The twelve pictures Davenport has given us and the tale they tell play off of the story—better, stories—told by the sixteen blocks of text that accompany them. The account presented in what we might think of as the textual panels—bits of Russian history, Soviet history, Tatlin's history—is less straightforward than the one that can be derived from Davenport's artwork. The words, that is, do not illustrate the images. Rather, in the manner of a modernist collage, the different pieces, visual and textual, resonate more or less dissonantly and in doing so create a whole greater than the parts. As has been noted, Davenport's dissertation was on Pound (published in 1983 as *Cities on Hills: A Study of I-XXX of Ezra Pound's Cantos*). In "Tatlin!" Pound's influence can be seen in Davenport's arrangement of the pieces of his story, the pictures and blocks of print (blocks of print that might themselves be collages of allusions, quotations, translations, and straightforward narration). Pound referred to such pieces as "luminous details" (Kenner 152). Most of Davenport's best stories take the form of luminous details expertly organized into what he called *assemblages*.

Told for the most part in simple prose (words of one syllable make up a large percentage of the story's vocabulary), "Tatlin!," though remarkably rich in reference, is less allusive than much of Davenport's work. Nevertheless, there is a great deal here to delight an active mind. Tatlin, pondering his great project, for example, remembers an earlier formalist: "*We must grasp nature*, Cézanne said, as *cylinder, sphere, cone*. Cézanne + Lenin = Konstruktivizm." Thus, "Tatlin's monument to the Third International was to have been a cylinder above a cone above a cube within a spiral half a mile tall." We know, of course, that this incredible edifice was never constructed, and we wonder whether a creation at once "a building, a sculpture, a painting, a poem, a book, a moving picture, a *construct*" ever could exist outside the mind of Tatlin, or a story of Davenport's (41). Even as we share Tatlin's enthusiasm (and Davenport's for Tatlin's project) we know—portraits of Stalin loom—the tale can have no happy ending.

In the last section of the story, headed "1953," we find Tatlin in internal exile, discussing with Viktor Shklovsky Stalin's death.

> —Will they publish your books, build my tower, open the jails?
> —It is only Stalin who is dead.
> —Aren't we all? (51)

Shklovsky leaves. We remain with Tatlin, contemplate a glider, "imagine it agile as a bat over rivers, lakes, and fields" (51). "If Tatlin had built his air bicycle," Davenport later remarked, "the first thing he would have done is flown across the border and gotten out of Stalin's Russia" (qtd. in Sullivan 64). Tatlin's "air bicycle" is far from being the last flying machine we encounter in this collection. Flight, and the freedom it implies, is one of the threads that makes *Tatlin!* not just a collection of stories but a unified work.

In twelve pictures and sixteen blocks of text, "Tatlin!" gives us the story of the life, from childhood to old age, of a little-known modernist artist. The next story in the collection, "The Aeroplanes at Brescia," is an account of just a few days in the life of a modernist who, but for accidents of history and fortunate friendships, might be as little known and celebrated today as Tatlin. The artist in question this time is Franz Kafka, the days in question those he spent at an air show in Brescia in 1909. Davenport writes,

> Kafka's account of this event is his first published writing, and as he could not in 1909 know the significance of what he had seen, I combined his newspaper article with Brod's memory of the occasion in his biography of Kafka, and with what I could discover of other people (D'Anunzio, Puccini) who were there, as well as of people who might have been there (Wittgenstein). To realize certain details I studied the contemporary photographs of Count Primoli, read histories of aviation, built a model of Blériot's Antoinette CV25, and collected as rich a gathering of allusions to the times as I could. I presided over the story like a Calvinist God who knew what would happen in the years to come. ("Ernst Machs Max Ernst" 374)

One would be forgiven for believing that such a weight of scholarship would break the back of a story not twenty pages long, but somehow it does not. In fact Davenport's research fortifies the fiction and does so in a way that has become increasingly rare. Feeling in our time is privileged over fact; Davenport, not a devotee of art as self-expression, reminds us that feeling is not necessarily first, that it is possible, in building stories, to eschew gushes of emotion in favor of information, all that one can take in through the senses and synthesize in the mind of the boom and buzz of the world.[3] In "Tatlin!," in "The Aeroplanes at Brescia," and in much of the rest of his fiction (as well as his essays) Davenport put to good use the information he had acquired about a subject after—as he described it— "falling in interest" with it (qtd. in Sullivan 64). His coinage parallels, of course, "falling in love," and with that in mind we understand that it was not some obsessive need to bone up that drove him but rather pleasure in knowing, a passion that was the seed that so often blossomed into fiction unique in the density of information it contained.

Knowledge as pleasure is a recurring motif in Davenport's work. One sees it throughout the remaining stories in this collection. In "Robot," for example, the account of the discovery of the cave paintings at Lascaux, we are privileged not only to learn about the archeologist Henri Breuil but also to encounter, in the course of Breuil's table-talk, an excellent exegesis of one of Picasso's masterpieces: "This man Picasso *is* a painter from the Reindeer Age. The *Guernica* with its wounded horse, its hieratic bull, its placing of images over images, is a prehistoric painting. It honors and grieves and stands in awe" (99). One doesn't know whether these are words Davenport put in Breuil's mouth or words he has encountered in the course of learning about Breuil (the latter, one suspects). Whatever their provenance, placed just so, they contribute to the overall liveliness of the tale Davenport tells. Equally rich in savory knowledge, the account of a sort of dim protoacademic meeting Herakleitos, "one of the local magicians or wise men or grammarians," gives us a sense of how the pre-Socratic "dark one" might have put his wisdom—his epigrams are scattered throughout the story—into practice in his life (113). And in the extrapolation on Poe's lie—he put it about that "he had gone to Saint Petersburg to enlist with some Russians to go and fight for Greek independence" (qtd. in Alpert 9)—we get an opening paragraph that is not only arresting but packed with information: "On the first night of the century Piazzi found the planet Ceres. It was in Saint Petersburg one bright morning when I was taking chocolate with the younger Prince Potyomkin of Tavris that I appreciated the flawless beauty of the Sicilian eye fulfilling the prognostications of Titius and Bode, whose mathematics indicated that there must be a planet whose orbit lies between Mars and Jupiter" (120). One may decide to find out immediately about Piazzi and Ceres (not to mention Titius and Bode) or make a note to look them up later or simply, caught up in the eccentric erudition, read on. Whichever road one chooses, one will be enriched.

Stuffed even fuller of erudition's plums than anything else in this very rich collection is the novella-length "The Dawn at Erewhon," the first published example of what Robert Kelly calls Davenport's idylls. He coins this term to use in opposition to the "inventions," the strand of Davenport's fiction we have examined thus far (Kelly 40). Kelly's taxonomy is useful. The idylls are significant and significantly different from stories such as those that precede "The Dawn at Erewhon" in *Tatlin!* Much that is nonexistent, barely hinted at, or left implicit in the inventions is, in the idylls, rolled out into the sun. Davenport unlocks his word hoard—peering through cracks, we have already seen hints of its riches: chirr, besom, peplum, and pinguid. He begins to elucidate a surprisingly romantic and inspiring utopianism, and, inextricable from that utopia, he begins to show us people—sometimes young people, sometimes, yes, children—who are freely and gleefully sexual.

"The Dawn at Erewhon" is written in two strands. One is set in a sort of contemporary Holland of the mind—it's not unlike the actual place but not entirely synonymous with it either—and the other is an account of a utopia that draws on elements of Charles Fourier's Harmony and Samuel Butler's Erewhon. Erewhon, of course, is nowhere, and as Davenport has pointed out, "Holland is the nether land" (qtd. in Alpert 10). In Davenport's Holland lives a philosopher called Adriaan Floris van Hovendaal,[4] who is, Davenport says, "Ludwig Wittgenstein opened up." He explains: "We know very little about Wittgenstein's sex life, but it seems to have been agonized and horrendous. And that he suffered a great deal because he could not absorb it. So I imagine a modern Dutchman who does express himself with his body as well as his mind and . . . (or at least I want to suggest this) he lands in Erewhon" (qtd. in Alpert 10). Thus we understand why the accounts of Hovendaal's life are mingled with tales of a traveler in a machine-free utopia, and we see, as the story proceeds, as Hovendaal jubilates in his body and his mind, that the two strands, separate at the beginning, must tangle and become one.

Late in the story Adriaan's friends and lovers Kaatje and Bruno are concluding a session of joyful sex while Adriaan, in the same room and not a bit uncomfortable, putters around preparing dinner: "Bruno withdrew, holding a deep tongue-winding kiss, a salamander wiggle for a coda. Adriaan lifted him up from licking his way down her tummy, swung him around swimming free, and set him balking and laughing before the fire" (238). Adriaan exchanges a few lines of banter with the lovers, and then we are in the Erewhon/Harmony, which has hitherto been kept apart from the sections about Hovendaal's life: "The children with Tartar sleeves rode their quaggas down a road that wound through fields of tall and yellow wheat. Larks whirred, butterflies zigzagged over the tassels, the red flags flounced and rippled like the hair of a noble horseman from the mythology of the Samoyeds" (238). We remain in this nether land for a couple of paragraphs and then we return to the room in the more real-seeming Holland, but we now perceive that this room is also Erewhon, a place where lovers are friends and don't know jealousy or pettiness, a place where history seldom intrudes—seldom, but not never.

Bruno and Adriaan, traveling in Greece, encounter some German tourists and react differently. "You saw Germans," Bruno says, "I saw neat bodies all tan and toned and hung like horses, and trim Italian bikes and rucksacks with all those buckles and snaps" (254). The bad history—Adriaan, but not Bruno, is old enough to remember Amsterdam during World War II—is displaced by the sensuality and friendship of the German boys (not to mention the exquisite design of Italian bicycles). Adriaan had been momentarily summoned by history away from Erewhon; Bruno, who brings him back to it, sees the Germans, as Adriaan observes, "with a lovely imagination, with Eros' own eyes" (254). Utopia—Bruno's vision rather than the darker one that had momentarily bewitched Adriaan—wins in "The Dawn at Erewhon," and this is, of course, no accident. Davenport is consciously creating for his characters an alternative: "I could have looked at it another way [he explained] and the story would be quite tragic and terrifying. But I chose to look at it through [Adriaan's] own eyes. That if he can have a moment of sensual pleasure, in his furtiveness, then I can zone away the world for a while" (qtd. in Alpert 10). The play of pronouns in the last sentence of the quotation is striking. Davenport, it seems, was creating an alternative not only for his characters but also for himself, an alternative always threatened (there recur, in the story, contrasted to the green and fecund earth, images of a lifeless moon). To take Davenport's words out of context, the beguiling Erewhonian alternative is "almost not there."

Da Vinci's Bicycle: Ten Stories (1979)

Mao Tse-tung, Richard Nixon, Leonardo da Vinci, Gertrude Stein, Alice Toklas: these are just a few of the figures who appear in Guy Davenport's second collection, Da Vinci's Bicycle. (Actually, they all appear in the first story.) Davenport continues here to construct assemblages made up of both fact and what he has called "necessary fiction" (qtd. in Hoepffner 122). Likewise, Davenport continues in these stories to arrange details, luminous and carefully selected, into patterns that delight. He has written that "a page, which I think of as a picture, is essentially a texture of images" ("Ernst Machs Max Ernst" 374), and the images and the textures he has made on these pages, the arrangements of information both visual and textual, are delightfully complex. Readers who know the pleasure of pursuing meaning, of sliding the pieces of a difficult text together for themselves, will find a great deal to relish in these stories.

Davenport, who felt that "all of my short-story volumes are books, rather than merely collections" (qtd. in Sullivan 69), suggested that the unifying principle of Da Vinci's Bicycle was his discovery "that dialogue is not responses but soliloquies, [that people] talk at each other, not to" (qtd. in Sullivan 76). This is certainly evident in the exchange between Richard Nixon and the Chinese government official, Marshal Yeh Chien-ying, which opens the first story in the collection, "The Richard Nixon Freischütz Rag." The story begins with Nixon's responses to what he is seeing in China: "I think you would have to conclude that this is a great wall," and later, "It is worth coming sixteen thousand miles to see the Wall." After visiting the tombs of the Ming emperors, he acknowledges, "It is worth coming to see these, too" (1). Yeh, perhaps growing tired of Nixon's constant and banal praise of monuments of Chinese antiquity, attempts to divert him into the present with an observation made by Nixon's counterpart: "Chairman Mao says . . . that the past is past" (1). Nixon is merely befuddled by this interruption of his soliloquy: "All over?" he wonders (1).

The exchange continues for a page or two and is, to be sure, funny ("We don't see many pictures of Engels in America, Richard Nixon explained" (3)), but where a lesser writer, having struck that humorous vein, might have mined it for many pages Davenport is not content with easy chuckles. Instead he moves his readers quickly on to the next panel in his *assemblage*, and entering that panel, we begin to understand the larger pattern of which Nixon's banalities—however amusing—are only a part.

We shift from Nixon and Yeh to Leonardo and his young protégé, Salai, and in so doing, we enter another world. Nixon's comments on the wall and the tombs are devoid of real content. He does not describe the places, gives us no sense of what they look like, smell like, feel like—no sense, in fact, that he took anything at all away from the experience of seeing them. One suspects that this is because, though he was in their presence, he never really saw them at all, and lack of attention, in Davenport's world, is the cardinal sin. Contrast Nixon's obliviousness with the detailed account of Leonardo's latest invention, something called a *due rote*: "You turned the pedals with your feet, which turned the big cog wheel, which pulled the chain forward, cog by cog, causing the smaller wheel to turn the hind *rota*, thereby propelling the whole machine forward" (4); or compare it to Leonardo's joy at what the morning light does to his studio's clutter: "Meadow grass from Fiesole, icosahedra, cogs, gears, plaster, maps, lutes, brushes, an adze, magic squares, pigments, a Roman head Brunelleschi and Donatello brought him from their excavations, the skeleton of a bird: how beautifully the Tuscan light gave him his things again every morning, even if the kite had been in his sleep" (3). It becomes clear that Davenport is showing us different ways of being in the world, and it is not hard to see which one he prefers. We remain in this better place, however, for only a few paragraphs. Davenport jars us out of Leonardo's Tuscany with: "Before flying to China Richard Nixon ordered a thousand targets in Laos and Cambodia bombed by squadrons of B-52s" (5), and from that harsh start we proceed to more sayings of Richard M. Nixon, such as, of his and Kissinger's flight to China, "We came by way of Guam," a line so good he repeats it (though he tells us nothing, really, of the flight or of Guam) (5, 6). We are grateful when the scene shifts once again to "Roses, buttons, thimbles, lace" (6), and we find ourselves with Stein and Toklas on an outing in Spain. The language, appropriately, turns Steinian and romantic: "When you smile, I say, I bite into peaches and Casals plays Corelli and my soul is a finch in cherries" (8). The story ends with one more Nixonian panel, his audience with Mao Tse-tung, and the shape of the story becomes clear. The structure of "The Richard Nixon Freischütz Rag" is A-B¹-A-B²-A where A stands for a Nixonian world, sexless, blind, banal, and at war, and B stands for alternatives: Leonardo with his learning and his delight in the young scamp Salai; Gertrude with her language and her happy companionship with Alice. Personal joys are set against the political ponderousness of Nixon and his Chinese counterparts, and—in Davenport's fictional world, anyway—personal joys win the day.

The story is its form: the placing of the A sections next to the B sections, the darkness the Nixonian panels cast over the utopian ones they surround. In making form integral to the story's meaning, Davenport once again demonstrates his allegiance to modernism. In fact, however, the form of "The Richard Nixon Freischütz Rag," as exquisitely done as it is, comes to seem simple next to some of the more complex designs he uses in this collection.

As and Bs such as those employed above are often called into play when discussing musical forms (and we were, in fact, examining a "rag"). As instrumental music is not *about* anything, we have no problem viewing it in purely formal terms, and those terms come in handy when considering formally elaborate literature. "Au Tombeau de Charles Fourier" is the most formally adventurous story in this very adventurous collection, and once again, musical analogies—not for the last time—spring to mind. "Au Tombeau" is a fuguelike composition as elaborate as any of J. S. Bach's. Themes are introduced, appear in different guises and mingle with their original iterations, disappear, reappear, mutate, and mingle again. Davenport has written of texts such as this one that, "no architectonic work is paraphrasable, for it differs from other narrative in that the meaning shapes into a web, or a globe, rather than along a line" ("Narrative Tone" 318). Thus one cannot paraphrase "Au Tombeau de Charles Fourier," for, like "The Richard Nixon Freischütz Rag," it is its form. That form can, however, be described.

And in fact, it is described in the story itself. Davenport is reputed to be an extraordinarily difficult author, but those who are willing to read his work with a modicum of care will find that often just a line or a paragraph or a page after a knotty bit there is an explanation of the arcane allusion, a translation of those sentences in Latin, a referent provided for the reference that seemed obscure. Readers wondering why "Au Tombeau" is made up, for example, of 266 parts will find an answer in the Dogon creation myth that makes up one of the subjects of this fugue:

Divide the table into quarters, north east south west. Divide each
quarter into sixty-four parts. Count them: you have two hundred and
fifty-six parts. Add two numbers for each crossline that first divided
the table into quarters, and two for the navel.

These are the two hundred sixty-six things out of which Amma made
the world. (81)

Eleven of the 266 things out of which "Au Tombeau" is made
are collages. The remaining 255 are blocks of text, all but one of
which is four lines long and all but three of which occur in sections
made up of nine four-line blocks. The effect, as Andre Furlani has
noted, is "a grid-like appearance . . . [that] . . . coincides with the
grid on which the Dogon map out the cosmos" ("When Novelists"
120). As for the content to be woven through this grid, Davenport
has explained that "Au Tombeau" is about "foraging and [the story]
proceeds like an Ernst collage to involve seven themes, or *involucra*,
which when opened disclose the theme of foraging in various senses
(Gertrude Stein and cubists; wasps; the Dogon and their forager
god Ogo; Charles Fourier and his utopian New Harmony; the flying
machine, a bionic wasp as developed by Blériot and the Wrights;
the French photographer Lartigue who made all his masterpieces
with a child's intuition before he reached adolescence; and myself)"
("Ernst Machs Max Ernst" 379-80).

The usual suspects are on hand, one might remark, noting again
the appearance of Stein, Fourier, and early aviators such as Blériot
and the Wright brothers. As always, however, Davenport finds new
things to tell us about them and new ways of telling. Of Fourier,
dead, he writes, "He lies under a slant stone bearing at its corners
parabola, hyperbola, circle, ellipse. Bones, buttons, dust of flesh.
High the jugal line would jut, and mortal holes gape where once there
had been the iambus of a wink, a dust of flowers sifted through his
ribs" (68). And of Ogo, the Dogon trickster: "You clabber the milk,
mother the beer, wart the hand, trip the runner, burn the roast,
lame the goat, blister the heel, pip the hen, crack the cistern, botch
the millet, scald the baby, sour the stew, knock stars from the sky,
and all for fun, all for fun" (86). One could, from this story, offer
253 more examples of the sparkle, wit, and invention of Davenport's
prose. The point, however, is made: Davenport's attention to form
is matched by genius at the level of the sentence, the word. He was
incapable of producing boring prose.

Davenport identified one of the themes of "Au Tombeau de Charles
Fourier" as "myself." A section of "Au Tombeau" is a straightforward
account of a conversation he had with Samuel Beckett, and that the
author, however sketchily, allows himself to appear is a rare event in
Davenport's fictional world. He was that increasingly extraordinary

thing: a writer less interested in himself than in the world of which he is a part. He included the anecdote because, he explained, it "belonged to the pattern I was making and not to autobiography" ("Ernst Machs Max Ernst" 380). "Ithaka," is also an account based on an actual experience, a meeting with Pound and Olga Rudge at a time when Pound had all but given up speaking. Davenport's appearance here is similar to that in "Au Tombeau" in that the events of his encounter with Pound and Rudge seem more fraught with symbols—a mouse in a tree, Pound swimming too far from the shore—than pure memoir could bear. "Ithaka" is the last time we will get anything this close to autobiographical fiction from Davenport. As fine as "Ithaka" and the fragment in "Au Tombeau" are, however, one never deplores Davenport's reticence. His fictional renderings of Victor Hugo and Robert Walser, of a stoic philosopher on a chain gang (who is also Ezra Pound), of a trip through Greece newly colonized by Rome, of the history of photography, of the various meanings a dove can have—to name as examples only the subjects treated in this collection—are more than enough to satisfy.

Eclogues: Eight Stories (1981)

Guy Davenport never wrote a novel.[5] He did, however, produce two novel-length series of stories, the first of which, begun in *Tatlin!* with "The Dawn at Erewhon," continues in *Eclogues* with "The Death of Picasso." The protagonist is once again the Dutch philosopher Adriaan Floris van Hovendaal, but Davenport's method has changed. In "The Dawn at Erewhon" Davenport combined entries from Adriaan's journal with third-person accounts of the philosopher's life. In "The Death of Picasso" Davenport dispenses with the narrator and makes his tale entirely out of pieces of the philosopher's journal. These pieces, these luminous details—a memory here, a philosophical musing there, the exegesis of a painting, a bit of day-to-day life—occurring in the seemingly random order in which they might appear in an actual journal, are, taken together, a portrait of Hovendaal. As we construct this portrait out of notes written in the *schetsboek*, fragments and shards, different views, we realize that we are reading not a story about Picasso but a story done in the manner of Picasso.

It is the bits of day-to-day life (think of the buttons, the mustaches, the bits of newspaper in a cubist portrait) weaving through Adriaan's more scholarly musings that provide the narrative that makes the journal entries cohere. Adriaan, we learn, has agreed to take into his custody a reforming juvenile delinquent—his "crimes" seem mostly sexual—called Sander. They spend three months together in a one-room cabin on a tiny island in the Baltic Sea, and we watch, through the lens of Adriaan's journal, friendship and passion grow up between them and see—sexual tension ever rising—the different ways they respond to these forces. The result is a narrative no less gripping than that of "Death in Venice," the tale that may have inspired it. Indeed, "The Death of Picasso" and "Death in Venice" appear to be mirror images, Mann's tale singing of decadence and death, Davenport's exuberance and life.

Though it needs to be teased out from the entries in Adriaan's journal, "The Death of Picasso" has a clear narrative line. This is far from being the case with "Lo Splendore della Luce a Bologna," a story that entirely dispenses with "story." It is made of seventeen sections linked not so much by causal or temporal progression as by the consciousness of T. E. Hulme and the light that illuminates the Bologna in which he finds himself. The importance of form is foregrounded as early as the second section, which reads in its entirety: "In the morning, sipping coffee, Mr. Hulme could find no proportion in the arcades, the buildings, the windows, the campanile, the duomi, the typography of the newspaper, that was not perfect. The children and the old people made him sad. All ideas rise like music from the physical" (125). Just as Davenport's Bologna is perfect in its windows, its newsprint, its campanile, so his story, in its luminous details—Ernst Mach talking about William James, Bolognese street scenes, Hulme explaining who's who in philosophy in England—is also exquisite. The proof of this is that, just as the formal excellence of Bologna produces, ultimately, a sadness in Hulme when he considers the old people and children living in its midst, so we begin to feel a sadness when we consider the fate of T. E. Hulme and the generation of which he would become emblematic. Davenport has written: "What the war blighted was a renaissance as brilliant as any in history which we can only know by the survivors and the early work of the dead—the Alain-Fourniers (Battle of the Meuse, 1914), Sant' Elias (Montfalcone, 1914), Apollinaires (1918), Gaudiers" ("Pound Vortex" 166). Between the Sant' Elias and the Apollinaires, in this catalog, one must place "the Hulmes (1917)."

It is not only ideas that rise like music from the physical. Emotions do too. The final section of the story reads, "The full moon rose over the pines like the red face of a jolly farmer above a hedge" (134). This is based on a line from Hulme's 1909 poem "Autumn," one of the twenty or so poems that comprise his complete poetic oeuvre (he was dead at thirty-two). To finish on that note, however, would be to give the impression that the entire effect of "Lo Splendore della Luce a Bologna" is gloom. It is not. Hulme and the philosophers among whom he finds himself—the city of Bologna too—are brimming with high spirits, humor, and hope for the new age that they believe is upon them. When the train carrying the philosophers arrives in Bologna, for example:

>—*Viva la filosofia!* cried the crowd.
>—*Portabagagli!*
>—*La bandiera rossa trionferà!*
>—*È vergine la mia sorella!*
>—*Benvenuto, stregoni!*
>—*A chi piace una banana?*
>—*Alle baricate!*
>—*Siempre Marconi!*
>—*Carrozze!*
>—*Viva la filosofia!* (125)

It is from this sort of high-spiritedness that—when we remember the fate of Hulme and his generation—the sadness, like music, rises. One may or may not agree with John Berger's assertion that "it is scarcely any longer possible to tell a straight story sequentially unfolding in time" (46), but what Davenport demonstrates conclusively in fictions such as "Lo Splendore" is that it is not necessary to do so and that choosing not to tell a "straight story" need not result in tales that forego laughter and tears. Nonlinear *assemblages* such as Davenport's are capable of producing both.

Laughter will be the predominant reaction to "Christ Preaching at the Henley Regatta," a sort of translation into prose of "Christ Preaching at the Cookham Regatta," an unfinished painting by the English artist Stanley Spencer. Davenport has written that Spencer's painting "was going to be a very crowded, Bosch-like tangle of people, picnicking, and punts. A great deal of eighteenth-century British humor," he explained, "comes from too many people in a space (Rowlandson, Hogarth, Smollet)" ("Stanley Spencer" 122). This describes well the humor of Davenport's very crowded tale. A paragraph will serve to give a sense of the story's exuberance:

> There milled and trod and eddied a flock of little girls with the faces of eager mice, a family from Guernsey all in yellow hats, Mr. C. S. Lewis of Belfast in belling, baggy, blown trousers and flexuous flopping jacket, his chins working like a bullfrog's, tars from the H.M.S. *Dogfish* with rolling shoulders and saucy eyes, pickpockets, top-hatted Etonians chatting each other in blipped English, a bishop in gaiters regarding with unbelieving mouth a Florentine philosopher peeing against a wall, Mallarmé wrapped in plaid shawl rapt. (95)

More quietly exuberant but just as celebratory is "On Some Lines of Virgil," the long idyll that closes out the collection. Davenport has explained that it is derived from Montaigne's essay of the same title, but "with [Davenport] translating [Montaigne's] Latin and

Greek examples of sexuality into action" (qtd. in Hoepffner 124). One assumes, given that it is a girl who orchestrates many of the revels in "Some Lines," that Davenport was thinking, for example, of *"adhuc ardens rigide tentigine vulve, / Et lassata viris, nondum satiata recessit,"* ("at last she retired, inflamed by a cunt stiffened by tense erections, exhausted by men but not yet satisfied"), or, since the actors are all teenaged or younger, of Horace's description of the vigor of young males: *"Cujus in indomito constantior inguine nervus, / Quam nova collibus arbor inhœret,"* ("in whose indomitable groin there is a tendon firmer far than a young tree planted on the hillside") (Montaigne 964, 1011).

Andre Furlani, however, opens his important essay, "Guy Davenport's Pastorals of Childhood Sexuality," not with a quotation from one of Montaigne's classical sources but from Montaigne himself: "Shall I say it, provided that I don't get throttled for it? It seems to me that love is not properly and naturally in its season except in the age next to infancy" (225). Davenport would appear, for complex reasons, to agree with Montaigne. "I think," he remarked, "that the awakening of sexuality is coterminous with the awakening of all sensibility," and, invoking Joyce, went on to point out that "the moment when Stephen Dedalus becomes an artist, he's looking at what most excites a Victorian, namely a woman's legs all the way up to the thigh" (qtd. in Sullivan 86). Thus in giving us a story in which two teenaged boys, a teenaged girl, and a barely pubescent boy gleefully engage in orgies of masturbation, copulation, and oral sex (and, one hastens to add, are damaged not a whit by these hijinks), he is giving us much more than "an easy method of learning the anatomy of the genitalia," as one critic suggested of Davenport's stories in this mode (Ehrenpreis), or "the cheerful porno scenario" another detects (Halliday 8). Rather, he is showing us "children [who] under the (non)guidance of an enlightened adult, may have a chance to escape the tethers of prejudice, superstition, greed, and priggishness" (Reece 33). Indeed, the young people in "Some Verses" demonstrate by their omnivorous sexual and intellectual energy and by the genuine regard they have for others that they are in little danger of ever succumbing to such ugliness. (The enlightened grown-ups in this tale, such as the scholar Tullio, suggest that it is not impossible for gifted adults to avoid these potential pitfalls as well.)

Thus we find passages such as this one, an encounter between the two teenaged boys: "My heart kicked, my testicles knotted tight, the back of my neck flushed hot. Interjoined, arms locked around each other's butts, we gave as we took, with deep breaths, hugging closer as we made headway, resolutely ungagging, grunting, thrashing heels, emboldened by doing" (234). But understand that for Jolivet this adventure with his friend Michel is but a part—an important part, to be sure—of a resolve he made at the beginning of the summer during which the story takes place. He tells his mother,

> This is the summer, Maman, that I'm going to learn all sorts of things that have nothing to do with school: art and Tullio's 'pataphysics, and politics. . . .

> And read the books I want to read. I'm going to build a World War I Spad and keep a notebook of exact observations, to examine emotions and focus ideas, and get brown as gingerbread, and shape up my body like Michel's, and make out like crazy with Jonquille when I can. (158-59)

The books Jolivet will read, the notebook he will keep of "exact observations," and the making out with Jonquille are, we understand, all of a piece, the birth of a human being alienated from neither body nor mind, excited about the world he is discovering. Readers who don't bridle at reading fiction that imagines what Davenport describes as "a morality transcending practically all present cultures" (qtd. in Furlani, "Guy Davenport's Pastorals" 226) will revel in the utopia the author gives us, and even those who might be inclined to take umbrage at the antics Davenport's young people get up to should be comforted by what Furlani calls the "flaunted artifice" ("Guy Davenport's Pastorals" 226) of it all: the heightened language, the pastoral conventions, the strict form (seventy-five sections each divided into five four-line blocks of text), and the impossible sophistication of the teenagers. This is not the real world or even a picture of it. It is a formally exquisite account of an Erewhon where coercion has no part in the youngsters' sexual play and where there are no Freudian traumas to be recovered years later with the help of dodgy analysts. Readers who don't mind considering a world where sexual mores are more humane than those currently in place, even if only in imagination, will find "Some Verses" a delight and will be happy to hear that Davenport continued in this vein in his next collection, *Apples and Pears.*

Apples and Pears and Other Stories (1984)

"I think it's taboo," Davenport remarked, "to write about any kind of happiness" (qtd. in Sullivan 71). In identifying this taboo, he highlighted an aspect of his idylls that sets them apart from the literary mainstream.[6] His utopian tales are full of people who jubilate in the interconnected pleasures of scholarship, of art, of friendship, of sport, and, of course, of sex. Not at all miserable in the best modern style, Davenport's people are at home in their minds and bodies and enjoy life in the world. This is certainly true of the characters who populate "Apples and Pears," the 233-page idyll in which we return to Davenport's Holland and to the characters we know from "The Dawn in Erewhon" and "The Death of Picasso." Divided into four parts, "Apples and Pears" is a continuous narrative in which we watch Adriaan and his loved ones work to create—successfully—an Erewhonian island in Amsterdam. For us to understand the goodness of this island and the life that is lived there, Davenport must make us feel the pleasures, small and large, that bejewel the more humane social arrangement he imagines.

As in "The Death of Picasso," the story is told in the form of entries from Adriaan's diary. "Other people bump into the world," a character remarks of this Dutch Epicurean, "Adriaan looks for things, finds them, knows them. I have been with him in Paris. He goes to a place and sits there putting it inside himself, atom by atom, smell by smell. Of course, in some wonderful way he brought the place with him, out of books, out of history, out of poems. He makes the place be" (280). And in his journals he makes his Erewhonian island be in such a way that we, Davenport's readers, know its attraction. He records, for example, a well-wrought room: "Canary yellow, white jug and basin, blue towel. Oval mirror on the wall above, plain unpainted walnut frame. Grietje's idea: a bit of the early century to relieve, as she says, some of the look of a barracks for reformed Calvinists" (222). He gives us friendship: " . . . Hans and Jan in their vermillion lifejackets as bright as pennies from the mint. They held hands, swapped gleeful glances, tossing hair from their eyes like foals" (143). And of course he sees and understands affectionate sex: "Tousled mops of heads held deep between brown, narrow, shifting thighs, a working of sharp shoulder blades, traveling of hands from pert butts along ribby flanks to virginal napes, a voluntary of restless caresses, hips hunched in slow exact pulsings" (154). This recounting of pleasures intellectual, aesthetic, social, and physical, is the heart of "Apples and Pears." We watch the *petite bande* around Adriaan grow—several children join and an adult or two—and we watch the group create a miniature society where they can live in the happiness they have made. At the end we learn that a baby will be born to the group. The utopia will regenerate, and so pleasantly addictive is the alternative world Davenport has painted that we are as delighted as the parents-to-be.

Davenport makes his gallery of pleasures something other than warm fuzzy mush by allowing us glimpses of the world outside the utopia. There are references throughout, for example, to the arms race in which the United States and the Soviet Union were then engaged, and, in case any reader misses the point of such grim information, we are reminded that "the punishment for killing a boy with an automobile, even if the driver is limber drunk, is six months in jail, whereas the punishment for loving a boy is thirty years hard labor" (263). Davenport is, however, less interested in an indictment of current social mores than he is in positing and illustrating, copiously and beautifully, what an alternative might look like.

"Apples and Pears" is the longest fiction Davenport published,[7] and thus the formal challenges it presents are of a different order from those he had faced in earlier works. There is too much material here for it to be organized into a fugue, even a seven-part one such as he had employed in "Au Tombeau de Charles Fourier." Thus he begins, in "Apples and Pears," to move toward the grander symphonic form he will perfect in "Wo es war, soll Ich werden," which would be published six years later. "Apples and Pears" lacks the symmetry of that piece and the elegance of the return in the final movement to themes introduced in the first, but still in its four-part structure and the disparity in the length, focus, and form of the sections, one senses the symphony lurking in the background as—however loosely—an organizing principle. The looseness, too, is easily explainable. "Apples and Pears," one feels, does not begin where it begins but rather way back in "The Dawn at Erewhon." And one feels, turning that last page, that it does not end where it ends but will be continued—the Erewhonian baby is not yet born—in future installments.

As in *Da Vinci's Bicycle*, Davenport balances the utopian idyll of "Apples and Pears" with what he takes to be one of the modern world's darkest moments, the loss of a generation in World War I. Among those lost was the sculptor Henri Gaudier-Brzeska, "whose hard, clean imagination was," in Davenport's estimation, "the firmest the world had seen since Paolo Uccello," and who Davenport believed to be "the first sculptor in a thousand years to work in modes that had been all that Homer, Ptahotep, Confucius and Sappho knew as beauty in stone" (Introduction). Davenport memorializes him in "The Bowmen of Shu," an *assemblage* built around pieces of Pound's poem "Song of the Bowmen of Shu" interwoven with excerpts from a letter Gaudier-Brzeska wrote from the trenches in December 1915 to a Russian journalist, John Cournos (Introduction).

The story, which takes the form of forty-two titled blocks of text, some as short as a line, none much longer than half a page, is among the most elliptical of Davenport's texts. His fictions are always packed with information, but the amount he manages to fit into this spare creation is astonishing. One need not have read Pound's poem or Gaudier-Brzeska's letter to enjoy this story and to learn from it. Doing so, however, equips one to appreciate the skill with which Davenport selects the telling details, adapts them where necessary, and weaves them into the *assemblage* he is making.

The story begins: "Here we are picking the first fern shoots and saying when shall we get back to our country, away from *das Trommelfeuer*, the gunners spent like winded dogs, white smoke and drizzle of sparks blowing across barbed wire in coils, the stink of cordite" (3). Pound's poem begins:

> Here we are, picking the first fern-shoots
> And saying: When shall we get back to our country?
> Here we are because we have the Ken-nin for our foemen,
> We have no comfort because of these Mongols. (Pound 64)

Thus in the first paragraph of his story Davenport places us with the sculptor in the trenches but also in Pound's China, a construct that—as Pound well knew—owes as much to the modern West as it does to the Asia of a millennium before Christ. Davenport goes on, continuing to tangle his sources with consummate skill: "Here we are because we have the Huns for our foemen. It's with pleasure, dear Cournos, that I've received news from you. We have no comfort because of these Mongols. You must have heard of my whereabouts from Ezra to whom I wrote some time ago" (3). The first sentence of this excerpt is a mix of Pound's poem and Gaudier-Brzeska's reality, the second a direct quotation from the sculptor's letter to the journalist Cournos, the third a direct quotation from the poem, the fourth a direct quotation from the letter. Davenport wrote in an essay on Pound, "Men who forget the past are doomed to repeat it, and the century has idiotically stumbled along repeating itself, its wars, its styles in the arts, its epidemics of unreason" ("Ezra Pound" 172). In this story inspired by Pound, in the few sentences of its first section, Davenport has illustrated this sad proposition with the immediacy of what Pound, and Davenport after him, would call an ideogram.

In addition to the poem and the letter, there are blocks of text devoted to other aspects of Gaudier-Brzeska's life: his relations with his wife, née Sophie Brzeska ("her story was a kind of badly constructed Russian novel" (12)), his education as an artist (a section entitled "THE BRITISH MUSEUM": "Out of the past, out of Assyria, China, Egypt, the new"; a section entitled "EPSTEIN, BRANCUSI, MODIGLIANI, ZADKINE": "Out of the new, a past" (15)), the milieu in which he and Pound moved, ("Sat with the god-like poet Brooke and the catatonically serious Middleton Murray, and the devout Tancred, Flint, FitzGerald, and the fair-minded skeptics, Wadsworth and Nevinson. The ale was good and Hulme chose his words with booming precision and attack" (11)).

This mesh of sources and information yields a picture of Gaudier-Brzeska that is perhaps not as complete as what one might find in a conventional biography but is, however, in its skillful ellipses and arrangement far richer in implication. Reading it we grasp, in a manner entirely visceral, that Gaudier-Brzeska's war was the same as the one to which Pound's Chinese source was responding. We see art present (Davenport's, Pound's), art past (the Chinese poet's), and art lost (the work Gaudier-Brzeska, killed in action at twenty-four, did not live to do). The last sentence of this, the first story in the collection, is Rimbaud's "*Il faut être absolument moderne*" (20). We can only respond to its exuberance with sadness, a sadness that makes us appreciate all the more the happiness of the last story in the collection, the idyll "Apples and Pears," which we considered above.

Apples and Pears is the last collection in which Davenport would use pictures as part of his *assemblages*. His reason for dropping them are evident when one looks at the uselessly tiny reductions of Davenport's renderings of the Gaudier-Brzeska works in "The Bowmen of Shu" and the botched collages included in "Apples and Pears." Davenport explains: "The designer [of *Apples and Pears*] understood the collages to be gratuitous illustrations having nothing to do with anything, reduced them all to burnt toast, framed them with nonsensical lines, and sabotaged my whole enterprise. I took this as a final defeat, and have not tried to combine drawing and writing in any later work of fiction" (*50 Drawings*). It is unfortunate that Davenport felt unable to continue with this aspect of his effort to make it new.

The Jules Verne Steam Balloon (1987)

In his next collection, *The Jules Verne Steam Balloon*, Davenport finds other ways to do so. He introduces, for example, new elements into his idylls: fantasy, in the form of daimons piloting a steam balloon, enters three of them; pain, in the form of heartbreak, enters the other. He essays a new form, a verse play composed entirely of decasyllabic lines, and, in a manner entirely different from that of "The Richard Nixon Freischütz Rag," in "Bronze Leaves and Red" he anatomizes a modern despot. Further, the tendrils spreading in this collection from one story to another grip especially firmly and establish links that are highly evocative, and these links don't stop at the boundaries of this book. They reach back to previous texts as well.

In the first tale in the collection, "The Meadow," we meet again Hans and Jan, Dutch adolescents introduced in "Apples and Pears" as members of the little horde that grows up around Adriaan. Now they are camping in a meadow in Denmark—meadows and their grasses are one of the tropes that, appearing in different guises in story after story, bind the pieces of *The Jules Verne Steam Balloon* together. They explore, with some young Danes, the wilderness in which they find themselves, and we see that their increasing knowledge of and pleasure in the natural world go hand-in-hand with their increasing knowledge of and pleasure in their minds and bodies. The forty-second of the forty-five blocks of text that comprise the story (its title is "Meadow") is a quotation from the French philosopher and poet Edgar Quinet. It helps us to understand the import of the blooming young people:

Aujourd'hui comme aux temps de Pline et de Columelle la jacinthe se plaît dans les Gaules, la pervenche en Illyrie, la marguerite sur les ruines de Numance et pendant qu'autour d'elles les villes ont changé de maîtres et de noms, que plusieurs sont entrées dans le néant, que les civilizations se sont choquées et brisées, leurs paisibles générations ont traversé les âges et sont arrivées jusqu'à nous, fraîches et riantes comme aux jours des batailles. (21)

In Richard Ellmann's translation:

Today as in the time of Pliny and Columella the hyacinth disports in Wales, the periwinkle in Illyria, the daisy on the ruins in Numantia and while around them the cities have changed masters and names, while some have ceased to exist, while the civilizations have collided with each other and smashed, their peaceful generations have passed through the ages and have come up to us, fresh and laughing as on the days of battles. (Ellmann 676)[8]

Nature, with its fresh and laughing pleasure, abides.

Even those troubled by Davenport's depictions of sex among the young will find that sentiment unexceptional, if not banal. As the story itself, however, is exceptional and anything but banal, we are reminded that texts in which form and the play of language take precedence over narrative are unparaphrasable. Davenport doesn't merely blurt out that the young people's discoveries in the meadow are important and good. He gives us an object the riches of which we are compelled to discover for ourselves. In teasing out the meaning, for example, of the untranslated, unattributed quotation above; in identifying the bits of Apollinaire, the poem by Emily Dickinson; in puzzling over the irruptions into the text of botanical and geological descriptions; in wondering about the titles that adorn some sections but often don't explain them; and in chuckling over the daimons—we won't immediately know that that's what they are—in their steam balloon, we don't just learn of the youngsters' pleasure and excitement. We share it.

In the second idyll in the collection, "The Bicycle Rider," we remain in Denmark. We will, in fact, return no more to Davenport's Holland, to Bruno and Sander and all the rest of the idyllic Dutch we have come to know. Adriaan, too, gives way to a Dane, Hugo Tvemunding, a classicist, theologian, and teacher (later headmaster) at a school called NFS Grundtvig.[9] In his discipline, perceptiveness, and intellect he resembles Adriaan, but he is different in one significant way: he is capable of being hurt. Beginning in "The Bicycle Rider" and continuing in "The Jules Verne Steam Balloon" and "The Ringdove Sign," we watch him experience the hurt—he had offered friendship to a young man; the young man preferred drugs—and gradually overcome it thanks, as he explains, to ". . . Mariana, that delightful girl, and my classical scholarship, and my Boy Scouts, and my sober round of reading, gymnastics, my thesis for the Theological Faculty at the university, my painting, teaching, learning" (88).

Hovering over the four idylls in this collection are the daimons in their outlandish craft. They watch the youngsters approvingly in "The Meadow," absent themselves from "The Bicycle Rider"—perhaps because Hugo is still as much in as out of misery—speak to Hugo in "The Jules Verne Steam Balloon," counseling him to "Be steadfast, patient, and silent" (112), and determine, in "The Ringdove Sign" that the "HQ" which has sent them is not really interested in Hugo and his circle: "A cute old man [Hugo's father], his tall randy son who can't keep his generator in his pants, one sprightly girl and her littler brother, and his friend. So Hugo is writing some gibberish, and teaches the old languages which he mispronounces, and has a loving heart, what's the bother?" (148). It is, the daimons surmise, a barely pubescent genius called Pascal—he returns in Davenport's masterpiece, "Wo es war, soll Ich werden"—whom they should be watching.

Readers will early on hazard guesses at what sort of beings the crew of the steam balloon are but will only begin to grow certain when they find, in the last few sections of the story, that Hugo's thesis is about the persistence of "daimons as angelic messengers" (139). We learn that "the daimon had, in one of the longest traditions we can trace in the Mediterranean, a bird form. A dove. More than any other folktale, Yeshua mentions the sign of Jonas. That is the sign of the dove. Jonas means dove . . ." (140). Reading this we recall that the third of the four idylls in this collection, "The Jules Verne Steam Balloon," closes with an allusion to the Old Testament book of Jonah—"What matters, Buckeye said, is that there are so many of them who don't know their right hand from their left" (121)—and that the story that comes between it and the concluding idyll is a retelling of that biblical tale. The weave binding the pieces of this collection is tight.

In the second of the idylls, "The Bicycle Rider," we find references to Buchenwald and to "the poet Mandelstam" (67). A tendril joins each of those references to other tales in the collection. In "Bronze Leaves and Red" we listen with mounting dismay as the narrator describes the unnamed leader of his country: "He knows everything. His study of Bolshevism, state finance, defense, racial purity, destiny, the German soul, music, city planning, military history, and nutrition has been profound" (45) and "He is a connoisseur of the fine arts and has frequently astounded the professors of aesthetics. He is fond of paintings of weeping clowns, a subject he maintains that Rembrandt would excel in were Rembrandt with us today" (46) and "He has an ear for the mighty line of Goethe. He is fond of dogs" (48). The juxtaposition of trivial details like the Führer's fondness for dogs with more alarming items such as "[he] gave a beautiful oration against Jewishness, communism, atheism, lies in the press, and flagrant immorality in entertainment and the arts" (47), taken together with the speaker's artless language and sinister naïveté and especially with the ghastly history not reported in the story but of which the reader will be all too aware, make this account devastating. We read it with horror and fascination.

The fascination we will feel reading "We Often Think of Lenin at the Clothespin Factory" will arise in large part from Davenport's deft use of a difficult form. Though we will be horrified when we remember the hard life that the protagonist, Nadezhda Mandelstam, was forced to lead, our predominant reaction to this verse play will be delight in Davenport's presentation, in unrhymed decasyllabic lines, of Mandelstam responding with wit and spirit to the younger party-line lunk who is the other actor in the drama. They come it is clear from two different worlds, two different times. Polden is a soldier who has never known anything but the Soviet Union and who has accepted the stories his leaders have told him about his country and its enemies. Notch (Nadezhda), on the other hand, cannot forget that there once was a life different from the one to which they are being subjected:

> Events happen again
> In memory, knowing, or narrative.
> Time rolls up as it goes along, bringing
> The past with it. Nothing is left behind. (41-42)

Far from being merely a nostalgic old woman, Mandelstam, we are aware, remembered with purpose: had she not memorized her husband's poetry much of it would have been lost.

One is reminded, too, by Notch and Polden's dialogue, of the revelation that informed *Da Vinci's Bicycle*, that people tend to talk past each other rather than to each other. Mandelstam tells Polden, for example, of the liveliness of the past:

Rilke and Lou Andreas Salome
Visited at Yasnaya Polyana.
They talked about Harriet Beecher Stowe.
Ah! the music, string quartets. Poetry.
You could meet someone who had seen Monet
At Giverny, beside the lily pond.
Proust. If you knocked on his door his servant
Had the same set speech for everybody:
Monsieur Proust wants you to know that there is
No waking hour when he is not thinking
Of you, but right now he is too busy
To see visitors. The Boratinskies,
Khlebnikov, Tatlin, Osip Mandelstam.
People who had been to Gertrude Stein's house.
Who recommended that you come? was what
She asked at the door. What a time that was,
Back then. (42)

"Parasites," Polden responds, for that is all that he can see in the world Mandelstam describes.
    The play ends with the following exchange:

NOTCH
Springtimes were sweeter, summers were greener.
The apple trees, the singing, and the gold.
There is no kindness now in the years.

POLDEN
But there are years.

NOTCH
Oh yes, the promised years,
Right on time. (43)

We know that Davenport read Borges; one of his last published essays was a long consideration of the Argentinean and his work. One wonders, therefore, if "We Often Think of Lenin at the Clothespin Factory" was inspired by Borges's "Funes the Memorious." Just as "The Death of Picasso" seems an inversion of Mann's "Death in Venice," so Davenport's verse play seems an inversion of Borges's tale. That "nothing is left behind" is a source of suffering for Funes; for Notch it is all the joy she has.

The Drummer of the Eleventh North Devonshire Fusiliers (1990)

"Colin Maillard," the story that opens this collection, is one of Davenport's most straightforward narratives. In it he gives us, as if in counterpoint to the loving boys who populate so many of his tales, boys who are brutal, who bully a smaller, younger child called Tristan, and who engage with each other in fights frightening in their savagery. Far from simply deploring this, however, Davenport paints the brutality, the savagery, as essential to what boys are, as necessary to the creation of the warmth, friendship, and love that can grow up among them. The contrast is startling: "With a porpoise heave and flop, Martin twisted from under Peder, jabbed his knee into his crotch, and pulled free. Peder's face was white with pain, his mouth making the shape of a scream. Martin was bleeding from the nose in spurts, and he was sobbing in convulsions, his shoulders jolting. He wiped the blood from his mouth, and fell on Peder with both fists hammering on his terrified face" (9). But just a few pages later we see, ". . . Bo carrying Tristan piggyback . . . Martin and Peder each with an arm around the other's shoulders, Ib and Bent skipping along behind" (12).

"Boys," Davenport noted, "do fight—as stupidly as nations" (Letter 4 Dec. 2002), and as this is the case, it is necessary for him to include this boyish stupidity in the picture he paints of them. He does so again in "Wo es war, soll Ich werden," the novella-length story that anchors the collection. Although the title is a quotation from Freud— "Where it was, there I shall begin to be"—this story is not, one will be relieved to hear, the sort of "psychological" fiction that exists only to illustrate the ideas of whatever analyst is currently popular among *littérateurs*. Rather, Davenport employs Freud's enigmatic notion as a sort of guiding motif (recall the boys' savagery in "Colin Maillard": where the fight was, comradeship begins to be). It is a starting point from which he moves off in unexpected directions.

Rilke's poem "The Bowl of Roses," for example, comes into the story when Hugo helps Holger, the biology teacher at Grudtvig, to understand it. The poem begins with a fight:

> You saw angry ones flare, saw two boys
> Clump themselves together into a something
> that was pure hate, thrashing in the dirt
> like an animal set upon by bees. (Rilke 27)

The something that was pure hate, however, is, at the beginning of the second stanza, transformed: "But now you know how these things are forgotten: / for here before you stands a full bowl of roses" (Rilke 27). The rest of the poem appears to be about those flowers. Rilke does not mention the thrashing boys again, but as Hugo explains to Holger, "The roses are the boys," and then, rhyming with Freud, "Where the boys were, roses are" (53). Davenport's story, too, begins with thrashing boys, but just as Rilke's poem quickly shifts from fight to flowers, so the quarrel in Davenport's tale is quickly displaced by the pleasures his idylls celebrate: the pleasure to be had in sex and scholarship, in art and nature, and most of all in friendship. The eighty-nine blocks of text that make up this tale are largely scenes from the interlocking friendships of its characters: Holger's with the twelve-year-old genius Pascal, Pascal's with Mariana's brother Franklin, Mariana's with her lover Hugo, and Hugo's with Pascal's friend Holger. The development of these friendships provides such narrative as "Wo es war" has and, in doing so, binds its luminous details together.

Also instrumental in making "Wo es war" cohere is its overall structure. It is a symphony in four movements. The first movement gives us the chaos of the fight, the middle movements the cosmos of the friendships, and the final movement returns us to a fight, but this time the fight does not, as the first did, suggest chaos. A theme returning late in a symphony is not—even when the notes are identical—the same as when it is first introduced, and this is the case here. The fight motif returns, but it is, as it were, in a different key.

The first sentence of the first section of the story reads: "—See? Pascal said, handing Housemaster Sigurjonsson a bunch of chicory and red valerian, they're flowers, for you, because Franklin brings them to Hugo Tvemunding, who puts them in a jar of water and says he likes them. They're sort of from the edge of fru Eglund's garden" (36). The first sentence of the last section reads: "—See? Pascal said, handing Holger a bunch of chicory and red valerian, they're flowers, for you, because Franklin brings them to Hugo, who puts them in a jar of water and says he likes them. They're sort of from the edge of fru Eglund's garden" (137). The small changes— Housemaster Sigurjonsson is now Holger, Hugo Tvemunding just Hugo—are merely the outward markers of larger ones, not only in the characters' relationships with each other but also in the way in which we read in the last section, having experienced the middle movements, this near repeat of an earlier paragraph.

We have seen, for example, Holger, with Hugo's friendly assistance, come to accept that where it was—an experience he had as a boy—is where he began to be—to be able, that is, to accept as an adult his loving relationship with a child, Pascal. And we have seen the birth, at last, of the Erewhonian baby hinted at in the last section of "Apples and Pears," albeit to different parents, to Hugo and Mariana rather than to Adriaan, Sander, and Grietje. "Wo es war, soll Ich werden" seems a sort of culmination of what might be called Davenport's Danish cycle, not only in the regeneration suggested by the appearance of the baby, Barnabus, but also in the consummate skill with which Davenport has shaped the materials his creative vigor and tremendous erudition have thrown up.

Like the first story in the collection, "Colin Maillard," and the last, "Wo es war," the three remaining tales in *The Drummer of the Eleventh North Devonshire Fusiliers* are concerned in one way or another with boys. In "Juno of the Veii" the eponymous idol is to be moved "from her countrified temple to Rome" and thus "pure youths" are needed to carry her (13). A group of potential candidates is assembled in the street, and, as they are being washed, they exchange banter friendlier than the bullying and violence the boys in "Colin Maillard" initially display but not entirely unrelated to it. The boys who are to carry the idol must be virgins. Remarks fly:

—Do goats count?
—You mean sisters, don't you?
—What about with the sergeant? (14)

When the Roman general, disdaining to bow to her, informs the idol that she is to be carried to Rome by "clean young men of pure morals" (15) one of the boys—still of an age, a purity, to see such things—reports that the idol smiled.

"A Gingham Dress," less than two-and-a-half pages long, is the only Davenport story aside from the juvenilia that can be characterized as Southern. It is one side of a dialogue between a country woman who has come to town to sell produce from her mountain farm and Mrs. Fant, the buyer. Much of the talk is about the country woman's son, Lattimer, who is "Going on nine and still won't wear nothing but a dress and bonnet" (16). Though not exactly an idyll, the story is in its way utopian. Lattimer, for example, is not bullied: "You'd think the boys would tease, but they don't. . . . One of the MacAlister boys, Harper, calls him his sweetheart," and Lattimer's father Leon, who "*will* sit in the car and talk to the dashboard," declares, through his more voluble wife, that "mountain people have always lived the way they want to" (17). He includes, it is clear, his son in this. The story ends with the mother announcing plans to make a gingham dress for Lattimer and then relaying her husband's observation that the homemade dress would be "cheaper than a pair of overalls" (18).

More ambitious than either "Juno of the Veii" or "A Gingham Dress" is "Badger." Unambiguously idyllic, it recounts a trip a twelve-year-old boy named Allen, shy and lonely, makes into Copenhagen, where he meets his imaginary dog, Badger. The trip, we come to see, is a step in Allen's growing away from his shyness, his loneliness, a part of his beginning (in the Freudian terms of "Wo es war") to be. Interspersed throughout the narrative, a block of text that may be a fantasy of Allen's—"The stranger facing Allen was blonde and trim," it begins (21, 22, 26, 31)—is repeated four times, and, more enigmatically, a quotation from Thoreau appears five times. The quotation reads: "I long ago lost a hound, a bay horse, and a turtledove, and am still on their trail. Many are the travelers I have spoken concerning them, describing their tracks and what calls they answered to. I have met one or two who have heard the hound, and the tramp of the horse, and even seen the dove disappear behind a cloud, and they seemed as anxious to recover them as if they had lost them themselves" (20, 23-24, 27, 32, 35). One can hazard guesses as to what this passage means and why it breaks into the narrative of Allen's day, and knowing, as Davenport discovered, that Thoreau was drawing on Mencius may help one arrive at some sort of solution (Renner). When one considers, however, that the passage is intentionally enigmatic even in *Walden*, perhaps it is well to keep in mind that for Davenport, "all Symbolism is subliminally perceived—is felt—without being arranged in a critic's museum display" (Letter 4 Dec. 2002). We will, in any case, have another opportunity to consider the quotation—and also some interpretations of it—as it is the centerpiece of "The Concord Sonata," a story included in Davenport's next collection, *A Table of Green Fields*.

A Table of Green Fields (1993)

B. Renner begins his interview with Davenport by noting that " 'The Concord Sonata' . . . features quite as much significant information about Thoreau as any biographical or literary essay and in a format which more effectively involves the reader."[10] This density of information—there's not "as much" information as is found in most biographical or literary essays; there's more—is characteristic of virtually all of Davenport's fiction. Readers averse to fact in their fiction—those, perhaps, who prefer feeling—may find this delightful barrage of knowledge off-putting; readers, on the other hand, who are eager to engage the world, to revel in the data it offers up, will find Davenport's fiction satisfying in a way that fiction—and scholarly essays—all too often are not.

"The Concord Sonata" begins with sentences pleasantly stuffed with facts: "At his small sanded white pine table in his cabin at Walden Pond on which he kept an arrowhead, an oak leaf, and an *Iliad* in Greek, Henry David Thoreau worked on two books at once. In one, *A Week on the Concord and Merrimac Rivers*, he wrote: Give me a sentence which no intelligence can understand. In the other, *Walden, or Life in the Woods*, he wrote three such sentences, a paragraph which no intelligence can understand . . ." (77). The paragraph in question is the cryptic account of the lost hound, bay horse, and turtledove. Davenport's story—readers wedded to convention will not recognize it as one—is a meditation on those sentences and includes apposite excerpts from John Burroughs, Stanley Cavell, and, of course, from Thoreau's own work—not just *Walden* and *A Week on the Concord* but also his less well known journals and natural history writings.

Burroughs, in the passage Davenport has selected, sees the enigmatic lines from *Walden* as being about longing. He quotes from Thoreau's journals, "The ultimate expression or fruit of any created thing is a fine effluence which only the most ingenious worshiper perceives at a reverent distance from its surface even," and then goes on to explain, "This *fine effluence* [Thoreau] was always reaching after, and often grasping or inhaling. This is the mythical hound and horse and turtledove which he says in *Walden* he long ago lost, and has been on their trail ever since" (77-78). Cavell, in his piece of this story, sees the quotation as being about loss and desire: "The writer comes to us from a sense of loss; the myth does not contain more than symbols because it is no set of desired things he has lost, but a connection with things, the track of desire itself" (78).

The desire, then, is to connect with the "fine effluence" of the world, but rather than simply telling us that it was this desire that drove Thoreau or even allowing the excerpts from Burroughs and Cavell on their own to suggest it, Davenport gives us anecdotes from Thoreau's life. The block of text that precedes the one titled "Stanley Cavell," for example, lets us see Thoreau puzzling over how a local boy could have heard geese during a season in which the birds should not have been in the vicinity. (After pondering the anomaly he guesses correctly that "at half past one Thursday a train had passed through with a crate of geese in the baggage car" (78).)

In a later section we learn that: "In *A Week on the Concord and Merrimac Rivers* Thoreau wrote: Mencius says: If one loses a fowl or a dog, he knows well how to seek them again; if one loses the sentiments of the heart, he does not know how to seek them again. The duties of all practical philosophy consist only in seeking after the sentiments of the heart which we have lost; that is all" (79). And then, having perceived that Mencius is the source of Thoreau's "sentences which no intelligence can understand," we are suddenly, in the next section, in China with the philosopher as he visits the court of Duke Hsuan of Qi. When Mencius tells the duke that "the benevolent have no enemies," the duke smiles. "Philosophers," he reflects, "were always saying idiotic things like that" (80), and we are reminded of the soliloquies of Nixon and Yeh.

In others of the blocks of texts that comprise the story we find epigrams ("Thoreau was most himself when he was Diogenes" (83)), a conversation (between Thoreau and a mouse), and observations

("The man under the enormous umbrella out in the snow storm
is Mr. Thoreau. Inspecting, as he says. Looking for his dove, his
hound, his horse" (84)). All of these pieces taken together don't
explain Thoreau or the quotation that is the story's subject. Rather,
in forcing the reader to slide the pieces back and forth, to consider
them in different combinations, Davenport compels the reader to
enter into the scholar's work of making sense of a jumble of sources.
He invites us to share in the scholar's excitement when pieces slide
smoothly together. And as he does so, he encourages us to join in
a more profound search as well: Thoreau's for the hound, the bay
horse, and the turtledove.

That this active exploration of the world is key is driven home in
the final three sections, the final three sentences, of the story:

W. E. B. DUBOIS
Lions have no historians.

WITTGENSTEIN
If a lion could talk, we could not understand him.

20
Fear not, thou drummer of the night, we shall be there. (86)

These are sentences that "no intelligence can understand" (and
one seems to be about an intelligence not understanding). Singly
or together they admit of no easy paraphrase, but in our desire to
comprehend what DuBois, Wittgenstein, and Thoreau are saying, to
understand Thoreau's quest and to understand Davenport's story,
we enter into a livelier engagement with the world. The story, in a
way that conventional fiction does not, digs deeper in us what Cavell
calls "the track of desire itself."

"August Blue" is comprised not of three sentences that intelligence cannot understand but of four sections, each of which is
perfectly comprehensible. What grips us this time—in addition to
the substantial charm of each of the four frames—is the effort to
determine how they fit together. The first is a story—augmented by
"necessary fiction"—drawn from the apocryphal Gospel of Thomas.
In it we see Jesus (Davenport prefers "Yeshua," the Aramaic form),
having magically picked figs from an unreachable tree, teaching
his teacher the true import of the Hebrew letter *alef*. The second
finds a Jewish professor, James Joseph Sylvester, attempting to
teach mathematics not long after the death of Jefferson to boorish
aristocrats at the University of Virginia. The third is a description
of the fenlands around Ely, near Cambridge, and the fourth is an
account—perhaps also apocryphal—of T. E. Lawrence visiting and
being painted by the English artist Henry Scott Tuke.

One sees—or makes—connections immediately.[11] Jewish teachers, for example, appear in the first two sections, and both have
their roles called into question. Jesus the student ends up making
a student of his teacher. The mathematician in Virginia is burdened
with "students" who, lacking all desire to learn, cannot be taught.
The first section and the fourth might be connected in that both are,
perhaps, apocryphal: Jesus picking unpickable figs and lecturing
his elders on *alef* derives from a Gospel excluded from the canon,
and Lawrence's "visit to Tuke at Falmouth in 1922 is unattested
except by Tuke's painting of him as Aircraftsman Ross at Clouds
Hill" (147). In addition, language as object and as tool of inquiry
binds the first three sections: Jesus lectures on *alef* in the first section, and *alef*, we learn in the last sentence of the second, is now
employed in mathematics "as a symbol of the transfinite." The third
section, the description of the Ely fenlands, is also, if more obliquely,
related to language, though it is difficult to see how unless we recall
(or read the note that Davenport has reluctantly provided[12]) that
Wittgenstein, who spent the better part of his life thinking about
language, is buried there. A final connection is the boys who run
through the stories of Jesus, of Sylvester, and of Tuke painting Lawrence. Remembering that Wittgenstein had a tortured interest in
young males, we can see boys in the description of Ely as well.

Viewing the four sections together, one notes that the first and
the fourth panels show boys and men and the societies in which
they live in a positive light—Jesus gets along well with his chums
and does not threaten his understandably less gifted teacher; Lawrence, Tuke, and the boys who are his models thrive in a homoerotic
idyll. Even the local vicar is tolerant: "A classical education gives
one a taste for the, ah, pastoral, don't you know" (14). The second
and third sections are bleaker—the boys in Virginia are ignorant
brutes; Wittgenstein was tormented by his homosexual impulses.
In addition, therefore, to the threads running from one section to
another there is, we perceive, an overall architectonic integrity that
binds them. When Lawrence is asked at the end of the final section
if he was "in this late, and one hopes last, terrible war," his reply is
"I was indeed in the war. . . . And it is not the last" (14). His answer
reminds us of the history to come. The next panel, were there one,
would be closer in spirit to the second and third than the first and
fourth.

In a different key "Belinda's World Tour" is pure whimsy, but,
appropriately, whimsy as if written by Franz Kafka. Except for
the first few paragraphs, which set the scene—a little girl has lost
Belinda, her doll; Kafka, to assuage the girl's grief, tells her the
doll has gone on a world tour—the story is made up entirely of
postcards ostensibly written by Belinda to her former owner, but

actually composed by Kafka. "There are streets here, all uphill," Belinda writes from San Francisco, "and with gold prospectors and their donkeys on them. There are saloons with swinging doors, and Flora Dora girls dancing inside. Everybody plays *Oh Suzanna!* on their banjos (everybody has one) and everywhere you see Choctaws in blankets and cowboys with six-shooters and Chinese and Mexicans and Esquimaux and Mormons" (19). This is not America, one perceives, but Amerika. "Some genius of a critic," Davenport speculated, "will one day show us how comic a writer Kafka is, how a sense of the ridiculous . . . informs all of his work" ("Hunter Gracchus" 18). In this story Davenport takes a large step toward doing so.

In "And" Davenport, once again, stretches the short-story form, this time making the matter of his tale the decipherment of a text. Like the first part of "August Blue," "And" considers apocrypha: "A papyrus fragment of a gospel written in the first century shows us Jesus on the bank of the Jordan with people around him" (62), and in "The Concord Sonata," Davenport entices his readers into engaging in a scholarly search for meaning, this time in the "fragment [that] is torn and hard to read" (62). "In the first line," Davenport writes, "Jesus is talking but we cannot make out what he's saying: too many letters are missing. . . . It's as if we were too far back to hear well" (62). In that "as if" a movement has begun that will carry the reader away from the text, the piece of papyrus almost impossible to read, to the place, the riverbank where a crowd has gathered around Jesus. We watch—we've forgotten we're reading—as Jesus throws seeds into the river, and the seeds sprout, become trees "hung with fruit, quinces, figs, apples, and pears" (62). And then we leave both the scratchings on the papyrus and the images they throw up: "We follow awhile in our imagination: the people running to keep up with the trees, as in a dream. Did the trees sink into the river? Did they flow out of sight, around a bend?" (62). There the story ends, and we have completed a journey from barely readable characters on a papyrus, to images evoked by those characters, to imagination unfettered in a story of just three-quarters of a page.

Looking at this story and others in this collection, we realize that the thread that joins them is language: sentences that no intelligence can understand, the *alef,* and marks on papyrus in the stories we have considered; in others a pregnant quotation from Dorothy Wordsworth's journal, the charged verse of Apollinaire, the language the protagonist of "O Gadjo Niglo" no longer, at the end of the tale, shares with the boy who was once his friend. And the title of the collection is also about language: a phrase from Shakespeare that, "as if we were too far back to hear well," we cannot be sure we have grasped.[13]

The Cardiff Team: Ten Stories (1996)

Davenport, in essays and fiction, wrote often about Franz Kafka, an artist whose work we can never be sure we've grasped. In "The Messengers," the story that opens *The Cardiff Team*, he gives us an account of Kafka's visit to a nudist spa in Austria. While at this spa, as is recounted in the story as well as in the essay "The Hunter Gracchus,"

> Kafka dreamed that two contingents of nudists were facing each other. One contingent was shouting at the other the insult "Lustron and Kastron!"
> The insult was considered so objectionable that they fought. They obliterated each other like the Calico Cat and the Gingham Dog, or like subatomic particles colliding into non-existence. ("Hunter Gracchus" 11)

The names or words "Lustron and Kastron" seem to be related to two Swedish boys, "twins . . . or cousins or brothers very close in age" whom Kafka sees at the spa (3). "Castor and Pollux" he calls them (3). Waking from his dream Kafka (or is it the narrator?) reflects on those nicknames and the insult he had heard in his dream:

> Latin endings rather than Greek would make the words into *castrum*, a castle, and *lustrum*, a cleansing. Pollux, *pollutum*, a defiling. Clean and filthy: antitheses. When antithetical particles in the atomic theory collide, they annihilate each other.
> Castor and Pollux could not exist simultaneously. One could live only while they other was dead, a swap made by loving brothers. (7)

"Dirty and clean, then, tref and kosher, motivated Kafka's dream," Davenport explains ("The Hunter Gracchus" 12), and another way of thinking about tref and kosher, dirty and clean, is as outside and inside. Pollution comes from outside the group; those on the inside must, to remain clean, defend against it. Kafka—both Davenport's and the real one—is "a nudist who wore bathing drawers, a non-observant Jew, a Czech who wrote in German, a man who was habitually engaged to be married and died a bachelor" ("Hunter Gracchus" 12). He was a man, that is, who, because he combined within himself antitheses, does not and cannot attain the purity of an insider and therefore can never quite receive the message that everyone else seems to understand. The messengers—prophets—fail to reach Kafka; Kafka, himself a prophet, was similarly unsuccessful. "Quite soon after the Second World War," Davenport wrote, "it was evident that with *The Castle* and *The Trial*, and especially 'In the Penal Colony,' Kafka was accurately describing the mechanics of totalitarian barbarity" ("Hunter Gracchus" 9). A message from an outsider, dirty, is not heeded.

That Davenport conveys so much—and so much more—in this ten-page story, that he is able to bring Kafka's diary together with a letter to Brod and the Bible, and then mix them with humorous accounts of 1912 health faddists and the Czech's conversations with the household god who shares his cabin is typical of the virtuosity that characterizes Davenport's work. Also typical is that the theme—insider/outsider, belonging/not belonging—reverberates throughout the collection. "All the stories in . . . *The Cardiff Team*," Davenport told the *Paris Review*, "are about belonging to a society, a team, a family—Lucien Lévy-Bruhl's theory that identity is one's sense of the tribe" (qtd. in Sullivan 69).

Team and family are at the fore in the idyll for which the collection is named, "The Cardiff Team." Though this title refers less to a Welsh rugby side than to an artwork, Robert Delaunay's painting of the same name, the story is rich in reflections on both teams and on Delaunay's creation. The two strands come together, for example, in the third of the story's forty-nine sections when Penny, a scholar working on the iconography of the painting, explains that "Social standing has no voice in sports, or family or class. Neither is language of any matter, or religion. . . . So here's a team of coal miners' sons playing football with the French rich, poor, and middle-class together. Their team's jerseys make them brothers in an equality hitherto unknown in the world" (92). Neither does social standing have a voice in the tribe that is at the center of this story: Penny and her son Walt; a girl named Bee (also known as Sam when she's masquerading as male); Penny's lover Marc, who is also Walt and Bee's tutor; Bee's mother Daisy, an artist; and by the end, Cyril, a sad, lonely, rich boy who joins Walt and Bee as a student at Marc's.

The story is largely an account of Walt, Bee, and Marc taking Cyril in hand and showing him how full the world is of pleasure. Cyril begins to get an inkling of this when, wandering Paris with Bee and Walt, he learns (to pick just a few items out of Davenport's tour de force page-long sentence):

> that sex is a kind of secret game and lots of fun . . . that iconography is the study of things in paintings, that Robert Delaunay was a painter scads of years ago, that Sam's mother had a neat friend named Christofer, a Norwegian who doesn't speak French too good but is seven feet tall, is hung like a horse, and is handsome, that they all had use of a house in the country, on weekends, where you run naked in the orchard . . . that Sam and Walt had read almost all of Jules Verne, that Penny was reading them a neat book called *King Matt the First* as a bedtime book, that flowers and trees and weeds have names which Sam and Walt knew and he didn't, that somebody named Lévi-Strauss

had left licorice out of a list of aromas and that somebody named Fourier hadn't, that the ancient Greeks loved boys and girls, that Penny, Daisy, and Marc owned no automobile nor television set . . . that there is a film and a recording of the poet Apollinaire . . . that Sam and Walt seemed to have endless conversations with their mothers; and that he was a very lonely little boy. (97-98)

The pleasure that Walt and Bee have known and Cyril has not, we see, is made of sex, books, art, scholarship, friendliness, knowledge, and nature, and these are the things that Walt, Bee, and Marc— only eighteen, but already an Adriaan-like, Hugo-like figure—set out to show him. No one writes better of pleasure than Davenport, and it's a grand pleasure to follow the garland of joys he stretches through his tale, to watch his tribe of characters—bastards (as Walt and Bee proudly call themselves), single mothers, poor little rich boy Cyril, and Marc, a self-made intellectual whose background is obscure—cohere. Toward the end Marc explains to Cyril, "Our real families are our friends, who of course may be family as well. Walt and Sam have not yet found the country they want to be citizens of. You and I, Cyril, are immigrants in the imaginary country Penny and Daisy founded, with a population of four" (159). These imaginary countries filled with pleasure strenuously pursued—Adriaan's in Amsterdam, Hugo's in Denmark—are offered as an alternative to that other one in which, the reborn Cyril observes, "there are forty-two wars raging right now, never mind the private unhappinesses everywhere, pain, disease, and hatred." He goes on to say, "We are here in this meadow. Even it has no reality we can know other than how our imagination perceives it" (160). As is usual in Davenport, the meadow and the imagination that perceives it triumph over that other less happy place. Once again, Davenport is "zon[ing] away the world for a while" (qtd. in Alpert 10).

Tribes and teams run though the rest of the book, too. "Boys Smell like Oranges" is a discussion between the missionary and ethnologist Maurice Leenhardt and the philosopher and anthropologist Lucien Lévy-Bruhl about myth and the primitive mind. Braided together with their conversation is the talk of two boys about the soccer team of which one is captain, the tribe of which he is chief. The parallels between the scholars' conversation and that of the boys are never simple and are all the more striking for that. "The River" and "Concert Champêtre in D Minor" are connected Danish idylls, in which the tribe is the bunch of boys that features so often in Davenport's fiction awakening to sex and the world. A long excerpt from *Robinson Crusoe*, titled "Home" and presented as a story in itself, follows them in the collection and is, one guesses, meant to be read as connected to them. We seem to have entered Daniel Defoe's book but may in fact have entered the mind of Adam, a character who reads *Robinson Crusoe* in "Concert Champêtre," the tale that precedes "Home."

In "Dinner at the Bank of England," Davenport's imagining of George Santayana's meal with the captain of the guard at that institution, the tribe is larger than just a gaggle of boys or a team of athletes. It is a society, the English. A literary visitor such as Santayana can, of course, see that tribe only with literary eyes. The room where he and Captain Stewart eat, Santayana says, is "Dickensian" (11); "It is England. The butler, fireplace, and mantel out of Cruikshank, the walnut chairs, the sporting prints, the polished brass candlesticks," and Stewart is "someone to be encountered in Thackeray or Kipling" (16). It is not only the setting and Captain Stewart, however, that are, in the best literary style, English. Davenport captures perfectly the jocular tone predominant in the English fiction Santayana would have known. Indeed, the Pickwickian humor is evident in the meal upon which they dine: "soup, mock turtle, and boiled halibut with egg sauce . . . mutton, gooseberry tart with cream, and anchovies on toast, to be washed down with these cold bottles " (12). In addition to the chuckles the story will provide, however, there is more. We have, for example, Santayana's wisdom: "The unexamined life is eminently worth living, were anyone so fortunate. It would be the life of an animal, brave and alert, with instincts instead of opinions and decisions, loyalty to mate and cubs, to the pack" (13). And there are, in this account of an older man's dinner with a handsome younger one, what Davenport calls "submerged depths": "Stewart would die on the Western front. GS, like Henry James, was a shy and circumspect admirer of young males. As a bread-and-butter gift GS sent Capt Stewart a copy of Charles Macomb Flandrau's *Viva Mexico!* (1908). They had met in Harvard Yard" (Letter 18 June 2004). There were, in Flandrau's life, "submerged depths" too.

The Cardiff Team was the last collection of short stories Guy Davenport would publish. He would, however, return to his Denmark twice more, in stories included in *The Death of Picasso: New and Selected Writing*.

The Death of Picasso: New and Selected Writing (2003)

"The Owl of Minerva" and "The Playing Field" are the last stories Davenport published in his lifetime, and as the two closely connected tales are populated by, for the most part, a new group of Danes (or the offspring of Danes met in previous tales), one wonders if they aren't the first two installments in what was to be a new cycle. At the center of the two stories are Magnus Rasmussen and Mikkel Rasmussen, a boy in need whom Magnus takes in and helps to become, in the best sense of the word, civilized. Davenport's tales, it will have been noted, often feature teachers who, through kindness and the sharing of pleasure, help younger boys move into a healthy engagement with the world. Magnus and Mikkel's relationship is another in this series.

"The Playing Field" is the more impressive of the two last stories, though so closely is it connected with "The Owl of Minerva" that one ought to think of them as two parts of a longer composition. Indeed, it would be difficult to entirely understand the second story without having read the first. In this first story Mikkel, now an adult and a major in the army, visits the old school where Magnus taught and where, thanks to Magnus, he had studied when they first came together. In Mikkel's discussion with the retired headmaster, Colonel Rask, we learn that Magnus and Mikkel had suddenly left the school, packing their things in the night and disappearing. Mikkel explains, "Magnus said later that he felt that something awful would have happened if we'd stayed, that the relationships we'd gotten into were potential disasters. They were daring adventures depending on trust and comradeship. . . . We were, as he said, too happy. . . . Nobody could ever understand" (13). Davenport, in his idylls, writes of utopias that exclude the world—almost. We sense here that it is the world and its disapproval of a boy sharing a bed with a man that drives them away from what Mikkel calls "our wonderful big room over the stables . . . the only home I'd ever had" (13). It is the nonutopian world, always hovering at the borders of Davenport's utopias, that they are fleeing.

In the second story we backtrack and, in a series of titled blocks of text, scenes from their time together, see Mikkel, apparently without family, creating a family—a tribe—with Magnus. Echoing Marc in "The Cardiff Team," Magnus counsels Mikkel, "We have to look around and find the people we're really kin to. They're only rarely our family" (28-29). We see the warmth that grows up as they discover their kinship:

> —Is love sex, Magnus?
> —Nope.
> —Silence. Wiggling.
> —Love is eating peapods out of the same bag. (30)

Later in the tale the adult Mikkel—Major Rasmussen—visits his old school again. Walking with Colonel Rask, he meets a boy on the playing field also called Mikkel. This Mikkel is, Rask tells him, Mikkel Havemand. *"Hej!* You were Dad's best friend! I'm *named* for you!" (35), Mikkel Havemand says, and the young Mikkel Rasmussen, we recall from "The Owl of Minerva," had been in love with a boy called Marcus Havemand.

And then the tale turns magical. At the end of the section of "The Owl of Minerva" that deals with Major Rasmussen's visit to his old school, Colonel Rask suggests, "we might take a turn around the grounds, for old times' sake" (14). Rasmussen declines: "I don't think I can, sir. I would see a twelve-year-old in a red-checked shirt, wide yellow braces, and stone-washed jeans with a brass-buttoned fly. I want to remember the quadrangle as he knew it. He was a very happy little boy" (14). When he meets Mikkel Havemand in "The Playing Field" he meets this happy boy. The boy who is at first Mikkel Havemand becomes the boy Mikkel Rasmussen; Mikkel Rasmussen, remembering himself young, talks with himself young. "You kept me," young Mikkel Rasmussen tells the older one, "and grew up around me" (36).

The penultimate section of "The Playing Field" ends with the older Mikkel saying, "The willow oak at Kastellet," to which the younger Mikkel responds, "A quintillion photons on every square centimeter of leaf per second" (36). This carries us back to the story's first section where the child Mikkel Rasmussen and Magnus lie under an oak tree and discuss the particles of light raining down on the leaves. The story, we see, has come full circle, and appreciating the formal beauty, we regret that Davenport retained the section he had added after the penultimate one at the behest of the editor of *Hotel Amerika*, the journal in which the story first appeared. The editor felt that the addition "would help *some*" (Letter 16 June 2003), and indeed, it surely did make the story more easily comprehensible, particularly for those readers who had not read "The Owl of Minerva," which first appeared in a different journal, the *Georgia Review*. With the stories next to each other in *The Death of Picasso*, however, the additional paragraph no longer seems necessary and indeed throws the delicate balance of Davenport's tale slightly out of tune.

The Critics

The best critic of Guy Davenport is Guy Davenport. No idiot savant (or any other kind of idiot), Davenport always knew exactly what he was doing in his writing and why. Further, he was not, like some authors, coy about explaining his work. He helped interested readers to understand his fiction in the letters he sent out to his many correspondents, in the published interviews, and especially in the essays. "My eighteen readers," Davenport remarked, "eventually learn that I do everything twice" (qtd. in Sullivan 69), and this often meant one time as a story and one time as an essay, with each illuminating the other. To offer just one example, it will be evident from the discussion above that the essay "The Hunter Gracchus" is tremendously helpful in reading the story "The Messengers."

Also essential are the essays "Narrative Tone and Form," in which Davenport discusses style and form in general, and "Ernst Machs Max Ernst," in which he discusses several of his early stories in particular.

The aesthetic that guided Davenport's writing guided his painting and drawing as well.[14] Thus it is no surprise to find that Erik Anderson Reece's *A Balance of Quinces: The Paintings and Drawings of Guy Davenport* is as necessary to one reading Davenport's fiction as it is to one viewing his paintings and drawings.

"I think," Davenport said, "the best critical take on all my writing is one Marjorie Perloff came up with in one of her books" (qtd. in Sullivan 68). She writes about Davenport's work in *The Dance of the Intellect: Studies in the Poetry of the Pound Tradition* and in *Wittgenstein's Ladder: Poetic Language and the Strangeness of the Ordinary*.

The quality of the two essays by Andre Furlani cited in this paper make one eager to read his forthcoming monograph, *Guy Davenport: Postmodern and After*, due out from Northwestern University Press in 2006.

Early in his career Davenport received a great deal of critical attention. At the time of the *Vort* interview (1976), for example, Davenport reported that *Tatlin!* had spawned sixty reviews, several critical essays, and a doctoral thesis (Alpert 11). This attention diminished book by book as Davenport's career continued and not because the work declined in quality: it never did. Samuel R. Delany in "The 'Gay' Writer / 'Gay Writing' . . . ?" collected in his *Shorter Views: Queer Thoughts and the Politics of the Paraliterary*, offers a possible explanation for the fact that today Andre Furlani appears to be the only scholar and critic paying sustained attention to Davenport's oeuvre.

Davenport once speculated that "[Hermann] Broch's . . . *The Death of Virgil* may be the final elegy closing the long duration of European literature from Homer to Joyce" ("Hunter Gracchus" 8). Those of us who reveled in the work of this Kentucky professor know that it was not. The long duration continued.

Guy Davenport died on 4 January 2005.[15]

Notes

[1] Davenport, when asked whether he reread his early stories, remarked, "Those as far as I know don't exist. They must have been awful" (qtd. in Alpert 11).

[2] Pictures are not only central to this story but also to its genesis. "'Tatlin!,'" Davenport told Barry Alpert, "began as an oil portrait of Tatlin

from an old photograph which is upstairs . . . " (Alpert 3).

[3] A fan envied Davenport's "ability to express himself." Davenport's response: "Yick!" (Letter 26 Feb. 2004)

[4] It should probably be noted that Hovendaal has lived only in Davenport's Holland, never in the real one. The note on the copyright page of *Tatlin!* that asserts that "parts of 'The Dawn at Erewhon' are excerpts translated from Adriaan van Hovendaal's *Het Erewhonisch Schetsboek* and *Higgs Reizen in Erewhonland*" has fooled more than one critic.

[5] Davenport: "I am not a novelist. Paul Klee was not a muralist. My ambition is to write as little as possible in the smallest possible space" (qtd. in Hoepffner 119).

[6] "Joyce Carol Oates," Davenport believed, "would burn her typewriter if she accidentally wrote about some happy people" (qtd. in Sullivan 71).

[7] Only the restored version of "Wo es war, soll Ich werden," sixty pages longer than the story as it was originally published in *The Drummer of the Eleventh North Devonshire Fusiliers*, comes close. Davenport stresses in the circumspectus to this restored version, published in 2004 in an edition of one hundred, that the restored version is not to be seen as the canonical one.

[8] As Davenport certainly knew, Joyce makes use of the same quotation in *Finnegans Wake*.

[9] Alert readers will catch a glimpse of Adriaan in *The Cardiff Team*.

[10] This interview is undated at the *Elimae* website. Renner believes it took place in 1998 (E-mail 23 Mar. 2005).

[11] When the *Paris Review* asked Davenport, "Does one create these rhymes, these affinities, or uncover them?" his response was "I probably make them up" (qtd. in Sullivan 82).

[12] Davenport: "I'd rather not provide notes to stories. [Publisher James] Laughlin wanted them" (Letter 18 June 2004)

[13] The phrase "a table of green fields," from Mistress Quickly's account of Falstaff's death in *Henry V*, has been considered by scholars to be a scribal error and is often amended to "a babbled of green fields." Davenport was not convinced. He believed Falstaff was referring to a *tableau*—a picture—of green fields, noting that Shakespeare twice used "table" in this manner ("Scholar as Critic" 86-87).

[14] "A really clever critic," Davenport remarked, "will find a way to conflate my abstracts . . . with my imagery and sentence structure" (Letter 22 Sept. 2004).

[15] The author would like to acknowledge the hospitality of David Eisenman. Guy Davenport reader number nineteen, he never hesitated to share bibliographical information and hard-to-find Davenportiana. Duncan Baker, by dragging his fine-toothed comb through it, also helped to make this essay better.

Works Cited

Alpert, Barry. Interview with Guy Davenport. *Vort* 3:3 (1976): 3-17.

Berger, John. "The Changing View of Man in the Portrait." *The*

Moment of Cubism and Other Essays. London: Weidenfeld and Nicolson, 1969. 35-42.

Davenport, Guy. *Apples and Pears and Other Stories*. San Francisco: North Point Press, 1984.

—. *The Cardiff Team: Ten Stories*. New York: New Directions, 1996.

—. Circumspectus. *Wo es war, soll Ich werden: The Restored Original Text*. Champaign: Finial Press, 2004.

—. *Da Vinci's Bicycle: Ten Stories*. 1979. New York: New Directions Classic, 1997.

—. *The Death of Picasso: New & Selected Writing*. Washington: Shoemaker & Hoard, 2003.

—. *The Drummer of the Eleventh North Devonshire Fusiliers*. San Francisco: North Point Press, 1990.

—. *Eclogues: Eight Stories*. San Francisco: North Point Press, 1981.

—. "Ernst Machs Max Ernst." *The Geography of the Imagination*. Boston: David R. Godine, 1997. 373-84.

—. "Ezra Pound 1885-1972." *The Geography of the Imagination*. Boston: David R. Godine, 1997. 169-76.

—. *50 Drawings*. New York: Dim Gray Bar Press, 1996.

—. "The Hunter Gracchus." *The Hunter Gracchus and Other Papers on Literature and Art*. Washington: Counterpoint, 1996. 1-18.

—. "The Illuminations of Bernard Faucon and Anthony Goicolea." *Georgia Review* 56 (2002): 961-86.

—. Introduction. *Ezra's Bowmen of Shu*. By Henri Gaudier-Brzeska. Cambridge: Adams House and Lowell House Printers, 1965. N. pag.

—. *The Jules Verne Steam Balloon*. San Francisco: North Point Press, 1987.

—. Letter to the author. 4 Dec. 2002.

—. Letter to the author. 16 June 2003.

—. Letter to the author. 26 Feb. 2004.

—. Letter to the author. 18 June 2004.

—. Letter to the author. 22 Sept. 2004.

—. "The Life of the Mind." Letter. *New York Review of Books* 20 Feb. 1975. < http://www.nybooks.com/articles/9262>.

—. "Narrative Tone and Form." *The Geography of the Imagination*. Boston: David R. Godine, 1997. 308-18.

—. "The Pound Vortex." *The Geography of the Imagination*. Boston: David R. Godine, 1997. 165-68.

—. "The Scholar as Critic." *Every Force Evolves a Form*. San Francisco: North Point Press, 1987. 84-98.

—. "Stanley Spencer and David Jones." *The Hunter Gracchus and Other Papers on Literature and Art*. Washington: Counterpoint, 1996. 112-26.

—. *A Table of Green Fields*. San Francisco: North Point Press, 1993.

—. *Tatlin!* New York: Scribner's, 1974.

Delany, Samuel R. *Shorter Views: Queer Thoughts and the Politics of the Paraliterary.* Hanover: Wesleyan UP, 1999.

Ehrenpreis, Irwin. "Enigma Variations." *New York Review of Books* 12 Dec. 1974. <http://nybooks.com/articles/9316>.

Ellmann, Richard. *James Joyce.* New York: Oxford UP, 1959.

Furlani, Andre. "Guy Davenport's Pastorals of Childhood Sexuality." *Curiouser: On the Queerness of Children.* Ed. Steven Bruhm and Natasha Hurley. Minneapolis: U of Minnesota P, 2004. 225-44.

—. "When Novelists Become Cubists: The Prose Ideograms of Guy Davenport." *Style* 36.1 (2002): 111-30.

Halliday, Bob. "Guy Davenport's Terrestrial Paradise." *Washington Post Book World* 20 Jan. 1985: 8.

Hoepffner. Bernard. Interview with Guy Davenport. *Conjunctions* 24 (1995): 118-26.

Kelly, Robert. Rev. of *The Death of Picasso: New and Selected Writings*, by Guy Davenport. *Bookforum* Fall 2003: 40.

Kenner, Hugh. *The Pound Era.* Berkeley: U of California P, 1971.

Mason, Wyatt. "There Must I Begin to Be: The Heretical Fictions of Guy Davenport." *Harper's* April 2004: 87-92.

Montaigne, Michel de. "On Some Lines of Virgil." *The Complete Essays.* Trans. M. A. Screech. London: Penguin, 1991. 947-1016.

Pound, Ezra. "Song of the Bowmen of Shu." *Selected Poems: 1908-1969.* Rev. ed. London: Faber & Faber, 1977.

Reece, Erik Anderson. *A Balance of Quinces: The Paintings and Drawings of Guy Davenport.* New York: New Directions, 1996.

Renner, B. Interview with Guy Davenport. *Elimae.* 1998. <http://www.elimae.com/interviews/davenport.html>.

—. E-mail to the author. 23 Mar. 2005.

Rilke, Rainer Maria. "The Bowl of Roses." *The Essential Rilke.* Trans. Galway Kinnell and Hannah Liebmann. Rev. ed. New York: Ecco Press-HarperCollins, 2000. 27-31.

Sullivan, John Jeremiah. Interview with Guy Davenport. *Paris Review* Fall 2002: 42-87.

A Guy Davenport Checklist

Fiction

Tatlin! New York: Scribner's, 1974; Baltimore: Johns Hopkins UP, 1982.

Da Vinci's Bicycle: Ten Stories. Baltimore: Johns Hopkins UP, 1979; New York: New Directions Classic, 1997.

Eclogues: Eight Stories. San Francisco: North Point Press, 1981; Baltimore: Johns Hopkins UP, 1993.

Apples and Pears and Other Stories. San Francisco: North Point Press, 1984.

The Jules Verne Steam Balloon. San Francisco: North Point Press, 1987; Baltimore: Johns Hopkins UP, 1993.

The Drummer of the Eleventh North Devonshire Fusiliers. San Francisco: North Point Press, 1990.

A Table of Green Fields. San Francisco: North Point Press, 1993.

The Cardiff Team: Ten Stories. New York: New Directions, 1996.

12 Stories. New York: Counterpoint, 1997.[*]

The Death of Picasso: New & Selected Writing. Washington: Shoemaker & Hoard, 2003.

Wo es war, soll Ich werden: The Restored Original Text. Champaign, Illinois: Finial Press, 2004.

Nonfiction

Every Force Evolves a Form. San Francisco: North Point Press, 1987.

The Hunter Gracchus and Other Papers on Literature and Art. Washington: Counterpoint, 1996.

The Geography of the Imagination. Boston: David R. Godine, 1997.

[*] There is no new fiction in *12 Stories.* Each of the twelve stories included appeared in previously published collections.

Aldous Huxley

David Garrett Izzo

> *He thought of the millions who had been and were still being slaughtered. . . . he thought of their pain, all the countless separate pains of them; pain incommunicable, individual, beyond the reach of sympathy . . . pain without sense or object, bringing with it no hope and no redemption, futile, unnecessary, stupid. In one supreme apocalyptic moment he saw, he felt the universe in all its horror.*
>
> —Aldous Huxley,
> "Farcical History of Richard Greenow" (109)

> *I have frequently been accused, by reviewers in public and by unprofessional readers in private correspondence, both of vulgarity and wickedness—on the grounds, so far as I have been able to discover, that I reported my investigations into certain phenomena in plain English and in a novel. The fact that many people should be shocked by what he writes practically imposes it as a duty upon the writer to go on shocking them. For those who are shocked by truth are not only stupid, but morally reprehensible as well; the stupid should be educated, the wicked punished and reformed.*
>
> —Huxley,
> *Vulgarity in Literature* (21)

Many people know the name Aldous Huxley in connection with his landmark 1932 novel *Brave New World*. Few know much more than this and that at one time Huxley was one of the most revered and respected figures in twentieth-century literature and philosophy. An irony of his present neglect can be found by noting that the day he died—22 November 1963—was the day John F. Kennedy was murdered; hence, Huxley's passing was ignored. On any other day, his death would have likely been acknowledged with front-page articles and a retrospective of his life and work. The highlight of this work, *Brave New World*, is often selected as one of the greatest novels in all of literature, but there was much, much more to Huxley as a writer, philosopher, and influence.

There is not a writer who came after Huxley who does not owe to him directly or indirectly the new tangent in the history of the novel that his work impelled. There is not a person who learned about Eastern philosophy in the 1960s who is not directly or indirectly indebted to Huxley the philosopher. Anyone who admires the philosophy of Horkheimer and Adorno, particularly their essay "The Culture Industry," is actually influenced by Huxley, as these two German refugees from Hitler acknowledged that their ideas came from Huxley. There *is* an academic Aldous Huxley Society with a home base in Münster, Germany, that *does* appreciate his impact on our world and spreads the gospel of Huxley through a book-length *Huxley Annual* and a conference every year so that he will not be forgotten. His friend and fellow philosopher Gerald Heard called Huxley "The Poignant Prophet" (101), and he was certainly a godfather of the New Age. And with all of his accomplishments, perhaps the most enduring was how endearing he was to those who knew him and adored his wit, his kindness, and, finally, his profound humanity.

Aldous Leonard Huxley was born on 26 July 1894 to Leonard Huxley and Julia Francis Arnold Huxley. He was the third child of four—two elder brothers, Julian and Trevenen, and a younger sister, Margaret. His father was the son of the great scientist and disseminator of Darwin, T. H. Huxley; Julia was the great-niece of the Victorian era's preeminent man of letters, poet-philosopher Matthew Arnold. Hence, it was unlikely that Aldous would not be born clever; just how clever, however, no one could have foreseen. His childhood was advantaged, and he took the most advantage of it, achieving a classical education in the public schools. In Britain the misnomer "public" really means private schools where anyone among the "public" who can afford them is allowed to attend. On 29 November 1908 his mother died from cancer; she was forty-seven. Aldous adored her and was devastated. In a final letter to her son written on her deathbed, she told him, "Don't be too critical of people and love much" (qtd. in Huxley, *Letters* 83). Huxley later added in 1915, " . . . I have come to see more and more how wise that advice was. It's her warning against a rather conceited and selfish fault of my own and it's a whole philosophy of life" (*Letters* 83). In the 1920s his cynicism prevailed, but, indeed, in the 1930s he began to formulize this "philosophy of life."

In the spring of 1911 Aldous contracted the eye ailment *keratitis punctata* and was blinded for over a year. His father and doctors feared that he might never recover his sight. Tutors were engaged, one for Braille, one for his schoolwork. During this period, his older brother Trevenen was his greatest comfort, sitting with him frequently and reading to him. His vision improved ever so slightly enough for him to function in the world. In 1913 Aldous stayed with Trevenen in Oxford. Trev, as he was called, was the most outgoing of the Huxley brothers and very popular with his school chums although he had a stammer. Perhaps the fact of dealing with it good-naturedly had encouraged his more effusive personality. In

August 1914, after a very difficult year at school, the sensitive Trev had an affair with a young woman he cared for but who was not of his social class, which was then still an impossible barrier. Filled with guilt, Trev went missing. After seven terrible days, he was found in a wood, hanging dead from a tree.

Aldous endured tragedy once again, and thus began his abhorrence for the strictures of class divisions, which would become the main target for his relentless pen through fiction and essays. Aldous felt somewhat adrift. His father had remarried in 1912 and was leading his own life. In 1915 seventeen-year-old Maria Nys and her family, émigrés from Belgium fleeing the war, came to England to stay at Garsington, the celebrated estate of Philip and Ottoline Morrell. Garsington was a first or second home to artists, intellectuals, and conscientious objectors who had officially received alternative work deferments and "worked" on the manor. Here, Aldous met Maria and fell in love; they married on 10 July 1919 in her home of Bellem, Belgium. Their only child, Matthew, would be born 19 April 1920.[1]

For the next eight years, Huxley lived the life of the struggling writer. He worked as an editor and contributing essayist for periodicals that ranged from the very literary *Athenaeum* to the less literary *House & Garden*. His more serious essays were in the manner of the devastating *Prejudices* written by the American social commentator H. L. Mencken, with whom Huxley corresponded. He often worked at more than one position, for example, editing *H & G* all day while attending the theater at night to write reviews for the *Westminster Gazette*. Meanwhile he published poems and short stories, leading to his first book of stories, *Limbo*, and his first widely published book of poems, *Leda*, both in 1920 for Chatto & Windus. More poems and short stories followed and in 1921 his first novel, *Crome Yellow*. This novel's sharply satiric look at his Garsington days attracted the attention of a small but arch readership that enjoyed the darts Huxley threw at the pretensions of the upper class. Lady Ottoline did not speak to him for a long time.

This limited success encouraged Chatto to give Huxley his first three-year contract, one that included, of all things for a struggling writer, yearly advances, albeit small ones. The Huxleys packed their bags and traveled to Florence, Italy, where they could stretch that advance more than in England and where they saw the emergence of Mussolini's fascists and the tools of media propaganda. Huxley now would write only what he wanted to write. From 1922 to 1928 he wrote four more volumes of short stories (*Brief Candles, Two or Three Graces, Little Mexican, Mortal Coils*), two more novels (*Antic Hay, Those Barren Leaves*), two philosophical travel books (*Along the Road, Jesting Pilate*), and many essays collected in numerous volumes.

Huxley slowly increased his devoted following. Sales were modest, but steady; reviews were either full of praise from those who welcomed his savage wit or full of hate from the traditional critics who were among those Huxley pierced with his sharp darts. As the twenties progressed and the postwar era began to see changes in British traditions, he gained new readers from the young intellectuals who were adolescents in 1920 but who were now rebellious iconoclasts at Oxford and Cambridge. Huxley's targets were the same masters and dons, the same parents, the same aristocrats, the same bourgeois element that the university intellectuals raged against. With his 1928 novel, *Point Counter Point*, an international success, Huxley reached a much wider readership. His fifth novel, *Brave New World* (1932), while well received, was not quite so revered at that time as it became after World War II, precisely because there had never been anything like it before and some critics didn't know what to make of it. Who could believe in such a future—one that is already upon us?

Huxley's novels have been called "novels of ideas," and they certainly cover a wide range of literary, social, political, cultural, and philosophic topics. In 1936 Huxley published *Eyeless in Gaza*, with its complex alternating time shifts in the life of the main character, Anthony Beavis; in it Huxley advocated his pacifist beliefs. His title was, in part, homage to author Conrad Aiken, who had written a time-shifting novel, *Great Circle*, in 1933, in which he twice used Milton's line "eyeless in Gaza."

Huxley relocated to Los Angeles in 1937 with his family and best friend, the philosopher Gerald Heard. Huxley's writing in America became increasingly philosophical, and fiction works became extensions of his nonfiction books and essays. His 1939 novel, *After Many a Summer Dies the Swan*, tackles a William Randolph Hearst-like character and influenced Orson Welles's 1941 film classic *Citizen Kane*. In 1945 Huxley's anthology with commentary, *The Perennial Philosophy*, helped popularize mysticism in the United States and abroad. His 1944 novel *Time Must Have a Stop* incorporated the Perennial Philosophy into its narrative.

Huxley's wife, Maria, died in 1955. A year later Huxley married concert violinist Laura Archera. His novel *The Genius and the Goddess* was published in 1955. Huxley developed throat cancer in 1960. On 4 November 1963 Christopher Isherwood saw Huxley for the last time: "Aldous was in obvious discomfort, but there was nothing poignant or desperate in his manner, and he clearly didn't want to talk about death. . . . I touched on subject after subject, at random. Each time I did so, Aldous commented acutely, or remembered an appropriate quotation. I came away with the picture of a great noble vessel sinking quietly into the deep; many of its delicate marvelous mechanisms still in perfect order, all its lights still shining" (*My Guru* 259-60).

Huxley died of throat cancer on 22 November 1963. His ashes were initially buried in California but were later interred in Britain with his parents. In 1968, his 1962 utopian novel of ideas, *Island*, was reprinted and became a best-seller of over a million copies. Huxley wrote a great deal of nonfiction that far exceeded his creative writing. This writer has fully examined the nonfiction in his study, *Aldous Huxley and W. H. Auden on Language.*

Huxley was *The Man* in British Literature in the 1920s, much more so than Eliot was, although Eliot's reputation has fared better since then. His influence was enormous directly or indirectly in the United Kingdom and the United States. Undergraduates made sure to read him in the 1920s. When Christopher Isherwood was a student at Cambridge, his mid-1920s *Mortmere* story, "Prefatory Epistle to My Godson on the Study of History," has a Mr. Starn proclaim, sounding Huxleyesque, that "man is the sole and supreme irrelevance. He is without method, without order, without proportion. His childish passions, enthusiasms, and beliefs are unsightly protuberances in the surface of the Universal Curve. . . . [H]ow perfect would be the evolutions of nature in a world unpeopled" (Isherwood and Upward 171). Starn also warns his godson to be skeptical of the New Testament saying, "I refer to this exploded forgery with all due reference to Professor Pillard, who has, by the Historical Method, clearly proved that it is the work of Mr. Aldous Huxley" (171).

The cult of Aldous Huxley was afoot as he dared to write down what other artists and intellectuals would have loved to have said, particularly regarding class pretension and snobbishness. Indeed, his subject matter itself was innovative—and widely imitated. Isherwood's first two novels in 1928 and 1932 are Huxleyesque attacks on the bourgeois middle and upper classes or, as Isherwood called them, *The Others*. Later, in Isherwood and Auden's 1935 satirical play *The Dog beneath the Skin*, it is clear from the following lines that they had read *Brave New World*: "No family love. Sons would inform against their fathers, cheerfully send them to the execution cellars. No romance. Even the peasant must beget that standard child under laboratory conditions. Motherhood would be by license. Truth and Beauty would be proscribed as dangerously obstructive. No books, no art, no music" (167). Huxley in the 1920s and 1930s was a marked man by The Others, who considered him the most cynical of the postwar cynics. As the epigraph from *Vulgarity in Literature* makes quite clear, someone needed to tell the truth and puncture complacent bubbles. If he needed to get personal, so be it.

The nihilistic tone of T. S. Eliot's, *The Waste Land* (1922) is the tone of Huxley's essays, his first novel, and the early short stories, which had preceded the poem that is now much more remembered. Huxley's own nihilism matches in vitriol any post-World War II writers, or angry young men as they were labeled. One can also point out that even if autobiographical fiction became more prevalent after World War II, it was far from unprecedented. Huxley's first novel, the satire *Crome Yellow*, is based on his days at Garsington Manor. Huxley's breakthrough best-seller *Point Counter Point* featured, with fictitious names, D. H. Lawrence, the British fascist Sir Oswald Mosley, shipbuilding heiress Nancy Cunard, and Huxley himself as Philip Quarles, the aloof, too intellectual author who drives his wife into the arms of the Mosley surrogate (which did *not* happen in real life). Philip's son, the same age, seven, as Huxley's son Matthew, becomes horribly ill and dies—punishment for the illicit affair (which in fact is planned but never consummated). Huxley's wife Maria was not pleased. *Eyeless in Gaza* features another Huxley surrogate, Anthony Beavis, whose father (Huxley's father) does not come off very well. There is also a detailed account of Anthony's best friend who has a stammer and is very fragile, as was Huxley's brother Trevenen. The character, as did Trevenen, kills himself, causing more woe among Huxley family members. This would be Huxley's last roman à clef, and perhaps his switch to less familiar and familial subjects, starting with *Brave New World*, was not accidental.

Brave New World in 1932 was the first of two "before/after" dividing lines in Huxley's career. The second was his emigration from Britain to America in 1937. *Brave New World* followed four parlor satires of the upper class that largely took place in people's drawing rooms and preceded his more directly philosophical novels of ideas, which is not to say that the parlor satires were not full of ideas, but they were presented more discretely within the novel format than Huxley would choose to do later. The move to the United States and sunny California opened his eyes to a world much different from Europe and, through his initial interest in the Vedanta Society of Southern California, enhanced and codified his already existing predilection for mysticism.

Huxley's critical reception first generated immense praise among progressive critics when he was a wunderkind in the 1920s. These were the same critics who supported Forster, Joyce, Eliot, Woolf, and their peers in critiquing post-World War I society. With *Point Counter Point* Huxley graduated from an avant-garde darling to international acclaim as a writer and thinker. His subsequent books were highly anticipated, with the 1930s and 1940s perhaps a peak of esteem. The 1950s began to see him as a revered old master who was still quite interesting but not quite up to pre-World-War II standards. Huxley's reputation took a bit of a hit in the 1950s when he experimented with LSD and mescaline, which were then legal—he did so under Dr. Humphrey Osmond's scrutiny. He described these experiences in *The Doors of Perception* (1954) (from which the 1960s rock band The Doors took its name) and *Heaven and Hell* (1956). Indeed, even as late as 18 October 1958, the very sedate and respected *Saturday Evening Post* featured Huxley's front-page headlined essay, "Drugs that Shape Men's Minds." Had Huxley lived past 1963, he would have enjoyed a second coming with his best-selling utopian novel *Island*, considered a handbook for New Age thought. Through the 1960s and 1970s Huxley remained an iconic figure for his New Age thinking, which had preceded the actual New Age. In the 1980s, with the 1960s no longer such a strong influence, the conservative wave that took over from the New Age found Huxley's reputation and direct influence waning in terms of cultural appreciation, even while his indirect influence was—and is—as strong as ever. This waning engendered an article by John Derbyshire in London's *New Criterion* of 21 February 2000, titled, "What Happened to Aldous Huxley?" Derbyshire wrote:

> Metaphysics is out of fashion. . . . Living as we do in such an unmetaphysical age, we are in a poor frame of mind to approach the writer [Huxley] who said the following thing, and who took it as a premise for his work through most of a long literary career.
>
> It is impossible to live without a metaphysic. The choice that is given us is not between some kind of metaphysic and no metaphysic; it is always between a good metaphysic and a bad metaphysic.

Derbyshire is correct. As early as 1916, in a letter to his brother Julian, Huxley wrote, "I have come to agree with Thomas Aquinas that individuality in the animal kingdom if you like is nothing more than a question of mere matter. We are potentially at least, though the habit of matter has separated us, unanimous. One cannot escape mysticism; it positively thrusts itself, the only possibility, upon one" (*Letters* 88). And in 1925, "I love the inner world as much or more than the outer. When the outer vexes me, I retire to the rational simplicities of the spirit" (*Along the Road* 110). The quest for choosing between a "good metaphysic and a bad metaphysic" and forming a way to live around the good metaphysic is the fulcrum from which Huxley's entire body of fiction and nonfiction was launched. Even when he was at his most cynical and satirically sarcastic, this was a cry by an angry young man who depicted the worst so that one could try to imagine something better to take its place. He spent his entire life seeking the "something better" and knew it would be found in the world of the metaphysic over the physic. This itself from 1920 to 1963 was the major innovation of his work—only the presentations changed, as Huxley grew older, wiser—and less angry.

Huxley's novels of ideas are always about moral dilemmas that need to be sorted out. In the 1920s his characters wallow in the philosophy of meaninglessness with sarcasm as their defense veiling a prevalent despair. The other side of a cynical man is a fallen hero— or an aspiring hero. The characters secretly—or openly—seek a vehicle that can give meaning to a world that has realized that science, technology, and industry are not the answers. Huxley's protagonists evolve as either upward seekers of the Perennial Philosophy of mysticism or they devolve downward into an even greater disaffected nihilism.

Crome Yellow (1921)

Since its initial publication in 1921, Huxley's first roman à clef, *Crome Yellow,* has delighted readers with its ironic wit aimed at a diverse carnival of pretentious upper-class characters. *Crome Yellow* was Huxley's first novel, and it will receive here a full discussion as it presents in nascent form both his new approach to the novel and the thematic concerns that would evolve through the rest of his career. *Crome Yellow* exposes the social hypocrisy of a rigidly class-conscious British establishment that was trying to forget World War I had ever happened and thus ensure that the circumstances would repeat themselves, as it turns out they did in World War II. His characters hide their insecurities behind masks of pseudo-intellectuality. Even the book's title is a clever metaphor implying the stark differences between appearance and reality. The personas depicted by Huxley are not what they seem at first glance, but they do represent human nature's duality of public and private faces.

Since human nature does not change, *Crome Yellow*'s humor is just as relevant today as it was in 1921 when the novel earned Huxley a deserved reputation as a sharp-tongued social commentator. He was compared to H. L. Mencken, a writer Huxley admired and corresponded with. As for essays, Huxley wrote them copiously during the 1920s, and his inspiration for their acerbic, take-no-prisoners style resulted directly from Mencken's famous commentaries, or, as Mencken called them, *Prejudices,* which indicates their pointed intentions. In a review of 2 January 1920 Huxley wrote of Mencken, "we have sore need of critics who hate humbug, who are not afraid of putting out their tongues at pretentiousness however noble an aspect it may wear, who do not mind being *vulgar* at need, and who, finally, know not only how to make us think, but how to make us laugh as well" (qtd. in Bradshaw, *Aldous Huxley* 3). This became the guideline for Huxley's technique in his first four novels culminating in *Point Counter Point.* Before Huxley became a cult-hero on his own, he had a correspondence with Mencken to express his approval of the

Baltimore sage's attitude, one which Huxley emulated in the early
to mid-twenties when he made his living much more from writing
essays than art. In his first letter to Mencken, of 10 January 1920,
he wrote, "May I be allowed, as a humble fellow critic, to express my
great admiration for 'Prejudices' which I had the pleasure of reviewing recently for 'The Athenaeum.' I only wish we had a few more
people in this country capable of producing anything as good and,
at need, as destructive in the way of criticism" (qtd. in Bradshaw,
Aldous Huxley 3).

Mencken's manner became Huxley's, and the tone of these biting
essays continued in his fiction. *Crome Yellow* created a stir among
intellectuals. Upon its publication, U.S. critic Malcolm Cowley would
say, "the Aldous Huxley craze starts quietly" (243). The novel's title,
which refers to the fictitious estate called Crome where the story
takes place, is itself a bit of subversive wit. The term "crome yellow"
describes a yellow pigment that has an initial brightness that tends
to fade when exposed to sunlight and turns brown or green over
time. Hence, the title symbolically refers to the novel's characters,
who at first appear flashy but will soon turn dark or fade away into
a yellowish green hue. As Peter Bowering has said of the novel, "the
'yellow' of *Crome* is more than a little jaundiced" (35).

The novel is plotless: things happen, but there is no particular
conflict needing to be resolved at novel's end. *Crome Yellow* is like
life—just characters randomly talking—and its randomness is a
shared innovation for 1920. There is no linear inevitability of plot;
instead there are evocations of "streams of consciousness," with
thoughts tumbling one after another. In this, Huxley joined Joyce,
Woolf, and others as modern practitioners. Randomization is the
inverse of routine. The former defines the latter by its absence. For
Huxley routine is established so that randomization can assert
itself. In melodramatic fiction, interruptions of already tragic lives
are not quite so abrupt and affecting to readers as the interruptions
that disturb the commonplace of realistic, Wholly Truthful lives.

The characters in *Crome* are a bit sick under their superficial
surface sheen. They are a bizarre group, especially when observed
secretly by Denis, the pseudo-poet: "Denis peeped at them discretely
from the window. . . . His eyes were suddenly become innocent, childlike, unprejudiced. They seemed, these people, inconceivably fantastic. And yet they really existed, they functioned by themselves, they
were conscious, they had minds. Moreover, he was like them. Could
one believe it? But the evidence of the red notebook was conclusive"
(131). The red notebook belongs to Jenny, an almost deaf (or is she
really?), nearly mute young woman who records her contempt for
everyone at Crome in it. Denis opens Jenny's red notebook surrep-
titiously and sees the nastily accurate caricatured drawings and

vicious verbal descriptions of him and the others: "And so this, he reflected, was how Jenny employed the leisure hours in her ivory tower apart. And he had thought her a simple-minded, uncritical creature" (121). Foolishness is exactly what Huxley wishes to expose.

Huxley's main theme is like the distorting and fading colors of crome yellow pigment. First impressions do not last. He depicts men who indulge in exercises of intellectual futility and women who are Freudian moderns or Victorian predators or both. Huxley views the Crome estate as a microcosm of the much larger macrocosm that was Great Britain. He also sees in the characters that populate Crome personalities that are recognizable in any society past or present. His characters exhibit humanity's foibles and follies that we can all recognize and laugh over. Readers will perceive the more serious and painful repercussions of their behaviors that the satire implies between the lines.

The characters are vividly drawn from Huxley's experiences. Denis exemplifies the man who agonizingly analyzes every action and reaction while trying to imagine what others are thinking. He is a hopeless romantic who feels and thinks *too* much to ever relax and be happy, saying, "I can take nothing for granted, I can enjoy nothing as it comes along. Beauty, pleasure, art, women—I have to invent an excuse, a justification for everything that's delightful" (18). Anne is the "liberated" but cynical femme fatale who responds to Denis's equivocations with matter-of-fact smugness: "One enjoys the pleasant things, avoids the nasty ones. There's nothing more to be said" (18). Of course, there is much more to be said, but being rich and spoiled simplifies Anne's view of reality. Mary is also "liberated" and a reader of Freud and Havelock Ellis, the then-shocking sex researcher. She is an amateur psychologist who analyzes her own subconscious: "I constantly dream that I'm falling down wells; and sometimes I even dream that I'm climbing ladders. . . . The symptoms are only too clear. . . . One may become a nymphomaniac if one's not careful" (31). What actually seems clear is that Mary is not sure if she's coming or going. Mr. Barbecue-Smith is the pseudo-mystic who has won over Mrs. Wimbush, Crome's owner, with his books of saccharine aphorisms with titles like *Humble Heroisms* and *Pipe Lines to the Infinite*. He repeats to Denis such "gems" of wisdom as, "The flame of a candle gives Light but it also Burns," and "The Things that Really Matter happen in the Heart" (28). It is hard to imagine that anyone could take Mr. Barbecue-Smith seriously, but Huxley's point is exactly that he *is* taken seriously. Huxley disapproved of fake mystics because they diverted truth-seekers from real mysticism.

Huxley's superficial idealists are contrasted with the equally superficial pessimists Mr. Wimbush, Mr. Bodiham, and Mr. Scogan.

Wimbush makes memorials of the past because his present is such a bore. Bodiham is the fire-and-brimstone rector of Crome who believes in an angry God. His God is also spiteful, vindictive, and wants everyone to burn in hell. Finally, Mr. Scogan is the cold rationalist who is the forecaster of a *Brave New World*. In Scogan's future there will be three cloned types of humans: "Directing Intelligences," who will con the "Men of Faith" into convincing the remaining "Herd" to follow blindly. Scogan argues that the "men of intelligence must combine, must conspire, and seize power from the imbeciles and maniacs who now direct us. They must found the Rational State" (113). Through Scogan, Huxley hints at the coming of fascism, as well as his future novel.

In the 1920s Huxley's books were sharply attacked by those who resented his criticisms of British society. Huxley was also criticized for his then unprecedented discussion of previously unmentioned topics such as British traditions, upper-class arrogance, class divisions, religion, psychoanalysis, and especially sex. He considered it his duty to respond to these critics. He did not hesitate to challenge the complacency of post-World War I England. There has to be a tearing down of the old to the point that there is a vacuum that needs to be filled. The cynical void Huxley creates points out the complete folly to readers who then intuitively want—if often subconsciously—to fill the vacuum with antithetical solutions. In *Lord Jim* Conrad called this the Destructive Element into which one must immerse oneself and confront the demons of past and present until he has no choice but to either re-create himself or drown. The re-creation comes after a tearing-down of past influences so one can begin a building up of a better future. In *Crome Yellow* Huxley introduces a group of character types that will reprise their roles in his later work with just the names and nuances changing and their complexities developing with greater intricacy and depth.

Shortly after *Crome Yellow*'s publication, Eliot published *The Waste Land*, now considered the landmark definition of modern post-World War I despair and alienation. *Crome*'s satirical cynicism set the tone that helped prepare readers for Eliot's verse rendition of angst-ridden nihilism. Many authors in the 1920s, including Virginia Woolf, E. M. Forster, and Conrad Aiken, followed Huxley with their own fiction that was critical of British society.

Huxley's influence in the 1920s cannot be understated. Besides fiction, Huxley also expressed his opinions in essays. After World War I, he wrote that authors should tell the truth in a simple and realistic way that emphasized substance over style rather than style over substance that was a leftover from the fin de siècle floridity exemplified in Oscar Wilde. In essays such as "The Subject-Matter of Poetry" and "Tragedy and the Whole Truth," Huxley made two assertions: 1) everything and anything between the mundane and the magnificent could and should be suitable subject matter for literature if the artist writes about it as sincere truth; 2) the artist's striving for reality in art is not new but a mode that is as old as classical antiquity. Writing in 1923, Huxley said,

> [Writers today] are at liberty to do what Homer did—to write freely about the immediately moving facts of everyday life. Where Homer wrote of horses and tamers of horses [we] write of trains, automobiles, and the various species of . . . bohunks who control the horse-power. Much too much stress has been laid on the newness of the new poetry; its newness is simply a return from the jeweled exquisiteness of the eighteen-nineties to the facts and feelings of ordinary life. There is nothing intrinsically novel or surprising in the introduction into poetry of machinery and industrialism, of labour unrest and modern psychology: these things belong to us, they affect us daily as enjoying and suffering beings; they are part of our lives, just as the kings, the warriors, the horses and chariots, the picturesque were part of Homer's life. . . . The critics who would have us believe that there is something essentially unpoetical about a bohunk (whatever a bohunk may be) and something essentially poetical about Sir Lancelot of the Lake are, of course, simply negligible. . . . ("The Subject-Matter of Poetry" 32-34)

(The poet who used "bohunk" was Carl Sandburg.)

Of the "ordinary, everyday things," Huxley writes that the commonplace and the tragic can be combined into a synthesis he called "Wholly Truthful" art:

> What are the values of Wholly Truthful art? . . . *Wholly Truthful* art overflows the limits of tragedy and shows us, if only by hints and implications, what happened before the tragic story began, what will happen after it is over, what is happening simultaneously elsewhere (and "elsewhere" includes all those parts of the minds and bodies of the protagonists not immediately engaged in the tragic struggle). Tragedy is an isolated eddy on the surface of a vast river that flows majestically, irresistibly, around, beneath, and to either side of it. Wholly Truthful art contrives to imply the existence of the entire river as well as the eddy. . . . Consequently, Wholly Truthful art produces in us an effect quite different from that produced by tragedy. Our mood when we have read a Wholly Truthful book is never one of heroic exultation; it is one of resignation, of acceptance. (Acceptance can also be heroic.) . . . The catharsis of tragedy is violent and apocalyptic; but the milder catharsis of Wholly Truthful literature is more lasting. . . . There is no reason why the two kinds of literature should not exist simultaneously. . . . The human spirit has need of both. ("Tragedy and the Whole Truth" 14-15)

Wholly Truthful art reflects the "tea-tabling" technique of writing. To tea-table is to reveal important and even emotional information without resorting to a traditionally histrionic tragic scene—but to do so instead over afternoon tea or during some other mundane moment. Jane Austen had mastered tea-tabling a century earlier. Huxley recognized that much of life occurs, however emotional the situation, quietly more often than loudly. In *Crome Yellow* Denis reads the apocalyptic red notebook in complete silence but with profound shock. No one else finds out that Denis has read it. Yet even if someone had seen him read the notebook, he or she would have simply witnessed him engaged in the quite ordinary act of reading a book. Nonetheless, in this act the commonplace and the tragic are combined. In *Crome Yellow* the tragedy of Crome's cursed past is conveyed in a dry, matter-of-fact manner. The cold, unemotional tone with which Sir Henry Wimbush tells the story renders the terrible details even more horrible (and they will not be revealed here).

Crome Yellow is a satire of understated comic efficiency that evokes from its readers sly smiles rather than loud laughter. Even so, the novel's pervasive slyness becomes more penetrating in its cumulative effect as it demonstrates for the reader the oddities of human relations. *Crome Yellow* is a wry, allusive, and masterfully erudite novel that displays the lengths to which people will go to escape reality by hiding behind various neuroses and psychoses.

Behind the satire and the cynicism, Huxley was attempting to understand the human spirit so that he could learn how to improve himself and influence others to improve themselves. Huxley's questing after spirit in his art and essays is now a major font of study in Europe, particularly in Germany, where metaphysical approaches to literature resonate with great importance. Throughout his life, Huxley belied the cynicism of his fiction by actually being a thoughtful, kind, and generous soul who thought that the money he earned was meant to help others, and he gave it away to good causes and good people.

Christopher Isherwood joined Huxley in America in 1939. Isherwood and Huxley became very close, with Huxley seeing Isherwood as an occasionally wayward younger brother. Isherwood adored Huxley, as is seen in his diaries, and did not tolerate others' criticism of Huxley. In a diary entry of 1943 he recounts a meeting with Bertolt Brecht and notes Brecht's disparagement of the Perennial Philosophy, which he endures as funny until Brecht attacks Huxley: "I was so angry I nearly got up and the left the house at once. I did leave shortly afterwards. . . . What I object to is his claim to be more honest than a man like Aldous" (*Diaries* 318-19). And what kind of man was he? Isherwood wrote of Huxley in 1939, "How kind, how shy he is—searching painfully through the darkness of this world's ignorance with his blind, mild, deep-sea eye. He has a pained, bewildered smile of despair at all human activity. 'It's inconceivable,' he repeatedly begins, 'how anyone in their senses could *possibly* imagine—' But they *do* imagine—and Aldous is very, very sorry" (*Diaries* 77).

In this light *Crome Yellow* is written with the very tone that Isherwood describes, and its bitter wit is just as relevant now as it was when Huxley wrote it. Haves and have-nots still exist. Corrupt politicians still thrive. Pretentious artists and intellectuals still sell their recycled ideas as if they were new. Wars still happen. Huxley hopes to instruct us while we laugh—even if through tears—and *Crome Yellow* is, in its final lesson, just as humane as Huxley himself.

From *Crome Yellow* forward, Huxley wished to expose human nature in order to change it. *Crome Yellow* was the first of the 1920s novels that were pointed satires of British bourgeois life, and it was followed by *Antic Hay* and *These Barren Leaves*. In these novels following *Crome* the satire inveighed more serious social concerns, and with each, the serious themes became more pronounced and the satire more deadly. The zenith—and last—of these drawing room novels is *Point Counter Point*.

Point Counter Point (1928)

Huxley was . . . equipped with the scientist's tireless curiosity and passion for classifying. Point Counter Point, *the best of his literary novels, is almost comically a "novel of types"—the equivalent of Ponchielli's opera* La Gioconda, *which has six precisely equiponderant roles, one for each major vocal category.*

—John Derbyshire

Novel of ideas. The character of each personage must be implied, as far as possible, in the ideas of which he is the mouthpiece. In so far as theories are rationalizations, of sentiments, instincts, dispositions of soul, this is feasible. The chief defect of the novel of ideas is that you must write about people who have ideas to express—which excludes all but .01 percent of the human race. Hence the real, the congenital novelists don't write such books. But then, I never pretended to be a congenital novelist. . . .

The great defect of the novel of ideas is that it is a made-up affair. Necessarily; for people who can reel off neatly formulated notions aren't quite real; they're slightly monstrous.

—Huxley (as the character Philip Quarles),
Point Counter Point (294-95)

In 1936 Malcolm Cowley said of the literary world of 1928 that "*Point Counter Point* . . . [was] compulsory reading" (247). One could say that prior to *Point Counter Point* Huxley's fiction and essays were cumulative steps up a ladder that, as Huxley climbed higher, gave him the fullest perspective from which he could culminate his criticisms of upper-class British society. This novel of ideas can be read correlatively with Huxley's nonfiction of the preceding years, and one sees these essays "fictionalized" so that this novel of ideas deeply resonates with Huxley's social concerns. Prior to writing *Point Counter Point*, Huxley had made an extended sojourn to the Far East, which became his "travel" book *Jesting Pilate*, in which much philosophy is derived from his experiences. In *Point Counter Point* the Huxley surrogate, Philip Quarles, is just returning from a trip to India. Through Philip, Huxley expresses his own views on diverse subjects, particularly his friendship with D. H. Lawrence.

The notorious Lawrence, the working-class scholarship lad who had married an aristocrat—unheard of—had a great influence on Huxley from 1926 until his death from tuberculosis in 1930. Lawrence is Mark Rampion in *Point Counter Point*, and he is the spokesperson for ending class divisions and living life with intuitive feelings rather than British stiff-upper-lip constraint. As a contrast, the leading British fascist, Sir Oswald Mosley, is portrayed with his name barely changed to Sir Everard Webley. No doubt, in Huxley's book Webley is vivisected in public. Others make the cut as well: Lawrence as Rampion, Katherine Mansfield, her husband John Middleton Murray, and Nancy Cunard as Lucy Tantamount, with her name not too subtly implying that Lucy was tantamount to Cunard, the shipbuilding heiress and a femme fatale who had once thrown Huxley over to be heaped upon a stack of other bodies trampled in her wake.

In his novel Huxley spared no one, including himself. He is the novel's novelist, Philip Quarles, who, with his aloof detachment and otherworldly perambulation into esoteric abstraction, pushes his wife Elinor into the arms of—yes, of all people—Webley. (Maria Huxley, one can be assured, is not Elinor, although she wouldn't disagree that Aldous was sometimes Philip, but a tamed version under her pragmatic Belgian earth-mother spirit that matched in quiet fire her husband's ice cool brilliance.)

In 1928 *Point Counter Point* shocked readers with the then unheard of portrayals of infidelity, sexuality, and the pretensions of artists and intellectuals. Marjorie Carling leaves her husband to live with—and get pregnant by—her lover Walter Bidlake who becomes bored with Marjorie and pursues Lucy, the voracious "modern woman" who seeks constant stimulation with no thought to the pain she causes, since other people's desires are not her responsibility. The "characters" are the same types as in *Crome Yellow*, but they are more rounded, detailed, and complex. The satire here is less humorous and more angst-ridden. The analysis of the motives behind the characters is profoundly current, as Huxley makes clear in this 1929 essay:

> Human nature does not change, or, at any rate, history is too short for any changes to be perceptible. The earliest known specimens of art and literature are still comprehensible. The fact that we can understand them all and can recognize in some of them an unsurpassed artistic excellence is proof enough that not only men's feelings and instincts, but their intellectual and imaginative powers, were in remotest times precisely what they are now. In the fine arts, it is only the convention, the form, the incidentals that change: the fundamentals of passion, of intellect and imagination remain unaltered.
>
> It is the same with the arts of life as with the fine arts. Conventions and traditions, prejudices and ideals and religious beliefs, moral systems, and codes of good manners, varying according to the geographical and historical circumstances, mould into different forms the unchanging material of human instinct, passion, and desire.
>
> At any given moment human behaviour is a compromise (enforced from without by law and custom, from within by belief in religious or philosophical myths) between the raw instinct on the one hand and the unattainable ideal on the other. (*Do What You Will* 130)

Raw vs. ideal, body vs. mind, intuition vs. reason, science vs. spirit—ultimately, these cause enormous conflict in the human psyche; yet, if these oppositions could be balanced in a perfect harmony of an undifferentiated unity (mystical unity) then humanity would strive and not just survive. The novel opens with this epigraph:

> *Oh, wearisome conditions of humanity!*
> *Born under one law, to another bound,*
> *Vainly begot and yet forbidden vanity:*
> *Created sick, commanded to be sound.*
> *What meaneth Nature by these diverse laws—*
> *Passion and reason, self-division's cause?*
> *—Fulke-Greville*

Huxley is clear that this novel will be about the albatross of duality in human nature, which is an invention of the individual ego. Language itself in the sense of "I am I; *you* are not I" is a great separator, for each person uses language to proclaim his or her uniqueness more than to nurture unanimity. It is not accidental that mystics meditate in silence or chant in unison to achieve a sense of undifferentiated unity. As Huxley puts it, "For in spite of language, in spite of intelligence and intuition and sympathy, one can never really communicate anything to anybody. The essential substance of every thought and feeling remains incommunicable, locked up in the impenetrable strong-room of the individual soul and body. Our life is a sentence of perpetual solitary confinement" ("Sermons in Cats" 211).

No one really knows what another person is really thinking. Words are an inadequate outcome of a lifetime's accumulation of experiences and emotions. Words are outcomes that are meant to protect one's ego from vulnerability. In *Point Counter Point* the incommensurateness of two people really connecting is a theme and a technique. Huxley depicts minds in opposition, as each mind will not say what it really means so that each person is dancing a pas de deux of misinformation that leads to greater confusion and separation. For Huxley this ineffability is aggravated by the British stiff-upper-lip constraint that will not discuss inner emotions. With this ineffectual exchange of misinformation there is a constant slippage between what is said and what is meant—and this does not even begin to account for the deceptions of deliberate lies. Huxley wrote copiously on the nature of personal language and language used for propaganda—see *Brave New World*. Art, Huxley believed, was one of the vehicles by which people sought to bridge the gap of ineffability. Another bridge was the very recent development of psychoanalysis. In the 1920s, Virginia and Leonard Woolf's Hogarth Press had begun translating Freud into English and intellectuals read him avidly, learning that everything is about sex and that sexual repression was a bad thing; hence, lots of people, married or not, were having open relationships long before the 1960s.

In addition to Freud, another influence on Huxley's views of art and language was Nietzsche, and in a novel of ideas Huxley borrowed some from the very best. Nietzsche wrote, concerning the formative power of opposition and the role of language coextensive with opposition, that,

> To demand of strength that it should not express itself as strength, that it should not be a desire to overcome, a desire to throw down, a desire to become a master, a thirst for enemies and resistances and triumphs is just as absurd as to demand of weakness that it should express itself as strength. A quantum of force is equivalent to a quantum of drive, will, effect—more, it is nothing other than precisely this driving, willing, effecting, and only owing to the seduction of language (and of the fundamental errors of reason that are petrified in it) which conceives and misconceives all effects as conditioned by something that causes effects, by a "subject," can it appear otherwise. . . .
> There is only a perspective seeing, only a perspective "knowing"; and the more effects we allow to speak about one thing, the more eyes, different eyes, we can use to observe one thing, the more complete will be our "concept" of this thing, our "objectivity," be. (25, 79).

Huxley, as Philip Quarles, extrapolates Nietzsche, "the essence of the new way of looking is multiplicity. Multiplicity of eyes and multiplicity of aspects seen. For instance, one person interprets events in terms of bishops. . . . And then there's the biologist, the chemist, the physicist, the historian. Each sees . . . a different aspect of the event, a different layer of reality. What I want to do is to look with all those eyes at once" (192).

Many of the conceptions and misconceptions of language and, by extension, extrapolation and evolution, the life experiences that are strongly influenced by language's pervasively collective subjectivity, are the result of conflict and opposition between "strong" and "weak." For Nietzsche, these terms of "strong" and "weak," just like "good" and "evil," are among the "fundamental errors" pervasive within the *is*ness of language and life. (The *is*ness is not in error because it just *is*; only acts of cognition can err or seek to overcome error.) Any value of the words *strong, weak, good, evil* cannot be understood through static definition, which, for these words, is an impossibility. These words can only be understood in terms of causation and opposition. These words cause opposition by the very fact that they are intangibly subjective concepts, and their interpretation depends on which end of the power structure the perspectival eye of the beholder is looking out from. Language "conceives and misconceives" with the inevitable conflicts of what is meant and what is said in perpetual opposition.

For example, Walter Bidlake is chasing Lucy Tantamount and forsaking Marjorie Carling who has left her husband and become pregnant via Walter. Remember, this was a far different era from ours, where such things are commonplace. Marjorie's choices were considered scandalous; thus she had sacrificed her reputation for Walter's sake. Walter, the aspiring writer, tells Marjorie he is going out to see an editor—not true and she knows it. He is going to see Lucy. She whiningly asks him not to go. Walter is ashamed but undeterred:

> "Don't go," he heard her repeating. How that refined and drawling shrillness got on his nerves! "Please don't go, Walter."
> There was a sob in her voice. More blackmail. Ah, how could he be so base? And yet, in spite of his shame and, in a sense, because of it, he continued to feel the shameful emotions with an intensity that seemed to increase rather than diminish. His dislike of her grew because he was ashamed of it; the painful feelings of shame and self-hatred, which she caused him to feel, constituted for him yet another ground of dislike. Resentment bred shame, and shame in its turn bred more resentment. (4)

Huxley does not mean mere resentment; he meant what Nietzsche called *ressentiment:*

> The slave revolt in morality begins when *ressentiment* itself becomes
> creative and gives birth to values: the *ressentiment* of natures that are
> denied the true reaction, that of deeds, and compensate themselves
> with an imaginary revenge. While every noble morality develops from
> triumphant affirmation of itself, slave morality from the outset says No
> to what is "outside," what is "different," what is not "itself": and this
> No is its creative deed. This inversion of the value-positing eye—this
> need to direct one's view outward instead of back on oneself—is of the
> essence of *ressentiment*. (19)

Walter is a slave to his desire for Lucy and his "inversion of the
value-positing eye—this need to direct one's view outward instead
of back on itself," is what he does by his ressentiment of the shame
he feels by turning this inner shame outward toward Marjorie (or
others) in the form of resentful anger. This also applies to his role
as a book reviewer: "On paper Walter was all he failed to be in
life. His reviews were epigrammatically ruthless. Poor earnest spin-
sters, when they read what he had written of their heartfelt poems
about God and Passion and the Beauties of Nature, were cut to the
quick by his brutal contempt" (162). These poor poets get the wrath
he wants to direct at Marjorie. *Ressentiment* can be an individual
subjectivity but even more so a collective subjectivity as per Mr. Sita
Ram whom Philip Quarles meets in India: "Dere is one law for the
English," he said, " and anoder for de Indians, one for the oppressors
and anoder for the oppressed. De word justice has eider disappeared
from your vocab'lary, or else it has changed its meaning" (69-70). In
Nietzsche's purview, words like "justice" are not so much defined by
any intrinsic logic but by who is in power at any given time.

This pattern of individual and collective *ressentiment* will evolve
throughout the novel for many of the characters, who, like Walter,
feel guilt. Some, however, feel no guilt at all, particularly Maurice
Spandrell and Lucy; she, as well as other "modern" women, enjoys
the opportunity to turn the tables on men by acting as they believe
men act toward them:

> "Do you enjoy tormenting him?" Spandrell enquired. . . .
> "Tormenting whom?" said Lucy. "Walter? But I don't."
> "But you don't let him sleep with you?" . . . Lucy shook her head.
> "And then you say you don't torment him! Poor wretch!"
> "But why should I have him, if I don't want to?"
> "Why indeed? Meanwhile, however, keeping him dangling's mere
> torture."
> ". . . I assure you, I don't torment him. He torments himself. . . ."
> "Still, he only gets what's due to him. . . . He's the real type of
> murderee. . . . It takes two to make a murder. There are born victims.
> . . . Walter's the obvious victim; he fairly invites maltreatment. . . . And
> it's one's duty . . . to see that he gets it." (150-51)

This is sport for the idle rich who have too much time on their hands. Yet even Spandrell knows there could be a reckoning. Huxley here invokes the Destructive Element as well as earlier novels, J. K. Huysman's *A Rebours* and Oscar Wilde's *The Picture of Dorian Gray*.[2] For Spandrell,

> Time and habit had taken the wrongness out of all the acts he had once thought sinful. He performed them as unenthusiastically as he would have performed the act of catching the morning train to the city. "Some people . . . can only realize goodness by offending against it." But when the old offences have ceased to be felt as offences, what then? The argument pursued itself internally. The only solution seemed to be to commit new and progressively more serious offences, to have all the experiences, as Lucy would say in her jargon. "One way of knowing God" he concluded slowly, is to deny him. . . . [I]f you're equally unaware of goodness and offence against goodness, what *is* the point of having the sort of experiences the police interfere with?"
>
> Lucy shrugged her shoulders. "Curiosity. One's bored." (155)

Everyone's bored. That is, everyone's bored who has the money to be idle and bored: "Yes, yes. There's something peculiarly base and ignoble and diseased about the rich. Money breeds a kind of gangrened insensitiveness. It's inevitable. Jesus understood. The bit about the camel and the needle's eye is a mere statement of fact. And remember that other bit about loving your neighbours" (53).

Conversely, the poor and working class chafe at the insensitiveness of the rich's attitude of condescending noblesse oblige. Illidge is the working-class assistant to Lord Edward Tantamount, the scientist who conducts experiments that may be clever but are ultimately of no service to humanity: "But being unpleasant to and about the rich, besides being a pleasure, was also, in Illidge's eyes, a sacred duty. He owed it to his class, to society at large, to the future, to the cause of justice. . . . He thought of his brother Tom, who had weak lungs and worked a . . . machine in a motor factory. . . . He remembered washing days and the pink crinkled skin of his mother's water-sodden hands" (59-60). Indeed, Huxley from *Crome Yellow* forward, and peaking with *Point Counter Point*, castigates the rich for selfish behavior. He equally attacks the world of science that had objectified humanity to serve the ends of science and industry instead of being the means by which humanity could be served and improved. Certainly ameliorating the squalid conditions of the working class, like Illidge's brother Tom, would be an end worth scientific means.

Not all is negative in *Point Counter Point*. One can listen to Bach and feel something good:

> There are grand things in the world. . . .
>
> John Sebastian puts the case. The Rondeau begins, exquisitely and simply melodious, almost a folk song. . . . His [Bach's] is a slow and lovely meditation on the beauty (in spite of squalor and stupidity), the profound goodness (in spite of all the evil), the oneness (in spite of such bewildering diversity) of the world. It is a beauty, a goodness, a unity that no intellectual research can discover, that analysis dispels, but of whose reality the spirit is from time to time suddenly and overwhelmingly convinced. . . .
>
> The music was infinitely sad; and yet it consoled. . . . [I]t was able to affirm—deliberately, quietly . . . that everything was in some way right, acceptable. It included the sadness within some vaster, more comprehensive happiness. (23-25)

Early in the novel Huxley introduces his duality of a mystically spiritual basis that is juxtaposed to the physical reality of pain and sadness. The spirit cannot be gained by intellectuality, by trying to codify it and rationalize it. The spirit must be gained intuitively, without discursive reasoning. In *Point Counter Point* the exemplar of balanced reason and intuition is Rampion who is also the spokesperson for ending class divisions so that a meritocracy would be favored over an aristocracy.

Huxley's characters are not too happy and not too likable except for the happily married Mark and Mary Rampion, who provide the book's moral clarity of reason and passion in a workable balance. The others suffer from too much of one or the other, leading to failed love, envy, class hatred, infidelity, and murder, as Huxley juxtaposes one point of view against another. Through the surrogate of Mark Rampion, Huxley portrays D. H. Lawrence's personality and his ideas in this novel of ideas. Rampion says what he thinks and means what he says as a deliberate confutation of British restraint, which he considers a tourniquet against the flow of honest feelings. He says, "I don't suffer fools gladly" (94). In this mode he is the novel's conscience. He also echoes Illidge: "For Rampion there was also a kind of moral compulsion to live the life of the poor. Even when he was making quite a reasonable income. . . . To live like the rich, in a comfortable abstraction from material cares would be, he felt, a kind of betrayal of his class, of his own people. If he sat still and paid servants to work for him he would somehow be insulting his mother's memory, he would be posthumously telling her that he was too good to lead the life she had led" (110-11). And Huxley as Quarles thinks, "After a few hours in Mark Rampion's company he really believed in noble savagery; he felt convinced that the proudly conscious intellect ought to humble itself a little and admit the claims of the heart—aye, and the bowels, the loins, the bones and skin and muscles—to a fair share of life. The heart again!" (195).

Lidan Lin writes: "Huxley shared Lawrence's rejection . . . of being subservient to the order of mind and his espousal of the Dionysian mode of being that responds to the spontaneous impulses of the blood and the flesh. Both men agreed that things were going wrong, and neither Christianity nor a philosophy that was to replace it could offer solutions. Both men felt the need to return to a more immediate experience of being by connecting the self to the dark mystery of the Other surrounding us. But Huxley did not agree with Lawrence that science and intellect were wholly useless since Huxley believed that both could be made to serve the good of the world."

In this novel of ideas the very concept of a "novel of ideas" is an innovation that was and still is imitated. Recent examples include Don DeLillo's *Underworld*—as close to *Point Counter Point* in essaying ideas as is possible—and Paul Auster's *City of Glass*. Huxley's perspectives on politics, ecology, art, science, language, and much more are profoundly prescient. Lucy's father, Lord Edward Tantamount, the scientist (in part J. B. S. Haldane), discusses finite natural resources with the fascist Webley, who wants to take over Britain: " 'No doubt,' he said, 'you think you can make good the loss with phosphate rocks. But what'll you do when the deposits are exhausted?' He poked Everard in the shirt front. 'What then? Only two hundred years and they'll be finished. You think we're being progressive because we're living on our capital Phosphates, coal, petroleum, nitre—squander them all. That's your policy. And meanwhile you go round trying to make our flesh creep with talk about revolutions' " (57). When Webley asks Lord Edward if he wants a revolution, Tantamount wants to know if this would reduce the population, which would then use fewer resources. Assured it would, Tantamount responds, " 'Then certainly I want a revolution.' The Old Man thought in terms of geology and was not afraid of logical conclusions" (57-58).

Huxley's lifelong concern with the duality between passion and reason is fully explored in *Point Counter Point*. Multiple aspects of experience are juxtaposed—point counterpointed in the musical sense—to achieve the clearest depiction of what happens when passion and reason are not in accord. Huxley believed as early as age twenty-one that the path to true balance and an end of duality would in some way be found through a mystical consciousness, which he discusses at length in his 1931 anthology of poetry *Texts and Pretexts*, but not yet in the formula that he would embrace after he came to America. In *Brave New World*, however, Huxley would not yet end his discussion of conflicted duality, but he would use his future dystopia as the ultimate argument of how a cold scientific reasoning without human passion would be the end of human progress, even while this science mistakenly believed it had acted for human progress.

Brave New World (1932)

> [I have been writing] a comic, or at least satirical, novel about the future, showing the appallingness (at any rate by our standards) of Utopia and adumbrating the effects on thought and feeling of such quite possible biological inventions as the production of children in bottles (with consequent abolition of the family and of all the Freudian "complexes" for which family relationships are responsible), the prolongation of youth, the devising of some harmless but effective substitute for alcohol, cocaine, opium, etc—and also the effects of sociological reforms as Pavlovian conditioning of all children from and before birth, universal peace, security and stability.
> —Huxley, in a letter to his father, 24 August 1931

> "God," said St. Augustine, "who made us without our help will not save us without our consent." Propaganda, like the sword, attempts to eliminate consent or dissent and, in our age magical language, has to a great extent replaced the sword.
> I can imagine, though I know, thank God, that it will never happen, the following situation. A group of pious multi-millionaires buy time on radio and TV at a moment when the Church happens to have at its disposal a number of brilliant demagogic evangelists, who know all the tricks of appeal. Bombarded by sermons, religious movies and musicals, the public are persuaded that to go to church is to be with it, so presently all the churches are full every Sunday. What will this signify? Neither more nor less than the forcible conversions of the Barbarians in the eighth and ninth centuries.
> —W. H. Auden (129-30)

> O, wonder!
> How many goodly creatures are there here!
> How beauteous mankind is! O brave new world,
> That has such people in't!
> —Shakespeare, The Tempest

How influential is Huxley's 1932 novel Brave New World? The title, while originally from Shakespeare's The Tempest, is recognized from Huxley's novel, and today these three words are a catch phrase for any person or idea that is cutting edge and may have a possible positive/negative duality.

If one Googles "brave new world" (as of 11 May 2005) there are 953,000 hits and the majority are not about Huxley's novel. Examples: "The Brave New World of Customer Centricity," "Mental Health Review, Brave New World," "Iraq embraces a brave new world of democracy," "Brave New World Astrology Alive!," "The Brave New World of E-Showbiz," "Computer Intelligence: A Brave New World," "Politics in a Brave New World," "Koreans Discover Brave New World of Blog," "Brave New World Surf Shop." No other twentieth-century novel title has become such a ubiquitous term. The meaning of the phrase as Huxley intended is now both ubiquitous and threatening, as can be seen in an essay written in 2000:

> Human nature itself lies on the operating table, ready for alteration, "enhancement," and wholesale redesign.
> Some transforming powers are already here. The pill. In vitro fertilization. Bottled embryos. Surrogate wombs. Cloning. Genetic screening. Organ harvests. Mechanical spare parts. Chimeras. Brain implants. Ritalin for the young, Viagra for the old, and Prozac for everyone. And, to leave this vale of tears, a little extra morphine accompanied by Muzak. What? You still have troubles? Not to worry. As the vaudevillians used to say, "You ain't seen nothin' yet!"
> Years ago Aldous Huxley saw it coming. More important, he knew what it meant and, in his charming but disturbing novel, *Brave New World*, Huxley made it strikingly visible for all to see. *Brave New World*'s . . . power increases with each rereading, and coming generations of readers should—and I hope will—find it still more compelling. For unlike other frightening futuristic novels of the past century, such as Orwell's already dated *Nineteen Eighty-four*, Huxley shows us a dystopia that goes with, rather than against, the human grain—indeed, it is animated by modernity's most humane and progressive aspirations. Following those aspirations to their ultimate realization, Huxley enables us to recognize those less obvious but often more pernicious evils that are inextricably linked to successful attainment of partial goods. And he strongly suggests that we must choose: either our misery-ridden but still richly human world, or the squalid happiness of the biotechnical world to come. In this satirical novel, Huxley paints human life seven centuries hence, living under the gentle hand of a compassionate humanitarianism that has been rendered fully competent by genetic manipulation, psychopharmacology, hypnopeaedia, and high-tech amusements. At long last, mankind has succeeded in eliminating disease, aggression, war, pain, anxiety, suffering, hatred, guilt, envy, and grief. But this victory comes at a heavy price: homogenization, mediocrity, pacification, spurious contentment, trivial pursuits, shallow attachments, debasement of tastes, and souls without loves or longings. (Kass 51-52)

Huxley's world of "human life seven centuries hence" is already upon us. Huxley himself recognized it long before the year 2000, first in his introduction to the 1946 edition of *Brave New World* and then in book-length form for 1958's nonfiction evaluation *Brave New World Revisited.* This novel, the precursor for the modern genre of science fiction,[3] is still telling the future, and as Kass signifies, the threats it depicts are now more reality than fantasy: "brave new man will be cursed to acquire precisely what he wished for only to discover—painfully and too late—that what he wished for is not exactly what he wanted. Or, Huxley implies . . . he may be so dehumanized that he will not even recognize that in aspiring to be perfect he is no longer even human (52).

In Huxley's *Brave New World* the duality of reason and passion is explicitly out of balance. There is no emotional passion whatsoever; the world is run by Mustapha Mond. John the Savage enters this world and almost turns it upside down. The novel shows us the two squaring off. Mond argues, "The world's stable now. People are happy; they get what they want, and they never want what they can't get. They're well off; they're safe; they're never ill; they're not afraid of death; they're blissfully ignorant of passion and old age; they're plagued with no mothers or fathers; they've got no wives, or children, or lovers to feel strongly about; they're so conditioned that they practically can't help behaving as they ought to behave. And if anything should go wrong, there's *soma*" (220). *Soma* is the all-purpose feel good drug that fixes everything; a populace in a stupor is not inclined to be rebellious. John the Savage counters,

> "But I don't want comfort. I want God, I want poetry, I want real danger, I want freedom, I want goodness. I want sin."
> "In fact," said Mustapha Mond, "you're claiming the right to be unhappy."
> "All right then," said the Savage defiantly, "I'm claiming the right to be unhappy." (240)

John is actually claiming the right to have free will, choices, initiative, and spiritual freedom. In this world the people are the types that Huxley first had Scogan describe in *Crome Yellow.* They are conditioned to fill and accept certain roles genetically and with "educational" conditioning that amounts to brainwashing. The masses are pacified to believe they want for nothing. All is good—so they believe—nothing is bad. There is no sense of comparison. They are lazy, not just of body but also of mind—their ability to think independently has nearly disappeared. While the collective body of the people was pacified, the collective mind was falling into apathy and ignorance. The world was becoming soulless, and without soul and sprit, in Huxley's vision, there would be no progress toward the evolution of consciousness—and that is much more important than being pacified by the constant sensuous satiety of food, sex, and drugs.

If there is no dark, one cannot truly appreciate the light and think about why the light and dark need to be compared. Light and dark, strong and weak, good and evil have no meaning without contrast, and it is from thinking on their meanings that the collective mind moves toward an evolving spiritual consciousness. The mystics call this the Reconciliation of Opposites. The friction and fission of these opposites rubbing against each other create the energy needed for consciousness to evolve. Without a Reconciliation of Opposites the body may be satisfied, but the spirit knows nothing of what it means to be good, to be strong, to be heroic and noble. And without this knowledge life has no meaning. Moreover, the Reconciliation of Opposites explains the force of what Huxley would later call upward transcendence, the desire to move toward the world of spirit. Downward transcendence occurs when one thinks too much of oneself and not for the good of the whole. If all good is given instead of chosen, there would be no effort to learn the difference and no progress toward the evolution of consciousness.

This is Huxley's first novel to have a plot. The novel was written relatively quickly to fulfill a contractual obligation to his publisher. Huxley had been having difficulties with another social novel and knew he wouldn't complete it on time. The novel opens 600 years hence in 2632 A.F. (which means After Ford, as in Henry Ford, the father of mass production and the god of the New World), and after civilization was largely destroyed by a world war. Dictatorship by the tyranny of the boot-on-the-neck approach did not work—repression through force eventually collapses under its own effort to maintain it, as it did in the Soviet Union in 1989. A second war follows, and the formation of the Brave New World begins; it achieves stability through pleasure instead of fear, conditioning the mass to believe it is happy. Society has a scientifically engineered and cloned caste system. The five highest castes are Scogan's superior beings, while the rest perform the drudgework. Ten Controllers run the world, and stability is enforced by brainwashing minds from infancy to accept their roles and by tranquilizing adults with *soma*. Feelings of passion and the expiation of passion are limited to a permitted sexual promiscuity; strong feelings for any single individual are in no way encouraged. Independent thinking is repressed. Any sign of it means exile for the thinker. Science and "reason" exert control. Marriage and normal childbirth are not even remembered except as barbaric rites conducted long ago by primitive savages.

The novel begins with students being given a guided tour through the London Hatcheries that clone castes. Henry Foster and Lenina Crowne, who work there, have been seeing each other too regularly, which is against state rules. Emotional attachments are not in the state's best interests. Lenina's friend Fanny warns her to be careful and display a more socially acceptable promiscuity. Lenina follows Fanny's advice and decides to see Bernard Marx, who is very intelligent but a bit quirky and slightly nonconformist compared to the others of his caste. Lenina and Bernard go on a vacation to a Savage Reservation in New Mexico. (Huxley had been to New Mexico to visit D. H. Lawrence.) There, the inhabitants live primitively and engage in those barbaric practices of marriage and childbirth. Before Bernard leaves, he is warned by the Director of Hatcheries, Tomakin, that his eccentricities could get him exiled to Iceland.

In New Mexico, Lenina and Bernard meet Linda and her son, John the Savage. Bernard learns that long ago Linda had come to the Reservation with Tomakin, who had abandoned her there. Linda, pregnant by Tomakin, knew that she could not return to the "normal" world in such a disgraced state; she stayed on the Reservation and raised John. Bernard brings Linda and John back to Utopia. Tomakin, stunned, humiliated, and ridiculed, resigns. Bernard believes he has eluded exile to Iceland.

With Bernard as his keeper, John becomes a popular curiosity and amusement, and Bernard enjoys the attention that John brings him along with the women who had previously not been interested in him. John is repulsed by the ways of the New World. He will not take *soma*, because he knows it is a fool's cure. Lenina is attracted to John and tries to seduce him—which is normal in her world. John, who read Shakespeare on the Reservation and believes in the plays' noble ideals, particularly romantic love over sexual promiscuity, resists his sexual attraction and rejects her advances. This scene is replete with a then unheard of striptease that Huxley implies by the repetition of "zip," as in Lenina undoing her zippered up outfit.

When his mother dies from a *soma* overdose—she had no qualms about taking it—John rebels. He tries to convert the others to his romantic ideals and briefly causes a stir that must be repressed. Bernard and his friend Helmholtz Watson are blamed for the small rebellion. When the two of them, along with John, are taken to Mustapha Mond, Bernard and Helmholtz are exiled, and John is retained for further experimentation. He resists and tries to flee into solitude, but the citizens of Utopia continue to hound him. In a fit of misery and depression, John hangs himself (as did Huxley's brother Trevenen when he too could not abide the world he lived in).

John the Savage is no more savage than Queequeg in Melville's *Moby-Dick*, which Huxley had read, as noted in a 1923 letter. Among his supposedly civilized crewmates, Queequeg, the Pacific Islander, was, in Ishmael's (and Melville's) view, more spiritually advanced. Queequeg and John the "Savage" are both looking for a balance of passion and reason.

D. H. Lawrence was the life force that inhabited *Point Counter Point*, and he is the spirit force that suffuses *Brave New World*. Lawrence died in 1930. He died in the presence of his wife Frieda and Aldous and Maria Huxley, whom he had asked to be with him. Lidan Lin writes, in reviewing Dana Sawyer's *Aldous Huxley: A Biography*, "Lawrence's influence contributed to the composition of the novel. . . . Huxley shared Lawrence's aversion for the process of industrialization that turns humans into mechanical objects. . . . As Sawyer writes, . . . 'Both Huxley and Lawrence believed that work . . . can cause us to shirk our first duty to life, which is to live.' Sawyer also illuminates the extent to which Huxley's disapproval of H. G. Wells' utopian novel *Men Like Gods*, and Henry Ford's autobiography *My Life and Work* spurred the composition of the novel."

Huxley, who had hoped to be a scientist like his grandfather and his brother Julian, could not because of his poor vision. This did not deter him from learning about science, which he did enthusiastically. With Julian's help he had access to the most cutting edge ideas, which included eugenics, the potential for conditioning humans through biological means. The research fascinated him but alarmed him as well. After the rise of Mussolini and Hitler, Huxley understood that dictators would use any means to subjugate a populace.

In 1929 Huxley met Gerald Heard, who would replace Lawrence as his best friend. Heard was already deeply involved with his philosophy of humanity being actually a spiritual species that had gone astray from its spiritual underpinnings. He affirmed Huxley's deepening interest in mysticism, and together they explored the potential for rejuvenating the latent spirit in human beings. Lawrence's lasting influence and Heard's living influence sustained the rest of Huxley's life.

In *Brave New World* spirit is absent. There is no need for God. Mustapha Mond quotes from the philosopher Maine de Biran (which means this is an idea that Huxley wants his readers to see):

"the religious sentiment tends to develop as we grow older; to develop because, as the passions grow calm, as the fancy and sensibilities are less excited and less excitable, our reason becomes less troubled in its working . . . whereupon God emerges as from behind a cloud; our soul feels, sees, turns towards the source of all light; turns naturally and inevitably; for now that all that gave to the world of sensations its life and charm has begun to leak away from us . . . we feel the need to lean on something that abides, something that will never play us false—a reality, an absolute and everlasting truth. Yes, we inevitably turn to God; for this religious sentiment is of its nature so pure, so delightful to the soul that experiences it, that it makes up to us for all our other losses." (274-75)

Peter Bowering writes of this passage, "For the citizens of the World-State there are no losses to compensate for; there is no need for a substitute for youthful desires when youthful desires remain to the end, therefore religious sentiment is rendered superfluous. And, if there is no need for God, then the values which human beings normally reverence are likewise irrelevant; self-denial and chastity, nobility and patience are also superfluous. There is no need for any civilized man to bear anything that is unpleasant. God and moral values are incompatible with machinery, scientific medicine and universal happiness" (110).

In Wholly Truthful art, tragedy is in conflict with routine; this gives everyday life its perspective about what is truly important. In a Brave New World of ceaseless pacification and sensual pleasure, there is no basis for comparison; stability is maintained, but the spirit's evolution toward consciousness is stalled. Only when individuals, then small groups, then larger groups, then towns, etc., seek to renew the life of the spirit can humanity reach its destiny—which is union with the divine ground of all being. This became Huxley's motivation thereafter in fiction and nonfiction, leading up to his most profound novel of the spirit, *Time Must Have a Stop*.

Time Must Have a Stop (1944)

Like *Brave New World*, *Time Must Have Stop* has a plot. Sebastian Barnack is the young man at the human center of Huxley's novel, but the search for a spiritual center is the novel's quest. The time frame is early Mussolini. Sebastian is a talented poet in his teens. He is very handsome, but he regrets his baby-faced looks, because they are in conflict with the serious, aspiring genius he wishes to be. His father is a humorously stern, stiff-upper-lip Briton and an uncompromising lawyer who talks a good game of socialist politics that he does not act on whatsoever. He silently resents how Sebastian looks like his late mother, a beauty of more outgoing but cheerful eccentricities. The father unconsciously (or is it consciously?) withholds from Sebastian material advantages, such as an evening suit suitable to his station, claiming that luxuries will spoil the boy. Sebastian must endure being with his wealthy British public school peers wearing hand-me-downs.

Consequently, Sebastian is thrilled when he is sent to Italy to visit Uncle Eustace, a courtly man who gives rather than withholds life's finer things and ideas, including a gift of a Degas painting and a promise of new clothes. Sebastian falls in love with a down-to-earth but mischievous caretaker at Eustace's mansion and is seduced by her. Eustace suddenly dies, and Sebastian, realizing he will not get his evening clothes, decides to swap the Degas for a new tuxedo, being greatly cheated in the process. An audit of the estate notes the missing Degas, and employees are accused. Sebastian says nothing; he knows he must get the Degas back. Unable to do so himself, he enlists the help of Uncle Bruno Rontini, a "flighty" spiritual enthusiast.

Uncle Bruno retrieves the painting, but by calling on certain friends for help, he inadvertently makes himself an enemy of the Italian Fascisti. The Fascist police imprison and mistreat him, thus hastening his declining health. When Bruno is released, a guilty and chastened Sebastian takes care of his dying uncle and is profoundly moved by the old man's spirituality, which is now no longer seen as flighty but essential. Bruno's spirituality begins a transformation in Sebastian toward a spiritual upward transcendence that teaches him awareness, maturity, love, and compassion for others. In his adulthood Bruno's effect on Sebastian is still felt, as an epilogue indicates. Years after World War II, and missing a leg, a mature Sebastian still writes poetry. This is the story, but what's innovative here is how Huxley writes a spiritual novel espousing a particular spiritual context, the Perennial Philosophy of mysticism.

Thus far, mysticism has been the intrinsic weave permeating Huxley's thought. At first it was unformed, just as Huxley was in his progress toward maturity. After *Brave New World* his next novel, *Eyeless in Gaza* (1936), was a study in the spiritual progress of Anthony Beavis, which included the pacifism Huxley embraced in the early-to-mid-1930s. Beavis knew, as Huxley knew, that pacifism was aligned with spirituality, but neither could define precisely how they were aligned. After coming to America in 1937 and moving to Hollywood in 1938, Huxley and Gerald Heard studied Vedanta, based on the ancient Hindu scriptures, the Bhagavad-Gita and Upanishads. Vedanta is the oldest known scripture by centuries and was based in an intuitive belief in human beings' integral mystical spirituality, which remains dormant until each individual chooses to awaken it. Huxley's first American novel, *After Many a Summer Dies the Swan* (1939), began to incorporate a more studied mysticism through the character of Mr. Propter (based on Heard) who explains it to others. In 1945 Huxley published his anthology *The Perennial Philosophy*, in which he correlated mystical writings from all eras and origins and showed, with his brilliant commentary, how they all expressed the same beliefs despite great separations of time and distance.

The plot of *Time Must Have a Stop* sounds simple, almost mundane; however, the philosophy in this novel of ideas is perhaps the most profound that was ever attempted to be conveyed in a fiction.

One can appreciate the novel without being an expert in the Perennial Philosophy, but one will be awed by it through understanding the Perennial Philosophy. One can even point to at least one conversion of a reader in a book titled *How I Became a Hindu*:

> I was born a Hindu. But I had ceased to be one by the time I came out of college at the age of 22 [in 1946]. I had become a Marxist and a militant atheist. I had come to believe that Hindu scriptures should be burnt in a bonfire if India was to be saved. . . .
>
> I was heading full steam into Communism when I received a severe jolt. It was a novel by Aldous Huxley, *Time Must Have A Stop*. . . . I had never read a book by Huxley so far. This one was quite a revelation of his unique genius. I was enraptured by one of its characters, Bruno, contemplating the dark destiny of an erudite scholar with great compassion. But what almost broke my Marxist spell was his demolition of the dogma of inevitable progress which was the bedrock of all Western thought, including Marxism, during the nineteenth century. He also questioned as a *"manipulative fallacy"* the repeated reconstruction of social, economic and political institutions to achieve a more equitable order of things. His conclusion was that the roots of social evils lay ultimately in human nature itself. . . .
>
> This book shook me very badly and its influence was to surface two years later. Meanwhile, I took to reading Huxley and finished his major novels as well as . . . *Ends and Means* and the *Perennial Philosophy*. I was preparing myself to dwell on a different dimension of thought and feeling. (Goel)

In a Huxleyan irony, a Briton taught an Indian how to be a Hindu, although not a modern ritualistic Hindu, rather, the Vedantic, mystical Hindu. Many more converts to mysticism would follow. Yet in 1945 mysticism was still a new venue for philosophy and more so for literature. *Time Must Have a Stop* and Isherwood's novel *Prater Violet* (1945) were philosophic parables. Few critics could grasp this because they had no clue about the underlying philosophical intentions of the authors. Bowering writes, "The critical reception of *Time Must Have a Stop* was largely one of unqualified mystification: one reviewer spoke of 'this immensely interesting, rather confusing, rather confused book'; another referred to 'the baffling mystical abstractions of Mr. Huxley's new faith,' concluding that 'much of its mystic message is incomprehensible' " (160-61). In today's post-1960s, post-New Age world, the message is no longer a mystery to the many who have learned the Perennial Philosophy, which will here be summarized as a necessary framework for understanding how Huxley's mystical predilection found its clearest voice in his work from 1945 forward.

> *But thought's the slave of life, and life's time fool,*
> *And time, that takes survey of all the world, Must have a stop.*
> —Shakespeare, *Henry IV, Part I*

> *Now there are some things we all know but we don't take'm*
> *out and look at'm very often. We all know something is*
> *eternal. And it ain't houses and it ain't names, and it ain't*
> *earth, and it ain't even stars—everybody knows in their*
> *bones that something is eternal, and that something has*
> *to do with human beings. All the greatest people ever lived*
> *been telling us that for five thousand years and yet you'd*
> *be surprised how many people are always letting go of that*
> *fact. There's something way down deep that's eternal about*
> *every human being. [People are] waitin' for something they*
> *feel is comin'. Something important and great . . . waitin'*
> *for the eternal part of them to come out. . . .*
> —Thornton Wilder, *Our Town* (44).

Huxley, despite his being called godless in the 1920s and 1930s, was far from being unspiritual. His cynical fiction was meant to display a world that was falling far short of the human potentiality that the mind, seeking rather than rejecting an intuitive spirituality, could fulfill in a world where spirit would overcome materialism. Since much less has been written about Huxley's American writings after 1939 than his British writings before 1939, the full importance of his belief in the Perennial Philosophy and this philosophy's meaning has been given little coverage, which means that his American work cannot be fully understood and appreciated. One cannot do justice to Huxley without a proper account of his mystical beliefs.

When he came to America in 1939 with Gerald Heard,[4] they both had been interested in the nature of evolving consciousness for many years. Heard and Huxley began attending the lectures at The Vedanta Society of Southern California. Vedanta, a mystical philosophy, is the basis for all subsequent mystical branches of the Hindu, Greek, Roman, Judaic, Islamic, and Christian religions. In 1945 Huxley anthologized the mystical writings of all religions in his book *The Perennial Philosophy*, augmented with his brilliant commentary. This book would lead to the booming renewal of interest in Eastern and mystical philosophy that is still prominent, with the 1960-1970s perhaps the zenith and with translations of the Vedas selling in the millions. The following elucidation of mystical philosophy is derived from Huxley's writings and from the original sources that he was writing about.

The Perennial Philosophy[5] (the philosophy of mysticism) has its seminal beginnings in the ancient Hindu sacred texts that are the first enunciations/elucidations of mysticism as an integral, continuous, contiguous, atomized essence within and without all existence, physically and psychically. Atoms move, but we can't see them; nevertheless, they exist. Consciousness evolves, but we can't see it; yet mystical philosophers believe it—beginning with the ancient texts. These texts—the Vedas—made their way from India to inform the East, then the West, through the derivatively evolving disciplines of Buddhism, Confucianism, Taoism, Platonism, Zen, Christian mysticism, German transcendentalism, British romanticism, American transcendentalism, Theosophy, and on the eve of the twentieth century came full circle in the revitalization and dissemination of the Vedas through the worldwide Vedanta Society. The Greeks may have been the cradle of Western civilization, but the Vedas are the womb of world civilization. The links in the chain are definitive and strong. This wisdom is perennial from some amorphous, indefinable beginning to some future, as yet indefinable end—and then it will start all over again in an endless cyclical regeneration. The Vedas' impetus of creation is exactly the big bang theory of an initial first cause that evolves as an ascending, widening spiral of the expanding universe, which scientists see as a physical process. The Vedas see it as both physical and metaphysical, that there is a corresponding, concurrent psychical expansion/evolution.

According to the Perennial Philosophy there are immutable constructs that change constantly in appearance but remain constant in their essence; yet, the changes are distinct and recognizable to nonmystically inclined perceivers, which causes these perceivers to see only flux as defined by the five senses. These senses and the individuals using them feel a separateness devised by eye and ear that assumes that one is never part of a whole because one cannot see oneself included with others without the aid of a picture or mirror—relatively recent methods—that have not yet quite caught up with the thousands of years of "I am I; you are not I." Indeed, the revelation of a primal group standing over their reflection in still water must have been as astounding as thunder and lightning. Separateness is man's physical condition; alienation is his assumption inculcated from his inability to see himself with others. Thus Vico theorized that humans created language to explain the disturbances to their senses (thunder, lightning), and the language, from which they developed fables, was initially inspired by their awe/fear of the natural world. Language was a creation that attempted to overcome both nature and separateness but in its development further separated individuals, as no two people interpret language in exactly the same way. Vico believed that these awe-sociations became fables, then became poetic wisdom, then became esoteric wisdom (philosophy) in an ever-ascending and widening spiral of complexity that became so far removed from the initial feelings of awe-sociation that individuals can no longer intimate feelings of awe solely from the natural world, as their childlike primitive ancestors did.

Feelings of awe are transcendent; the concentration upon the feeling of awe is systematic transcendence. Mystics meditate; artists create. Both are intuitive concentrations that hope and often succeed in evoking awesome transcendent feelings. The Katha Upanishad (1.2.22-24) explains the importance of intuiting the undifferentiated unity of the self: "The wise who knows the Self as bodiless within the bodies, as unchanging among changing things, as great and omnipresent, does never grieve. That self cannot be gained by the Veda, nor by understanding, nor by much learning. He whom the Self chooses, by him the Self can be gained. The Self chooses him (his body) as his own. But he who has not first turned away from his wickedness, who is not tranquil, and subdued, or whose mind is not at rest, he can never obtain the Self (even) by knowledge." Plainly, intuition is paramount; yet, spiritual intuition is less likely for the many that do not have any clue about achieving some form of inner self-understanding. Mystics and artists choose to pursue self-understanding.

Disciples or audiences wish to share in the awe-sociations of the mystic and artist. This desire has not changed since the earliest fable-makers created Viconian "fabula." The essence of awe has not changed either; the wise artist knows he is reflecting new images that are updated versions derived from the same long-evolving spiral begun by his ancestors. Fables to poetry to philosophy—all the same. Flux is a process, not the chaos that is seen in the material world; dialectics is a process, not an end. Consciousness evolves from the reconciliation of opposites as described in the Isha Upanishad and in the sixth chapter of the Bhagavad-Gita.

The Isha Upanishad teaches that evolving consciousness comes through the reconciliation of opposites, by the perception of essential Unity, of the apparently incompatible opposites, God and the world, renunciation and enjoyment, action and internal freedom, the one and the many, being and its becomings, the passive divine impersonality and the active divine personality, the knowledge and the ignorance, the becoming and the not-becoming. The Gita teaches that only the discerning man who chooses to be a calm center to life's hurricane and understands the reconciliation of opposites can hope to see the undifferentiated unity of the Ultimate Reality.

> He who regards
> With an eye that is equal
> Friends and comrades,

> The foe and the kinsman,
> The vile, the wicked,
> The men who judge him,
> And those who belong
> To neither faction: . . . He is the greatest. (81-82)

Through the fission of the reconciliation of opposites, activity creates graduated resolutions that proceed to another moment of the *eternal now* of "*is*ness," which is described by the Vedanta-influenced T. S. Eliot in "Burnt Norton" when Eliot echoes the Vedas and concludes, "And all is always now" (112).

The resolutions that graduate from the reconciliation of opposites exist in the *eternal now* and move fluidly without interruption to become the next sources of opposites needing to be reconciled while consciousness continues to move up the ascending spiral. The movement is fluid and imperceptible. The senses may see, hear, feel, touch, or taste the outcomes of these resolutions, but these physical outcomes are static. The outcomes are the residue of a movement after a particular movement is over. One drinks water, eats food, touches silk only after the process of their becoming reaches its material end; one is rarely conscious of the process and becomes focused only on the results. For the many, awareness of process, whether of an apple or consciousness, is rarely and barely thought about unless an aspect of process becomes an expedient necessity such as drought or famine. Necessity may be the mother of invention, but for the many, "mother" often doesn't speak until necessity is expedient and mandatory. Throughout history farsightedness has been in short supply and the barn door has been closed after the animals escaped. (Or a need to cut oil consumption is not seen as a necessity until chaos is recognized.) The many cannot grasp the hidden *all*ness of the bigger picture. What is misperceived to be linear, to be before/after, cause/effect, is finite and confined to an expedient present disconnected from the process of evolution. To the misperceiving majority events are dots on a line and the majority cannot see the continuity and contiguity of the present dots and how they are related to previous dots. The previous dots are forgotten or they are only memories or histories. The majority also cannot see the future that is ahead and too far off to consider or imagine. Conversely, to artists and mystics time is only a man-made construct to which we adhere slavishly and detrimentally.

Thornton Wilder wrote, "It is only in appearance that time is a river. It is a vast landscape, and it is only the eye of the beholder that moves" (*Eighth Day* 395). If one throws a rock into a pond, one can watch the process from the initial splash to the expanding circular ripples. If one could stand back far enough and see the big bang, one could see the first cause and follow the oval expansion of the universe moment-to-moment, *istgeist* to *istgeist* (*is*ness to *is*ness) and see the cause and effect of how each *is*ness ripples into the next *is*ness. From the expanding ripples in the pond to an expanding universe, these images—one real based on visible nature, one "metaphorized" as an extrapolation of invisible nature—help one's actual eyes to "see" an idea, like atoms, that the mind's eye can understand only by a leap of the imagination, even though atoms are real, not imagined. To imagine connotes "seeing" what isn't there; but atoms *are* there, spinning in a circle that is the ultimate microcosm of the larger microcosm of the pond, and both the atom and the pond are within the ultimate macrocosm of the expanding universe. All the sense-perceived microcosms seem differentiated, but if one sees as the mystic sees, then Ultimate Reality is both *is*ness and process. One sees a cloud that is made up of condensed water, from which drops of rain merge into an ocean. The drops are a process, a moment of *is*ness that flows from one *is*ness (cloud) to another *is*ness (ocean).

From the eye of the beholder who sees the vast landscape, one can see both the *is*ness and the process simultaneously and *Time Stops*:

> *Any given event in any part of the universe has as its determining conditions all previous and contemporary events in all parts of the universe.*

Imagination (intuition) can allow us to see the timeless interrelations. But imagination is not just about seeing what isn't real; it is equally about "seeing" what *is* real—atoms. Imagination leads to the discovery of what is physically real and can be measured (science). Imagination also leads to the discovery of what is metaphysically real and can be "metaphorized" (art). Science and art are about seeing what previously was not seen but was imagined (intuited), after which the scientist and artist take what was imagined and make it into an outcome that *can* be seen or heard. Michael Polanyi said, "*We know much more than we can tell*" (25).[6] *Telling* is an outcome of what is already known, even when that telling might be imagining what is not yet known. (A science-fiction writer takes the known to imagine what an unknown future might be like. He or she wishes to transcend the known through the creative impulse.) Art is one vehicle for transcendence. Humans have a compelling desire for transcendence, which for most is an unconscious need without a cognitive, let alone a philosophical, basis. There are forms of upward transcendence and downward transcendence.[7] Upward transcendence is more conscious of its own ambitions; downward transcendence is often crudely unconscious. Upward: mysticism, art, spirituality, love (mystic love for the individual as *eros* then transformed to the transcendently awesome love for all existence of *agape*). Downward: addictions (drugs, alcohol, sex, religious dogma and fanaticism, nationalistic fanaticism).

Transcendence, conscious or unconscious, is the desire of humanity; transcendence is the design of the Perennial Philosophy, first recorded in the Vedas. Still, long before the 3,000-year-old Vedas, awe-sociations were recorded by the primitive fabulists described in Vico's *New Science*. The creative impulse of art/literature is the reflective dialectical synthesis of moments in space. These moments re-create awe and evoke a sense of unicity that seeks to overcome feelings of separation. Unity with the Ultimate Reality is the goal of the Perennial Philosophy. The continuum of the statement above starting "any given event" includes the evolution of man's consciousness. The metaphysical basis for the quotation and its assertion of an overall perpetual continuum of existence is contained within the Perennial Philosophy.

Within this philosophy is the concept of an Ultimate Reality or Ground of Being (perhaps divine) that is both the first cause of the continuum and the continuum itself. An artistic perspective as grounded in the Perennial Philosophy is just now becoming a view that some critics, particularly in Europe and Russia—and Satya Mohanty in America—have begun to apply to literature, seeing certain writers as exponents who have consciously or unconsciously incorporated this philosophy into their art.

The vast literature of mysticism that reflects the Perennial Philosophy has been given an encapsulated form by Huxley. The "any given event" aphorism is a good basis for understanding what Huxley called *The Minimum Working Hypothesis*, which summarizes the common denominators of the Perennial Philosophy into four basic tenets that were first stated in his introduction to the 1944 Isherwood/Prabhavananda translation of *The Bhagavad Gita*. To consider these tenets as a prelude to the American Huxley is to make the same metaphysical leap that philosophers and writers have made in their careers. If the reader is also able to make this leap even temporarily, then Huxley's American fiction and nonfiction will fit into a much clearer context:

Minimum Working Hypothesis
1. the phenomenal world of matter and of individualized consciousness—the world of things and animals and even gods—is the manifestation of a Divine Ground within which all partial realities have their being, and apart from which they would be non-existent.
2. human beings are capable not merely of knowing about the Divine Ground by inference [intimating the awe-sociations]; they can also realize its existence by a direct intuition [i.e., meditation, art] superior

to discursive reasoning. This immediate knowledge unites the knower with that which is known.

3. man possesses a double nature, a phenomenal ego and an eternal self, which is the inner man, the spirit, the spark of divinity within the soul. It is possible for a man, if he so desires, to identify himself with this spirit and therefore with the Divine Ground which is of the same or like nature with the spirit.

4. man's life on earth has only one end and purpose: to identify himself with his eternal self and so come to unitive knowledge of the Divine Ground of all existence. (7)

The key to Huxley's hypothesis is the role of intuition as a guide to knowledge that cannot be otherwise found empirically:

It is the task of philosophy to try to translate and understand analytically in terms of thought or conceptual thinking what has been presented in the living experience of intuition. It must start from experience and it must recognize experience to be the goal of all philosophy. Philosophy cannot give us an experience of the actual—it attempts to show what is possible, not what *is* but what *may be*. The merely possible demands verification or rather an actualization in concrete experience. This is supplied by intuition. A philosophy that does not base itself on this solid footing of perfect experience is a merely barren speculation that moves in the sphere of ideas alone, detached from Reality. This is what distinguishes Hegel's Idea from Sankara's Brahman. The latter is a concrete experience in ecstatic intuition, while the former is only the highest achievement of reason. (Brahma 167)

Intuition drives the inspiration of the creative impulse even if hard work follows to see that impulse through to the art's completion. Art is a means to the end for the artist and his audience to intimate the *awe*-sociations that are harbored in the unconscious in order to identify with and come to "unitive knowledge" of the "Divine Ground of all existence."

In *Time Must Have a Stop* Huxley intends to introduce the Perennial Philosophy to readers and also to write of Uncle Eustace's dying in terms of the Tibetan Book of the Dead (the Bardo Thodol), a Mayahana Buddhist text that describes the transitional state between the death of one body and the spirit of that body having a rebirth in a new body. A body is a suitcase that carries the spirit around; suitcases may wear down or change, but the spiritual contents remain. The fact that Sebastian loses a leg is meant to signify that while his body has changed; his spirit has grown and this is what measures his existence, not his body.

The first half of the novel sets the stage for the second half. Huxley as narrator very early indicates where he is heading in this passage on Sebastian, "he had read Nietzsche, and since then had known that he must Love his Fate. *Amor fati*—but tempered with a healthy cynicism" (2). At seventeen, one can intellectualize *amor fati*, but its reality requires trials more severe than just teen-age angst. Huxley introduces Nietzsche here but is also nodding at Nietzsche's mentor, Schopenhauer, who was the first notable Western philosopher to be thoroughly guided by Vedanta philosophy. To love fate is to accept that one's finite corporeal existence and that existence's travails are secondary to one's infinite spiritual existence. Hence, immediately in the novel, Huxley in an incidental way foreshadows the very serious considerations of fate and spirituality that are forthcoming.

Readers first learn of Bruno Rontini in a conversation about him while he is not yet present. Eustace says that "Bruno's the last person to gossip about a man when his back is turned. . . . There's nothing that so effectively ruins conversation as charitableness. After all, no one can be amusing about other people's virtues" (70). Bruno's good nature is here explained; he is in fact, an exemplar of Vedanta's two simple rules of ethical conduct: do no harm and compassion for all. Two pages later Eustace reads aloud a passage from a book he just purchased:

> "'Grace did not fail thee, but thou wast wanting to grace. God did not deprive thee of the operation of his love, but thou didst deprive his love of thy co-operation. God would never have rejected thee, if thou hadst not rejected him.' Golly!" He turned back to the title page. "*Treatise of the Love of God* by St. François de Sales," he read. "Pity it isn't de Sade." (72)

Eustace's pithy cynicism dots the text, which is counterpoint to his spiritual experience in the novel's second half. The message that Eustace reads in de Sales is that one chooses to intuit God and seek upward transcendence; however, one may, like de Sade, choose downward transcendence away from God. One rejects God; God rejects no one.

Another character, Paul De Vries, an American from New England, (home of Vedanta-inspired American transcendentalism) is fascinated by Einstein (Huxley's reminder of the space-time possibilities that Einstein introduced) and seeks any evidence of an undifferentiated unity. He was hoping, "that some day one might get a hunch, an illuminating intuition of the greater synthesis. For a synthesis there undoubtedly must be, a thought-bridge that would permit the mind to march discursively and logically from telepathy to the four-dimensional continuum. . . . There was the ultimate all-embracing field—the Brahma of Sankara [Vedanta], the One of Plotinus, the Ground of Eckhart and Boehme [German mystics] . . ." (79). Huxley is giving readers an introduction to the Perennial Philosophy, which will be continued in Bruno's bookshop. A young man comes in and asks for a book on comparative religion. Bruno shows him the standard didactic selections, which the aspiring young philosopher buys. Bruno adds, " 'if ever you should get tired of this . . .' He hesitated; in their deep sockets the blue eyes twinkled with an almost mischievous light. '. . . This kind of learned frivolity . . . remember, I've got quite a considerable stock of really serious books on the subject. . . . Scupoli, the Bhagavatam, the Tao Teh Ching, the Theologica Germanica, the Graces of Interior Prayer . . ." (86). Thus does Huxley suggest texts if readers are so inclined to learn more.

Bruno becomes a source for felicitous thoughts that also teach; often, these thoughts come as pas de deux with the cynical Eustace, such as one on goodness. Bruno says,

> "if only people would realize that moral principles are like measles . . ."
> The soft voice trailed away into silence and a sigh.
> "Like measles?"
> "They have to be caught. And only the people who've got them can pass on the contagion. . . . One doesn't have to catch the infection of goodness, if one doesn't want to. The will is always free. . . . If only you could forgive the Good [that refutes Eustace's cynicism]. . . . Then you might allow yourself to be forgiven."
> "For what?" Eustace enquired.
> "For being what you are. For being a human being. Yes, God can forgive you even that, if you really want it. Can forgive your separateness so completely that you can be made one with him" (89).

The verbal duets between Eustace and Bruno are discussions of oppositions that need to be reconciled. Bruno's importuning to Eustace that he drop his cynicism and seriously consider his spiritual future takes on great significance when later Eustace is dying. Throughout the novel, passages both serious and lighthearted speak of the nature of the Perennial Philosophy and names many of its advocates, thinkers who are in Huxley's anthology, which would be published the year after *Time Must Have a Stop*, as if the latter was meant to introduce the former, which, in fact, it was.

The second half of the novel mainly concerns Eustace's dying. Bowering writes of this:

> The second half . . . is divided into three parts. . . . [T]he Chikhai Bardo which describes the happenings immediately after death; then, the

Chönyid Bardo which deals with karmic visions and hallucinations; and, finally, the Sidpa Bardo which is concerned with the events leading up to reincarnation. In the Chikhai Bardo the deceased is faced with the . . . Dharma-Kāya, or the Clear Light of the Void. This is symbolic of the purest and highest state of spiritual being which Huxley identifies with the Divine Ground or immanent Godhead of the Christian mystics. If, through a lack of spiritual insight, the dead person is unable to recognize the light as the manifestation of his own spiritual consciousness, karmic illusions begin to cloud his vision, the light is obscured and he enters into the second Bardo. In the Chönyid Bardo he is subjected to what Evans-Wentz calls "a solemn and mighty panorama" of "the consciousness-content of his personality." This will vary according to the life and religious beliefs of the individual concerned. . . . [I]f the deceased is spiritually immature and unable to recognize the fantasy world confronting him as the product of his own consciousness he will pass into . . . the Sipa Bardo [and] the dead person becomes aware that he no longer has a corporeal body and the desire for a new incarnation begins to dominate his consciousness. . . . As Jung points out . . . "freed from all illusion of genesis and decay . . . [l]ife in the *Bardo* brings no eternal rewards or punishments, but merely a descent into a new life which shall bear the individual nearer to his final goal [a final complete merging into spiritual consciousness]. . . . This . . . goal is what he himself brings to birth as the last and highest fruit of the labours and aspirations of earthly existence." This is the essential teaching of *Time Must Have a Stop*. (Bowering 167-68)

In the novel Huxley describes the death of Uncle Eustace:

And through ever-lengthening durations the light kept brightening from beauty into beauty. And the joy of knowing, the joy of being known, increased with every increment of that embracing and interpenetrating beauty.

Brighter, brighter, through succeeding durations, that expanded at last into an eternity of joy.

An eternity of radiant knowledge, of bliss unchanging in its ultimate intensity. For ever, for ever. (118).

Eustace was, just as Bruno knew, "spiritually immature at the time of his death." Sebastian, after learning mysticism from Uncle Bruno, is more advanced spiritually and further along in the path of evolving spiritual consciousness and union with the Divine Ground of all existence. In the epilogue Sebastian is looking through his notebook of thoughts and quotations concerning mystical spirituality. This notebook had its real counterpart, as Huxley was accumulating material for *The Perennial Philosophy*. Sebastian reads from his notebooks and readers lean more about mysticism.

Sebastian also remembers taking care of Bruno when he was dying of throat cancer and gradually lost his speech. There is great irony here as Huxley would die of throat cancer eighteen years later. Sebastian remembers Bruno's suffering: "But there had also been the spectacle of Bruno's joyful serenity, and even, at one remove, a kind of participation in the knowledge, of which that joy was the natural and inevitable expression—the knowledge of a timeless and infinite presence; the intuition, direct and infallible, that apart from the desire to be separate there was no separation, but an essential identity" (241). The last pages of Sebastian's notebook concern how time must have a stop in the mystical sense of the "vast landscape." These ruminations are followed by the Minimum Working Hypothesis, which by this juncture of the reader's mystical education resonates with the full import and impact of this spiritual novel.

In 1954 when Maria Huxley was dying and had reached the predeath state of unconsciousness, Huxley read to her from the Bardo.

Island (1962)

Huxley's last novel is a summation of his vast study in the ways that humanity might use science rather than abuse science and forsake a rabid capitalism for more of a spiritually motivated semisocialistic society. This novel of ideas has IDEAS writ large and the novel is merely a device for giving readers a look at a positive utopia rather than the dystopia of *Brave New World*. The innovation in this novel is in the ideas, rather than in the telling. In its way, *Island* is a refutation of *Brave New World*.

Will Farnaby works for industrialist Lord Joseph Aldehyde (formaldehyde); he deliberately crashes his small boat on the south sea island of Pala. The society on Pala seeks happiness as its goal rather than material success. Nearby, Rendang is scheming to take over the island for its untapped oil reserves. Crashing his boat, Will injures his knee and is left unconscious. He is found by two island children: Mary Sarojini and Tom Krishna MacPhail. They are the grandchildren of Dr. Robert MacPhail, Pala's co-founder with the Old Raja, who arrives with his assistant Vijaya Bhattacharya and Murugan Mailendra, a student. Will recognizes Murugan from his earlier visit with Colonel Dipa, the military dictator of Rendang, but Murugan seems to not want that information known, so Will played along. They carry him to the Dr. Robert's bungalow where he is bandaged. Susila MacPhail, Dr. Robert's daughter-in-law, and Mary Sarojini and Tom Krishna's mother treat him there for the pain by hypnotically transporting him to an internal place of rest. When he awakes he reads several chapters of the Old Raja's philosophical book, *Notes on What's What*. The Raja bears resemblance to Bruno Rontini in *Time Must Have a Stop*. Will is similar to Sebastian Barnack as he begins as a capitalist but is won over by Pala's joy and common sense approach to life. This is a New Age world where many of the ideas Huxley describes have since been developed and written about. In his conversion Will is taken, chapter by chapter, into Huxley's polemical descriptions of a potential paradise. So are readers. The novel's conflict is between a selfless utopia and selfish capitalist greed.

Will is shown around the island. He compares his own sad life with life on Pala, so readers feel the contrast between the failures of Will's world and the success of Pala's world. One must not dwell on guilt and remorse; one must live in the here and now, the eternal now. The island's mynah birds repeat, "Attention!" "Karuna, karuna." Be aware and care! Unlike the brainwashing of *Brave New World*, the repetitions on Pala are positive learning.

Western science works with the arts and education for a balanced equation of body and mind. Huxley details theory and practice based on his lifelong study. There is an Agricultural Experimental Station to breed better crops so that no one should go hungry. The educational and health care systems include the best of the East and West. Organized religion is not dogmatic but is based in mystical intuitive logic and self-experience. God is not an angry God used for propaganda as in the outside world, but a loving God who wishes all of his creation to love and be loved. Huxley's belief that human nature itself would need to be fundamentally reoriented through education is paramount in *Island*. Yet Huxley knew that the entrenched human nature that already existed would resist a common cause of universal love because the ego is self-serving and self-preserving rather than a vehicle for collective goodwill. There is an unhappy ending to the novel as Rendang invades Pala to take its oil.

Alex McDonald notes in a 2002 essay,

> The well-known etymology of "utopia" expresses a central problem in the interpretation of *Island*. Eu + topos means good place, and it is arguable that Pala is a good place which represents a triumphant positive conclusion to Huxley's life-long battle with dualism, that Will Farnaby's conversion from cynicism to utopian faith is the culmination of the progression of the earlier novels. On the other hand, ou + topos means no place, and it is equally arguable that *Island*, especially its horrific ending, represents the return of Huxley's profound pessimism, as David Bradshaw has claimed: "*Island* is perhaps Huxley's most pessimistic book. . . . [That] Pala's 'oasis of happiness' has little hope of survival" (viii.), in the real world. (75)

Bradshaw, as have many critics, do not understand Huxley's mysticism, and McDonald is overstating the case by saying "Huxley's lifelong battle with dualism." To a mystic there is no dualism. McDonald does say that in Huxley's 1935 novel, *Eyeless in Gaza*, "Anthony Beavis reaches a state of spiritual calm, suggesting the mystical experience, which can transcend the duality of the world. The basis for the leap beyond satire [of the novels up to and including *Brave New World*] to positive vision was elaborated in Huxley's spiritual anthology, *The Perennial Philosophy*" (75).

Many critics have misunderstood Huxley because they did not know of or did not understand the Perennial Philosophy and subsequently could not follow Huxley's logic. Bradshaw would have readers believe that Pala's positive experimentation with ways of living was a waste and a failure because the novel ends with the invasion. This is far from true. In a linear perception of time, it is imagined that Pala "ends" and something else begins. But when time is seen as the "vast landscape" within which all actions and reactions follow this dictum—*Any given event in any part of the universe has as its determining conditions all previous and contemporary events in all parts of the universe*—then the lessons learned on Pala have not ended or been wasted but have just been interrupted. Each person on Pala will take those lessons and in some form will affect others who will affect others. In the perpetual continuum there may yet be a future—even if eons hence—when the Pala experience can still be an impetus for change—who can say? Huxley's ending is a warning that only readers themselves can seek a better future and deter greed and selfishness. This is not the same as being pessimistic. Person by person, group, by group, society by society, change can take place. Time is humanity's enemy because humans can only consider their individual finite existences as the reality. Despite protestations otherwise about concern for the future, people see existence as that which begins and ends with their corporeal duration. People will say they love their children, but few parents consider how to take steps to insure a better world after they are gone. If they did, energy conservation and a clean environment would be front-burner issues so that their children and grandchildren will not face fuel rationing and pollution. This is why time must have a stop. When people begin to consider the totality of before and after as included with their present existence, when they do not limit their vision of existence to their own existences and see the vast landscape of eternity where time has stopped and they can include themselves in an encompassing vision of an eternal now, then we will care about the future of the collective spirit and not just care about our individual selves. Huxley believed in mysticism early and sustained this belief to the end of his own corporeal suitcase containing an ennobled spirit. His life itself is proof that he was right. He influenced countless people to believe in what he believed and to tell others who will tell others on and on.

This writer is one of those people and he has been telling you now how much he learned from Aldous Huxley, and in the telling, how much *you* have learned from Aldous Huxley.

Notes

[1] Matthew Huxley had his own distinguished career in public health. He died at age eighty-four on 12 February 2005.

[2] J. K. Huysmans (1848-1907), a Dutchman who lived in Paris, wrote *A Rebours* (*Against the Grain*) in 1884. It is autobiographical and depicts a protagonist, Des Esseintes, who, bored with life, indulges every decadent whim he can think of, denying God, as Spandrell puts it, but finally, when he has run out of self-destructive acts, realizes that there is nothing left *but* God and returns to the church. Oscar Wilde (1854-1900) took the story of *A Rebours*, a novel he greatly admired and, in fact, refers to, in his novel *The Picture of Dorian Gray* (1891), in which Gray, in an even more twisted path than Des Esseintes, pursues complete decadence. In his case, however, the ending is tragic.

[3] Examples: Orwell's *1984*, Bradbury's *Fahrenheit 451*, recent films such as *Total Recall, Gattaca,* and *Equilibrium*, and a 1998 TV miniseries of Huxley's *Brave New World*, that failed, as have previous versions, to get the point.

[4] Christopher Isherwood wrote in 1950 that "Gerald Heard is one of the very few who can properly be called philosophers; a man of brilliantly daring theory and devoted practice. I believe he has influenced the thought of our time, directly and indirectly, to an extent which will hardly be appreciated for another fifty years" (The Heard Collection, UCLA). Heard was an enormous influence on Isherwood, W. H. Auden, W. S. Maugham and many more. Of course, a principal figure among the "many more" is Aldous Huxley. In Heard, even more so than D. H. Lawrence, Huxley found a friend who was of a simpatico temperament and more so a train of thought that compelled them toward very similar approaches to what Heard called "intentional Living." That is, a way of living that took the part—the human mind—and integrated the individual mind with a world mind of evolving consciousness where each part acted in concert for the good of the whole. A tall order, but one that these two philosophical iconoclasts believed was the inevitable future of consciousness, if not in their lifetimes, in some future eon that would see the fruition of the impetus that they were a seminal factor in pushing forward. In Heard, Huxley found someone who agreed with much of his own thought, which allowed him to have a forum for further thought along the same lines. Heard befriended Huxley and Auden in 1929. Heard conveyed to Auden his theories on a universal evolving consciousness, which had won him a major prize from the British Academy that year for his breakthrough book *The Ascent of Humanity*. Books of fiction and nonfiction would follow almost yearly until his last in 1963 *The Five Ages of Man*. From 1929 to 1963, Heard was revered among an intellectual circle that would listen to and spread his ideas and then become better known than he was. There is compelling circumstantial evidence that Heard anonymously influenced the founder of Alcoholics Anonymous, Bill Wilson, with the handbook *Twelve Steps and Twelve Traditions*, which became the basis for the now ubiquitous Twelve-Step Recovery program that is based in the abnegation of the individual ego to a spiritual source that Heard referred to as

"this thing." (Heard's euphemism was meant to mean God without saying so.) Heard was a guru to gurus.

⁵ The term *philosophia perennis* first appeared in the Renaissance although its intended meaning is much older. The term *philosophia perennis* is associated with the philosopher Leibniz, in whose writings it appears and whose thought aims at many characteristics essential to it; however, he himself found it in Augustinus Steuchius, a theologian of the sixteenth century who in 1540 published the *De philosophia perenni sive veterum philosophorum cum theologia christiana consensu libri X*, a work that quickly passed through several editions. The term has also been applied retroactively to the Scholastics. Steuch's work returns to a revealed absolute truth made known to man before his fall. Leibniz in the next century and in the later years of his life took the term for the philosophy he was developing. Leibniz had already known of Steuch, noting him and his work in his journals. In these journals Leibniz gives a brief sketch of the contributions of the major schools and also makes a reference to the East.

⁶ Even science, that kingdom of supposed empirical objectivity, is dependent on language in order to learn it and make new discoveries about it. Since scientists are using language to explain discoveries and since language is a medium of subjective interpretation, science is not nearly so objective as might be assumed. Michael Polanyi, scientist and philosopher, makes this case in *Personal Knowledge* (an early salvo of postmodernism). All efforts to acquire knowledge are personal, meaning subjective, not objective. When Polanyi says that "we know more than we can say," he is asserting that language is merely the outcome or tip of a vast iceberg that is knowledge held both consciously and unconsciously in the mind and memory from which we reflexively make correlations that can be enunciated or acted upon. The above introduction to which this note refers is a synthesized outcome of much reading, research, and life experience that knows much more than it can say.

> We must conclude that the paradigmatic case of scientific knowledge, in which all faculties that are necessary for finding and holding scientific knowledge are fully developed, is the knowledge of approaching discovery.
>
> To hold such knowledge is an act deeply committed to the conviction that there is something there to be discovered. It is personal, in the sense of involving the personality of him who holds it, and also in the sense of being, as a rule, solitary; but there is no trace in it of self-indulgence. The discoverer is filled with a compelling sense of responsibility for the pursuit of a hidden truth, which demands his services for revealing it. His act of knowing exercises a personal judgment in relating evidence to an external reality, an aspect of which he is seeking to apprehend. (Polanyi 24-25)

⁷ Huxley discusses upward and downward transcendence in his book *Grey Eminence* (1941), a biography of Father Joseph, Cardinal Richelieu's spiritual advisor, a mystic who became corrupted by politics.

Works Cited

Auden, W. H. *Secondary Worlds*. New York: Random House, 1968.

Auden, W. H., and Christopher Isherwood. *The Dog beneath the Skin*. London: Faber & Faber, 1935.

The Bhagavad-Gita. Trans. Isherwood-Prabhavananda. Los Angeles: Marcel Rodd, 1944.

Bowering, Peter. *Aldous Huxley: A Study of the Major Novels*. London: Athlone Press, 1968.

Bradshaw, David. *Aldous Huxley between the Wars: Essays and Letters*. Chicago: Ivan R. Dee, 1994.

—. Introduction. *Island*. By Aldous Huxley. London: Flamingo, 1994.

Brahma, N. K. *Philosophy of Hindu Sadhana*. London: Kegan Paul Trench, Trubner, 1932; rev. ed, 1999.

Cowley, Malcolm. *After the Genteel Tradition*. New York: Norton, 1936.

Derbyshire, John. "What Happened to Aldous Huxley." *New Criterion*. 21 February 2003 <www.newcriterion.com> 18 May 2005.

Eliot, T. S. *The Complete Poems and Plays: 1909-1950*. New York: Harcourt, Brace & World, 1971.

Goel, Sita Ram. *How I Became a Hindu*. New Delhi, India: Voice of India, 2005. <voi.org/books/hibh/ch5.htm> 8 May 2005.

Heard, Gerald. "The Poignant Prophet." *Aldous Huxley 1894-1963: A Memorial Volume*. New York: Harper & Row, 1965.

Huxley, Aldous. *Along the Road*. London: Chatto & Windus, 1925.

—. *Brave New World*. London: Chatto & Windus, 1932.

—. *Crome Yellow*. 1921. Normal, IL: Dalkey Archive Press, 2001.

—. *Do What You Will*. London: Chatto & Windus, 1929.

—. "Farcical History of Richard Greenow." *Limbo*. London: Chatto & Windus, 1920. 1-115.

—. *Grey Eminence: A Study in Religion and Politics*. New York: Harper & Brothers, 1941.

—. Introduction. *The Bhagavad-Gita*. Trans. Isherwood-Prabhavananda. Los Angeles: Marcel Rodd, 1944.

—. *Island*. New York: Harper & Row, 1962.

—. *Letters of Aldous Huxley*. London: Chatto & Windus, 1969.

—. *Point Counter Point*. 1928. Normal, IL: Dalkey Archive Press, 1996.

—. "Sermons in Cats." *Music at Night*. London: Chatto & Windus, 1931. 258-69.

—. "The Subject-Matter of Poetry." *On the Margin*. London: Chatto & Windus, 1923. 26-38.

—. *Time Must Have a Stop*. 1944. Normal, IL: Dalkey Archive Press, 1998.

—. "Tragedy and the Whole Truth." *Music at Night*. London: Chatto & Windus, 1931. 3-18.

—. *Vulgarity in Literature*. London: Chatto & Windus, 1931.

Isherwood, Christopher. *Diaries, 1939-1960*. San Francisco: Harper, 1998.

—. *My Guru and His Disciple*. New York: Farrar, Straus & Giroux, 1980.

Isherwood, Christopher, and Edward Upward. "Prefatory Epistle to My Godson on the Study of History." *The Mortmere Stories*. London: Enitharmon Press, 1994.

Kass, Leon. "Aldous Huxley: *Brave New World*." *First Things* 101 (March 2000): 51-52. <www.firstthings.com/ftissues/ft0003/articles/huxley.html> 11 May 2005.

Lin, Lidan. "Aldous Huxley in an Age of Global Literary Studies." *International Fiction Review* Jan. 2004: 78-92. <infotrac.galegroup.com>. 18 May 2005.

McDonald, Alex. "Choosing Utopia: An Existential Reading of Aldous Huxley's *Island*." *Utopian Studies* 12.2 (2001): 103-14.

Nietzsche, Friedrich. *On the Genealogy of Morality*. Indianapolis: Hackett, 1998.

Polanyi, Michael. *The Tacit Dimension*, New York: Anchor, 1967.

Sawyer, Dana. *Aldous Huxley: A Biography*. New York: Crossroads, 2002.

—. " 'What Kind of a Mystic Was Aldous Huxley Anyway?' A Brief Appraisal of His Mysticism." *Aldous Huxley Annual* 2 (2002): 207–18.

Upanishads. Trans. Swami Prabhavananda and Frederick Manchester. New York: New American Library, 1957.

Wilder, Thornton. *The Eighth Day*. New York: Harper & Row, 1967.

—. *Our Town*. New York: Coward-McCann, 1939.

An Aldous Huxley Checklist

Novels

Crome Yellow. London: Chatto & Windus, 1921; Normal, IL: Dalkey Archive Press, 2001.

Antic Hay. London: Chatto & Windus, 1923; Normal, IL: Dalkey Archive Press, 1997.

Those Barren Leaves. London: Chatto & Windus, 1925; Normal, IL: Dalkey Archive Press, 1998.

Point Counter Point. London: Chatto & Windus, 1928; Normal, IL: Dalkey Archive Press, 1996.

Brave New World. London: Chatto & Windus, 1932; New York: Harper Collins, 2004.

Eyeless in Gaza. London: Chatto & Windus, 1936.

After Many a Summer Dies the Swan. New York: Harper, 1939; Chicago: Ivan R. Dee, 1993.

Time Must Have a Stop. New York: Harper, 1944; Normal, IL: Dalkey Archive Press, 1998.

Ape and Essence. New York: Harper, 1948; Chicago: Ivan R. Dee, 1992.

The Genius and the Goddess. New York: Harper, 1955.

Island. New York: Harper & Row, 1962; New York: Perennial, 2002.

Jacob's Hands. With Christopher Isherwood. New York: St. Martin's Press, 1998.

Short Stories

Limbo. London: Chatto & Windus, 1920.

Mortal Coils. London: Chatto & Windus, 1922.

Little Mexican. London: Chatto & Windus, 1924. (American title, *Young Archimedes and Other Stories.*)

Two or Three Graces. London: Chatto & Windus, 1926.

Brief Candles. London: Chatto & Windus, 1930.

The Gioconda Smile. London: Chatto & Windus, 1938.

Collected Short Stories. Chicago: Ivan R. Dee, 1992.

Children's Book

The Crows of Pearblossom. Illustrated by Barbara Cooney. New York: Random House, 1967.

Poetry

The Burning Wheel. London: Blackwell, 1916.
The Defeat of Youth. Oxford: B. H. Blackwell, 1918.
Leda. London: Chatto & Windus, 1920.
Arabia Infelix. New York: The Fountain Press, 1929.
The Cicadas. London: Chatto & Windus, 1931.
Collected Poetry of Aldous Huxley. New York, Harper & Row, 1971.

Plays

The World of Light, a Comedy in Three Acts. London: Chatto & Windus, 1931.
The Gioconda Smile: A Play. London: Chatto & Windus, 1948.
Now More than Ever. Austin: U of Texas P, 2000.
Brave New World. Aldous Huxley Annual 3 (2003): 33-128.
The Genius and the Goddess. Aldous Huxley Annual 4 (2004): 37-161.

Nonfiction

On the Margin. London, Chatto & Windus, 1923.
Along the Road. London: Chatto & Windus, 1925; New York: Ecco Press, 1989.
Jesting Pilate. London: Chatto & Windus, 1926; New York: Paragon House, 1991.
Proper Studies. London: Chatto & Windus, 1927.
Essays New and Old. New York: George H. Doran, 1927.
Do What You Will. London: Chatto & Windus, 1929.
Holy Face, and Other Essays. London: Fleuron, 1929; New York: Perennial, 2002.
Vulgarity in Literature. London: Chatto & Windus, 1931.
Music at Night, London: Chatto & Windus, 1931; Westport: Greenwood Press, 1975.
Texts and Pretexts. London: Chatto & Windus, 1932; Westport: Greenwood Press, 1976.
The Olive Tree. London: Chatto & Windus, 1936.
An Encyclopædia of Pacifism. London, Chatto & Windus, 1937; New York, Garland, 1972.
What Are You Going to Do About It? The Case for Constructive Peace. London: Chatto & Windus, 1936.
Ends and Means. New York: Harper, 1937; New York: Greenwood Press, 1969.
The Elder Peter Bruegel. New York, Willey, 1938.
Words and Their Meanings. Los Angeles: Ward Ritchie, 1940.

Grey Eminence: A Study in Religion and Politics. New York: Harper, 1941; Westport: Greenwood Press, 1975.

The Art of Seeing. New York: Harper, 1942; Seattle: Montana Books, 1975.

The Perennial Philosophy. New York: Harper, 1945; New York: Perennial Classics, 2004.

Science, Liberty and Peace. New York: Harper, 1946.

Prisons: With the "Carceri" Etchings. Philadelphia: Grey Falcon Press, 1949.

Themes and Variations. New York: Harper, 1950.

The Devils of Loudon. New York: Harper, 1952; New York: Carroll & Graf, 1996.

Tomorrow and Tomorrow and Tomorrow. New York: Harper, 1956.

The Doors of Perception. New York: Harper, 1954; *The Doors of Perception and Heaven and Hell.* New York: Perennial Classics, 2004.

Heaven and Hell. New York: Harper, 1956.

Literature and Science. New York: Harper & Row, 1963; Woodbridge: Ox Bow Press, 1991.

The Politics of Ecology: The Question of Survival. Santa Barbara: Center for the Study of Democratic Institutions, 1963.

Letters of Aldous Huxley. London: Chatto & Windus, 1969.

The Human Situation. New York: Harper & Row, 1977.

Aldous Huxley: Between the Wars. Chicago: Ivan R. Dee, 1994.

Complete Essays. Chicago: Ivan R. Dee, 2000-2002.

Book Reviews

Peter Weiss. *The Aesthetics of Resistance, Volume 1.* Trans. Joachim Neu-groschel. Foreword Fredric Jameson. Duke Univ. Press, 2005. 376 pp. Paper: $22.95.

Peter Weiss's monumental *The Aesthetics of Resistance* is a Marxist *Remembrance of Things Past*: a history of leftist politics from the end of the First World War to the Spanish civil war (where the first volume breaks off), as well as a bildungsroman concerning the education of its working-class narrator—particularly in what practical uses might be made of works of art. Written over the last ten years of Weiss's life, nearly a half-century after the events he records, it is both nostalgia and plea. The failed leftist (and modernist) revolution against capitalism and bourgeois society remains an uncompleted project, a reminder that something is missing, that the conditions of modern living do not satisfy the needs of life. Like Gaudí's Sagrada Familia cathedral in Barcelona, its dream today "retains its authenticity solely as a ruin." *The Aesthetics of Resistance* writes those who have been culturally and historically excluded back into the story of their time and demands—as modernism does—that we learn to read in a new way. It includes historical figures, like Bukharin, Nordahl Grieg, and Andres Nin; discussions of Picasso's *Guernica*, the Pergamum altar, and Géricault's *Raft of the Medusa*; and employs characteristic modernist techniques of montage, the document, the list, and the catalog. At the conclusion of a discussion of Munch's painting *Workers Returning Home*, the narrator leaves in a truck and looks back at a friend as he pulls away: "He stayed behind amid the gigantic domes and towers of Valencia, his laughter in his bright face, his waving, street ravines, boulevard along the shore, exit roads, low plateau, harvesters in the rice paddies." This, the last sentence of the first volume, is a description of a friend and a landscape, not of Munch or the Spanish civil war. We begin and end in that space. According to Weiss, art must always be seen in relation to life, writing in relation to action. This is a book not to read through from beginning to end, but one in which we should pause, as its narrator does, to consider an idea, event, or work of art in relation to our lives—"the trench warfare of thoughts," as Weiss puts it. Although Weiss was not himself working class, this novel could stand as its testimony: "What would I have become, how would I have developed if I had come from a proletarian home," he asks. The monuments of modernism today rise like Ozymandias' statue in the sand: *Ulysses*, Proust, Beckett, Pound's *Cantos*, *The Making of Americans*, *The Waste Land*. At last, we have an English translation of a work that stands alongside them. [Robert Buckeye]

Giorgio Manganelli. *Centuria: One Hundred Ouroboric Novels.* Trans. and preface Henry Martin. Preface by the author. McPherson, 2005. 214 pp. $24.00.

A friend once pointed out the fallacy of describing narratives as circular. A narrative can contain elements that are *recurrent,* but a truly *circular* narrative would be endlessly repetitive, with no beginning or end, pages around a central core like a novelistic Rolodex. (Joyce apparently envisioned something similar for *Finnegans Wake.*) This is worth keeping in mind while reading *Centuria,* whose subtitle, of course, promises 100 "ouroboric" novels (which average a page and a half and which could also be classified as short-shorts, exempla, fabliaux, or "novels from which all the air has been removed"). In precise and sometimes stiff prose (e.g., "the gentlemen's deaths . . . confute this putative salubrity of the air") most of the early novels describe "a gentleman" in dramatic if ordinary circumstances of love and indifference, of doubt and mistrust, of experiencing the relief that comes with romantic rejection. But soon, en masse, these gentlemen start dying at train stations, spontaneously crumbling to dust, and carrying their heads like saints. Then ghosts start to take center stage, and dragons, living spheres, and dinosaurs. Many of these figures recur in the other "novels," but don't strictly repeat, which brings us back to the ouroboros, the tail-biting snake of *Centuria's* subtitle. The eternally circular ouroboros is generally accepted to symbolize life's completion and renewal, but bear in mind that the ouroboros is actually *a snake that's eating itself* in a nihilistic, autophagous felo-de-se, and it seems that Manganelli might have envisioned *Centuria* not as circular (which it's not—its recurrent elements are more symphonic, like Curtis White's *Requiem* or even Calvino's *Invisible Cities*), but as ouroborically destructive. But it's a particular kind of destruction: as fire is cleansing, *Centuria* is metadestructive, immolating itself (and, by extension, its traditions), but leaving in its place something new and pure and often spellbinding. [Tim Feeney]

Cormac McCarthy. *No Country for Old Men.* Knopf, 2005. 309 pp. $24.95.

Over the past forty years, readers of McCarthy have watched as the author modulated his narrative voice, adjusting the contours of his language to fit his stories' terrain. This reviewer counts four specific alterations of style: the Gothic lyricism of his Appalachian novels; the Faulknerian maximalism of *Suttree*; the biblical rhetoric of his opus, *Blood Meridian*; and the harsh poeticism of his masterful *Border Trilogy*. With his latest book, set along the Texas border, McCarthy has metamorphosed his storytelling once again, creating a meticulously Spartan prose that many will compare to Hemingway, but which, to my mind, constitutes a kind of precision not yet encountered. The story is of Llewelyn Moss, a workingman who stumbles across a drug deal gone terribly wrong and who absconds with over two million in cash. Immediately, Moss is pursued by various parties—most important, the aging Sheriff Bell whose stunning monologues are interspersed throughout the book, and an intriguing contract killer named Anton Chigurh, a man unable to make himself vulnerable. McCarthy demonstrates how these two characters (one committed to Godly virtue, the other modeling himself after God) are the flipsides of not dissimilar coins. In the acknowledgments to *No Country*, McCarthy thanks the Santa Fe Institute—ground zero for the study of Chaos Theory—for a four-year residence, and critics would do well to pay close attention to how such notions play out in his latest work. Chance, design, the introduction of new variables—these are the principles out of which McCarthy composes a tale of immense terror and beauty, one which poses the most serious of moral questions even as it pushes the bounds of the literary thriller. The novel is an elegy in the truest sense. It shows a country forever lost, but leaves us with the dream of a new Byzantium, or in Sheriff Bell's words, "a fire somewhere out there in all that dark." [Aaron Gwyn]

Robert Walser. *Speaking to the Rose: Writings, 1912-1932*. Trans. and ed. Christopher Middleton. Univ. of Nebraska Press, 2005. 128 pp. Paper: $15.00.

In 1925, before voluntarily retreating to a mental institution for what would prove to be the remainder of his unhappy life, the eccentric Robert Walser wrote a sketch about a lion tamer. As Walser details the lonely figure who must confront the beauty and mayhem of menacing creatures compelled by unpredictable intent, the metaphor of the writer crystallizes: the tense confrontation with his material, the difficult struggle to maintain control of such energy, and most of all the evident loneliness of the job despite the very public spectacle. This sketch is one of dozens gathered here for the first time, splendidly translated by the inestimable Christopher Middleton, a poet and champion of Walser's. Indeed, much of the achievement here is Middleton's heroic effort to decode Walser's indecipherable pencil drafts, so crabbed that they were long thought to be in some kind of code. The translations are superlative—the sketches ring with emotional color. They range in topic from Walser's reinvention of characters from myth and the Bible (in one, he re-angles the story of the prodigal son by considering the plight of the faithful son who stayed at home); to sketches that capture everyday phenomena with elegant nuance (a lake, an alley, a woman in a garden); to essays on the writing profession (in one sumptuous sketch, he compares the cumulative dynamic of the writing process to the unfolding of a slow, shattering sunrise). The voice is unmistakably Walser's—the rich architecture of the sentences, the Kafkaesque cynicism, the fascination with the logic of paradox, the ability to infuse the banal with grace, the clawing loneliness. These reveries, of course, may not manage to coax Walser from the margins where he has so long lingered. But they remind us of the pleasure of his keen eye, his alert imagination, and his lyric voice. [Joseph Dewey]

Raymond Federman. *My Body in Nine Parts*. Starcherone Books, 2005. 133 pp. Paper: $16.00.

Just as there was a space- or atomic-age perspective, it might easily be said that we now look at the world through the lens of biology. This is especially true after the watershed that was Dolly the Sheep, when advances in bio-technique made many people rethink individuality and the self in terms of the body. Witness artists like John Coplands, whose large-format photos of his own aging body seem to exist in order to force viewers to *see*, to bear witness to the aging landscape that his flesh has become. Likewise, Kenneth Goldsmith's *Fidget* records the minutiae of his body's tics, wants, and needs over thirteen hours—performance art as prose poem. Raymond Federman's *My Body in Nine Parts* is very much in this vein. As indicated by its title, *My Body* is a collection of brief essay-fictions centered on nine parts of the author's body, each introduced by a stunning black-and-white photo by Steve Murez. The individual prose pieces are not so much about intense looking, à la Coplands: the photo for the chapter "My Sexual Organ" shows it wearing a fig leaf of Federman's own hands. Rather, the body parts are used as springboards to meditation: fact-fictions about the boy, the man, the seventy-five-year-old writer that is Federman looking back across a life and body-of-work through his scars, nose, hair style, and other corporeal features. A classic Federman theme emerges: a world where a life and the life of the imagination are a psychosomatic whole. When seen as critifictions—Federman's hybrid criticism-fictions—the pieces here might also be termed bio-fictions, bio being both biology and biography. The prose is simple, but the issues Federman raises are deceptively complex, as the author finds himself both at one and at odds with his body: a poignant place to arrive. [Steve Tomasula]

David Antin. *i never knew what time it was*. Univ. of California Press, 2005. 175 pp. Paper: $16.95.

When Muriel Rukeyser famously asserted, "The universe is made up of stories, not atoms," it was unlikely she was thinking about the kind of "talks" David Antin would perform from the sixties onward. But read-ing Antin's new collection, you begin to see precisely what she meant. *i never knew what time it was* is a collection of related texts that emerge from Antin's large oeuvre of performances over the last few decades. With various labels like improvisations, talk poems, or simply talks, these genre-busting pieces have been revised, remembered, and reconsidered for the written page. This new textual representation of Antin's talks reveal two crisscrossing themes that have obsessed him over the years: the experience of time, and its relation to narrative. Antin's tapestry of inter-related anecdotes, stories, meditations, narratives, musings, ruminations, philosophical investigations, psychological explorations, and linguistic experiments provide a complex and often delightful oral history of one man's journey through reality and consciousness via language. From a sex-obsessed Odysseus munching Viagra on Calypso Island to the execution of Romanian leader Ceausescu to stories of his son Blaise trying to arrange a prostitute for his grandfather's birthday, Antin covers a lot of ground. His characters, both real and imagined, are part of this poet-philosopher's complex verbal gymnastics, as well as, quite simply, his day-to-day life. Antin weaves his own personal life and family history with major events throughout time, and it is his seeming ease at making this connection that hooks us, as listeners and as readers, to what amounts to a poignant recollection of human experience. Perhaps what Antin makes us realize and believe most strongly is this assertion from the title piece: "the way we make sense of our lives is by telling stories about them stories which may or may not be true but making sense and telling the truth isn't exactly the same thing." [Mark Tursi]

James Salter. *Last Night*. Knopf, 2005. 133 pp. $20.00.

James Salter's new collection of stories doesn't offer much in the way of new themes; readers familiar with his work won't be surprised to find that many of the stories are about tortuous, and sometimes torturous, relationships between men and women. Salter's laconic, lingering prose hasn't changed much either; he is still able to concoct, in just a few words, authentic ambiences, as in "My Lord You"—the story of a woman who is unaccountably drawn to a dog owned by a local poet—which begins, "There were crumpled napkins on the table, wineglasses still with dark remnant in them, coffee stains, and plates with bits of hardened Brie. Beyond the bluish windows the garden lay motionless beneath the birdsong of summer morning. Daylight had come." The characters in Salter's stories are a rare breed, mixtures of WASP and epicurean, of the well-off and the aesthetically sensitive. But they are unmoored, subject to longings they can neither define nor deny. In "Comet" a man at a dinner party experiences a sudden bottoming out: "He stood up. He had done everything wrong, he realized, in the wrong order. He had scuttled his life." At times, Salter slips into caricature; there is a uniformity to his women, with their "thoroughbred" features. In the title story, which is the collection's best, a husband helps his wife commit suicide. Salter's wrought-iron style evokes the sine wave of emotion the man experiences, from agony to ecstasy, then back again. [Tayt J. Harlin]

Steve Stern. *The Angel of Forgetfulness*. Viking, 2005. 404 pp. $24.95.

This remarkable novel contains the following quotation from the mystical scholar Abraham Abulafia: "The end of forgetfulness is the beginning of remembrance . . ." If we take this statement as our entrance into this complex, secretive work, we can understand that endings (closures, deaths) are, in a sense, beginnings; that life seems to be a *circle* in which the present "signals" the past and vice versa. How to structure the unstructured? Is art more or less than life? Such questions are asked by Stern in an antic, philosophical way. There are sections named "Saul," "Nathan," and "Mocky." Saul is a young man who comes to New York—really the Lower East Side— to visit an old relative, Keni, who is alone, sick, "out of it." She mentions Nathan, who loved her, but couldn't *remain* with her. He was the writer of an unfinished manuscript entitled "The Angel of Forgetfulness." Saul is instructed to finish it (and, of course, to *translate* it from Yiddish to English). The novel concerns a half-man, half-angel named Nachman. Mocky, his father, has left paradise for Earth. Consider the oddities. Why leave paradise—and why desire to return if earthly life is, at times, *blossoming with possibilities*? The novel turns and turns as one character steps forward after another. We are continually surprised by the fact that they *echo* each other in their longings for wholeness, paralleling the others' desire for "the sense of an ending," but always failing to achieve it. Stern, who is their "father" or creator, remains invisible. He has given us a story about story, a creation that is itself about creation. We can say that the novels within the novel raise ontological questions. Here is one wonderful passage from Mocky: "With Nachman hugging my torso in a taut embrace, I renewed my resolve; I intended spiraling upward under cover of the fray to the third balcony, then out of a fire door into the soft evening air. In my mind we were almost there: I could smell already the aromatic herbs of the Garden . . ." Mocky is a word, not an angel, but often he becomes otherworldly. This novel is Stern's best—a miraculous mixture of joy and despair; it instructs us to live and die (and live) for higher ends. [Irving Malin]

———————

Paul West. *My Father's War.* McPherson, 2005. 187 pp. $24.00.

Since the interminable pontificate of Bill Cosby in the late 1980s, celebrities, usually uncomplicated by something to say, have, well, pontificated on fatherhood, that subgenre of memoir that's proliferated with the clumsy excess of pigeons. Each year around Father's Day, a gathering of titles celebrates paternity with the oily sincerity of greeting cards—books that testify (with unintended irony appropriate to the postfeminism era) that men can also serve up pabulum. What a find then to settle into Paul West's lyrical recollections of his father and to track West's adolescent evolution toward that stunning moment when a son realizes the complicated emotional circuitry of that figure long accepted as being as uncomplicated as a god. For most of his adult life, West's father, half blinded by his heroic service as a machine gunner in World War I, sorts through the psychological implications of that horrific experience. As England lurches toward yet another war to end all wars, and as father and son play at war games under the kitchen table, or share tense nights rocked by German fire during the Blitz, the son comes to see the difficult dynamics of the past and the hard dignity of a generous heart savagely bent by war. The delight, however, is the reading itself. Whether the subject is cricket, a pair of worn gloves, or a bloated sheep carcass, West invests the ordinary experiences of his adolescence with extraordinary dimension through the apparently effortless exertion of rich language that confers on these memories the sheen of significance. West's recollections are as loving and as engaging as they are painfully honest and quietly revelatory. It would be difficult to single out examples of West's elegant lyricism without quoting the entire volume, reading the pages aloud, delighting in their coaxing, musical lure. [Joseph Dewey]

Patrick Modiano. *Missing Person*. Trans. Daniel Weissbort. David R. Godine, 2005. 168 pp. Paper: $16.95. (Reprint)

Awarded France's Prix Goncourt in 1978, this existential mystery novel follows a Parisian amnesiac's quest for his own identity. During the ten years since he lost his memory, Guy Roland has worked for a sympathetic investigator named Hutte. When Hutte retires and dissolves their detective agency, Roland decides to pursue his forgotten past. This past only occasionally comes to dim light through encounters with people from such disparate locales as South America, Japan, Mauritius, Russia, and the United States. Complicating Roland's attempts to verify his identity is his own ethnically ambiguous appearance. In addition, he has a penchant for playing the chameleon. Almost every time he stumbles upon a lead, he takes on a new identity that he hopes will turn out to be authentic. But each time he does so, he ends up disappointed, fearing that, at heart, he may not have an identity at all: "Perhaps, after all, I never was this Pedro McEvoy, I was nothing, but waves passed through me, sometimes faint, sometimes stronger, and all these scattered echoes afloat in the air crystallized and there I was." Constantly doubting himself, he wonders, "Is it really my life I'm tracking down? Or someone else's into which I have somehow infiltrated myself?" Often, he projects this anxiety onto both his interlocutors and the absent subjects of his investigation, particularly the Russian lover he may or may not have lost while fleeing the Paris occupation. His identity-based anxieties have become familiar subject matter in postmodern fiction, but what makes Modiano's treatment stand out is the tone of Roland's narrative voice. As his uncertainties and anxieties become more and more acute, he faces them not with fatalistic indifference or self-indulgent outrage but rather with a gentle sympathy that extends beyond the confines of whatever his elusive self might be. [Thomas Hove]

Tibor Déry. *Love & Other Stories*. Various trans. New Directions, 2005. 254 pp. Paper: $17.95.

Nazi and Soviet occupation forms the backdrop to these superb stories of ordinary Hungarians struggling with the agents of their oppression. Blessed with courage and fortitude despite themselves, Déry's characters contrive novel ways to withstand the omnipresent threat of imminent destruction. A student radical of 1956 in "The Reckoning" arrives at the door of his former professor with a weapon to hide, his presumption initiating the old man's angry flight to join those streaming through a murderous winter storm toward the Austrian border. The bravura series of short tales composing "Games of the Underworld" depicts the uneasy society of the residents of a block of flats living communally in the cellar, while above ground Nazi death squads roam, ruthless and desperate as the Red Army pushes into Budapest. Even the Second World War avatars of "Philemon and Baucis," so frail and gentle one wonders how they have survived, are assailed by the implacable cruelty of destiny's minions. Comrade Bodi in "Behind the Brick Wall" tries to be a good Stakhanovite boss but finds doing so exacts a toll that is, finally, impossible to pay. Delicately lyrical in relating the release and return to his faithful wife of a shattered political prisoner, the title story's restraint and economy display Déry's genius in an altogether different light. "Two Women" probes the long-term relationship of the young wife of a political prisoner and his bedridden, nonagenarian mother, spending her last days faithfully awaiting her son's return from making his fortune in "America." In "The Circus," a willful brother and sister transform their village playmates into a mindless rabble, mimicking the manner of terrorists in their contempt for weakness and innocence, until death calls their bluff. By turns frightening and exalting, this representative selection should help introduce American readers to Déry's considerable craftsmanship and social conscience. [Michael Pinker]

Ander Monson. *Other Electricities*. Sarabande Books, 2005. 224 pp. Paper: $14.95.

It doesn't take more than a glance at Monson's debut work of fiction to see that its structure is progressive, ambitious. With its various charts, lists, and drawings, a quick flip through this slim volume will have you thinking of novels like Mark Danielewski's *House of Leaves* or Richard Grossman's *Book of Lazarus*. In between, however, you'll find something more like *Winesburg, Ohio*; that is, if Sherwood Anderson's seminal short-story cycle were written almost a century later in a setting about 700 miles north. Monson's narratives are set in a remote, snowbound community in Michigan's Upper Peninsula. This backdrop very much defines the characters of his stories, all of whom try to cope with the boredom, restlessness, and loss brought on by a barren, isolated environment. Our narrator's father has permanently retreated to the attic to be a ham radio operator; a diver finds reprieve from his young family in the freezing waters as he tags the various cars and snowmobiles that have inevitably fallen through the ice; our narrator himself taps into local phone lines to listen in on other people's conversations.

These stories can stand on their own—indeed, most of them were previously published—but the narrator holds them together. *Other Electricities*, as a collection, is a general lamentation about the narrator's community, but, moreover, it's about dealing with his own losses: the passing of his mother (to illness), his "X," Liz (herself a victim to thin ice), and his friend's sister (raped and murdered). Somehow, these stories aren't nearly as dark as they could be, given the subject matter. Monson provides levity with a wry wit and incredibly poetic, effectual prose style. His stories are so localized, both geographically and personally, that it's hard to imagine what his next endeavor will be—but a writer this talented and inventive is sure to endure, just as his hardened characters have in this stunning first effort. [Chris Paddock]

Nicole Brossard. *Yesterday, at the Hotel Clarendon.* Trans. Susanne De Lotbinière-Harwood. Coach House Books, 2005. 237 pp. $22.95.

A novelist is finishing a book fictionalizing her late father's life, intertwined with memories of her childhood reenactments of Descartes's last days. "I write (or read), therefore I am," could be the philosophy behind Nicole Brossard's *Yesterday, at the Hotel Clarendon*—the latest novel to arrive in English from the great French-Canadian practitioner of *écriture feminine*: a novel containing other novels. Over drinks at the Quebec City hotel, the novelist works through her novel with a character named "the narrator." "The narrator" in turn records these nighttime dialogues, transforming them into the nascent stages of *her* novel. The four female characters in *Yesterday*, all archivists by profession (an archaeologist, two writers, and a scientist), are inflicted by the trauma of memory and a nostalgia for "yesterday." "The narrator" catalogs antiquities at the Museum of Civilization; the death of her mother spurs her to record the present as well, transforming silence and wounds into fiction. Brossard is fascinated by language and writing, by how fiction penetrates reality and vice versa. The end of *Yesterday* follows the structure of a play. Words act as "fragments of mourning" to be archived in memory and savored on the tongue. Novels affect and infect her characters' lives, while implicating the reader in this exchange. Characters delight in the recitation of authors' names—Djuna Barnes, Joyce, Duras. One character marvels at Duras's use of pronouns as though objectifying a beautiful woman. Brossard's characters eroticize literature and the act of writing; sometimes literally, like a masturbation scene involving a "sapphic schoolgirl" passage from Violette Leduc. "The narrator" reads and rereads and replicates for the reader a found page of an abandoned novel. "Some days the meaning of the page seems obvious, on others it wavers like a conversation by the seashore . . ." Such can be the experience of reading Brossard's work, one that fluctuates between elusiveness and lucidity. [Kate Zambreno]

Thorvald Steen. *"Don Carlos" and "Giovanni."* Trans. James Anderson. Green Integer, 2004. 375 pp. Paper: $13.95.

These two short novels take the form of letters written by Giovanni Graciani, an Italian émigré living in Argentina, to his brother Roberto. *Don*

Carlos, set in 1833, introduces us to Giovanni, who is living hand-to-mouth as a shipyard worker in Buenos Aires. While the city is consumed by civil war, he finds an acquaintance and later a benefactor in a naturalist known as Don Carlos. Carlos turns out to be the young Charles Darwin, whose earnest scientific inquiries serve as a foil for Giovanni's increasingly vitriolic ruminations on personal and national destinies. *Giovanni* picks up the story several years later, after Argentina has been taken over by the dictatorship of Juan Manuel de Rosas. Implicated in a foiled assassination attempt on Rosas, Giovanni writes a second letter as he awaits capture. Steen's protagonist evokes both Borges and Sartre's Roquentin as he contemplates human idealism and the everyday brutality that belies it. Steen's choice of form is by no means incidental. Giovanni's letters juxtapose anecdote and history, lyricism and violence, to startling effect. "There is something about Don Carlos I find almost moving," he observes at one point. "While total chaos reigns in the world about him, he collects, sorts and classifies his finds." But the world Darwin classifies is no place for the likes of Giovanni: "I began to think of the cactus that feeds on itself like a flame. Burnt out and dry, it blooms. I am no cactus." Giovanni's fitness to survive is questionable, but his alternately ranting and resigned musings in this provocative pair of epistolary novels have a staying power all their own. [Pedro Ponce]

Yuri Andrukhovych. *Perverzion.* Trans. and intro. Michael M. Naydan. Northwestern Univ. Press, 2005. 326 pp. Paper: $25.95.

This novel purports to document the last week in the life of Stanislav Perfetsky, a young Ukrainian poet unexpectedly invited to speak at a seminar in Venice on "The Post-Carnival Absurditi of the World: What is on the Horizon?" in 1993. Tracing Perfetsky's circuitous path to his apparent suicide at the conclusion of this event, Andrukhovych, ostensibly the "publisher" of this phantasmagoric record of intimate access to the poet's thoughts, those of his companions (including dispatches to "the Monsignore"—evidently Lucifer—their boss), and various other papers, creates a startlingly carnivalesque narrative, replete with "learned" notes, numerous twists, and arcane lore. Larding so many singular voices and points of view into a game seemingly designed to outwit the reader, Andrukhovych keeps us from feeling entirely at ease with his ambitious sallies while beguiling us with japes and false leads: gateways to the Venice of his dreams. He makes this singular view of the city as much central to the action of his tale as his cast of characters, themselves curious specimens of contemporary excess. Among the more arresting scenes is a performance of "Orpheus in Venice," a mock-opera in which Perfetsky himself suddenly takes over the lead. If the principal storyline appears to be Perfetsky's seduction by agents of Lucifer, one of whom has become his lover, a mere *bolgia* away reside his hosts and fellow speakers, extravagantly sounding forth on male dominance, psychedelia, antiquarian mysteries, and erotic dance. His own near-abandonment to the hipness he mocks and mimics displays Andrukhovych's considerable range as well as an abiding affection for his bewildered hero. If occasionally so many bold leaps, sly winks, and outrageous plays on words threaten to go over the top, Andrukhovych's relentlessly in-your-face style keeps one alert throughout his fast-paced mystery-manqué. [Michael Pinker]

Kenneth Bernard. *The Man in the Stretcher.* Starcherone Books, 2005. 285 pp. Paper: $18.00.

Although Kenneth Bernard has received several awards for his astonishing plays and stories, he has never received the critical attention that he deserves. I am pleased that I can review his previously uncollected stories here. (These have appeared in such periodicals as the *New Yorker, Asylum, Confrontation,* and *Fiction International.*) "Chain-Saw" is an amazing creation: prose poem and dream-lecture. It blurs genres. "Let me tell you about my chain-saw." We note the seemingly common, plain style. We don't know who this narrator is; we feel that he has chosen *us* for his tale. We wonder what his *connection* is to us. And when he continues to give us the details of his "chain-saw," he terrifies us because we are not accustomed to read about—or listen to—the description of potential instruments of destruction. How to place the speaker? How to cope with his compulsive narration? And as he traces the purchase of the chain-saw and a pair of gloves, he sees the *problematics* of the sale. He then asks questions (which are numbered): "If I should lose a finger, whose fault would it be?" He philosophizes: "Considering the many unanswerable questions in this matter . . . can we ask whether or not it is *perhaps* the *nature* of things that *we are all out of context,* one way or *another?*" (My italics.) The narrator continues to broaden his questions, wondering whether we *know* "what, exactly, *is* a chain-saw?" or "What, for that matter, is a finger?" The madness increases: "Nevertheless I frequently fantasize that one of [my fingers] is missing." He has an "entirely different, alternate life" without the finger. In fact, how many lives does he have? The "last" lines: "Another life? How far can such a story or life go? I don't know. I don't want to know." If *you* follow *my* explanation of his thoughts, you—yes, you—are probably placing me in the same category as this mad narrator. Thus Bernard and I have seduced you into the cave of knowledge or nonknowledge. I'm sorry that I have brought you "here"—but where are we? Are we words or lives? Please investigate these "ridiculous" paths of thought. [Irving Malin]

Georges Perec. *Three by Perec.* Trans. Ian Monk. Intro. David Bellos. David R. Godine, 2004. 192 pp. Paper: $16.95.

Godine has done us all a service by making this gem of a collection available domestically under the umbrella of their attractive Verba Mundi series, and moreover as part of a long-overdue push to bring all of Perec's

book-length works in English translation back into print. We are in very
good hands indeed, as *Three* comes to us courtesy of Oulipian Ian Monk
and regular saint of Pereciana David Bellos—the former a poet and translator, the latter Perec's biographer and himself the heroic translator of
Life A User's Manual. Bellos's short introductions put each of the three
novellas collected here into context within the Perec oeuvre, while Monk's
translations are as ever gorgeous and eloquent, tackling the restlessly
playful French without the least sign of strain. (As wonderful as Gilbert
Adair's translation of the *E*-less *A Void* is, it's hard to deny that he "sweats
a little.") The first novella, *Which Moped with Chrome-Plated Handlebars
at the Back of the Yard?*, written before Perec joined the Oulipo, tells the
grim story of a group of Parisians trying to keep a friend doing his military service from being sent to the Algerian front, but in a rollicking comic
voice, incorporating as many absurdly fustian rhetorical styles as the
text can take (with a mocking partial index of these included at the end).
The second, *The Exeter Text: Jewels, Secrets, Sex*, is a salacious Sadean
entertainment—resembling at times the distorted "pornography" in Harry
Mathews's *Tlooth*—that uses only one vowel: purporting to gather up the
*E*s that Perec avoided in *A Void.* The last and arguably best of the trilogy is
A Gallery Portrait, which recalls the deadpan "academic" narration of the
author's *Le Voyage d'hiver*, telling a story of art-world intrigue through a
collection of quotations and succulent minutiae. Curious readers who want
to test the waters couldn't find a better introduction to the wealth and
charm of Perec's universe. Initiates, I hope, will need no encouragement.
[Jeremy M. Davies]

Marianne Hauser. *The Collected Short Fiction of Marianne Hauser.* FC2,
2004. 292 pp. Paper: $17.95.

The twenty-two stories gathered here are taken from throughout ninety-
three-year-old Marianne Hauser's nearly seven-decade career—from a
few pieces first published as early as the 1940s, to an introduction written
just before the collection was published. They are, generally speaking,
deft and light on their feet, and, like the stories of James Purdy, combine
an almost classical sensibility (particularly in their allusiveness) and a
love of story with subtle disruptive gestures and humor. In "Introduction," Hauser speaks frankly about aging and eros. "The Sheep" pursues a
mother and daughter's attraction to a mysterious Greek. "Weeds" concerns
a girl's obsession with another girl whose existence is open to question.
"The Seersucker Suit" moves marvelously and quite humorously from a
delusional narrator into the completely surreal. "The Missing Page" follows the peregrinations of a customs inspector obsessed with pornography, as his search for a missing calendar page moves in an unexpected
direction. Some of the later stories offer views of the war-torn Alsace that
Hauser left at a young age, giving insight into the borderland mentality
of the region. "A Lesson in Music," perhaps the strongest story in the
collection, follows a young student's sexualized obsession with her teacher,

Miss Stolz, and traces the way this obsession becomes a kind of hatred through being accidentally deflected. Add to these solid offerings the stories where Hauser manipulates narrative perspective—"ASHES," which is narrated by a dead man's ashes, and "Heartlands Beat," which pieces a story together through a range of different viewpoints—and the result is a rich collection that blends both an appreciation of tradition and a satisfying and continuing curiosity about where fiction can go. Though Hauser is best known as a novelist, this collection shows her to be a strong writer of stories as well. [Brian Evenson]

Eric Chevillard. *Palafox*. Trans. Wyatt Mason. Archipelago Books, 2004. 136 pp. Paper: $15.00.

Wyatt Mason's translation of Eric Chevillard's third novel *Palafox* elegantly captures the style and whimsy of the French original. Sentences caper musically to intricate patterns of wordplay and shifting, characterized narration from the first hatching of the title creature Palafox. With the aid of four scientists, Palafox's adoptive family attempts to keep the creature as pet and performing attraction. While the scientists fail to define him or predict his behavioral patterns, Palafox shifts between forms, ambiguously positioned between bird and fish, insect and mammal. He exists not as an embodied whole but in the shifting minutiae of his parts. Chevillard carefully catalogs the pieces of Palafox's composition even as they contradict each other, for a fragmented, cubist vision that leaves the reader never fully able to envision the creature—instead he's held together as a series of visceral fragments. Meanwhile each chapter turns on the meticulous description of process: either the scientific methods of the four experts, or that of Palafox's daily life—his upkeep, his escapades, his environmental preferences, all dealt with in scenes of increasing absurdity. As the family becomes increasingly frustrated with Palafox's ambiguity, their reactions become hostile, culminating in a stunning Palafox recipe section. Though Chevillard's writing is often compared to Samuel Beckett, in *Palafox* it is more reminiscent of Julio Cortázar's absurd processes in *Cronopios and Famas* or Borges's magical bestiary in his *The Book of Imaginary Beings*. Indefinable and untamable, Palafox is an impossible pet even when on his best behavior; he remains a wild beast—wildest perhaps in his blurriness and uncertainty. [Joanna Howard]

Michel Houellebecq. *H. P. Lovecraft: Against the World, Against Life*. Trans. Dorna Khazeni. Intro. Stephen King. Believer Books, 2005. 150 pp. Paper: $18.00.

Any essayist who attempts to explicate and illuminate a writer like H. P. Lovecraft must address the defects peculiar to this kind of creator. Lovecraft was definitely a homegrown talent—both a product of his times and existing outside of Time. He engaged in purple prose often redeemed by awe-inspiring breadth and depth of vision. He eschewed female and non-Caucasian characters, but this is of less consequence than the fact that he also disdained the usual nod to three-dimensional characterization, regardless of gender or race. (Lovecraft's generalist approach to racism, showing him recoiling from anything non-Caucasian, is mitigated by his specific relationships, including that with his Jewish wife.) In general, Michel Houellebecq's approach to Lovecraft is to play apologist for the *man*, while—in the book's more successful sections—providing astute analysis of the *work*. Although I must admit to partially sharing Angela Carter's negative opinion of Lovecraft as an arrested adolescent, I did come away from Houellebecq's essay with a renewed appreciation for those things Lovecraft does well. In defining Lovecraft's work as a monumental stand against the mundane, Houellebecq sets the foundation for a spirited appreciation of the classic Lovecraft story. This analysis makes a persuasive case as to how the supposed flaws in Lovecraft's work can be interpreted as strengths. Houellebecq successfully argues that Lovecraft required flat characterization to support his view of the universe as a cold and mechanistic place. His analysis of selections of Lovecraft's prose provide compelling evidence that the writer's florid style was actually highly controlled in his most important stories and that this style was the best way for him to create an awe-inspiring vision.

Houellebecq fares less well with statements like, "Those who love life do not read," reasoning that "the artistic universe is more or less entirely the preserve of those who are a little fed up with the world." Like most generalities about readers, books, or writers—and even if applied solely to Lovecraft—this statement seems more than a little suspect. While *H. P. Lovecraft: Against the World, Against Life* provides a spirited introduction to an influential author, it falls short of being a definitive work because of such generalities, and in its perhaps overly kind portrait of Lovecraft the person. [Jeff VanderMeer]

Jonathan Coe. *Like a Fiery Elephant*. Continuum, 2005. 486 pp. $29.95.

About his book *Trawl*, B. S. Johnson wrote, "It is a novel, I insisted and could prove; what it is not is fiction." Johnson's novels—with the exception of *House Mother Normal*, which comes the closest to sporting a wholly invented cast of characters—have much in common with autobiography: they take Johnson himself as the subject and his life as the plot. Jonathan Coe, in his remarkable book *Like a Fiery Elephant*, has done the opposite: he calls *biography* what reads like a novel. Though thorough in his seven years of research, Coe does not overexplain the deep genealogical or personal minutiae of Johnson's life, does not shy away from extrapolation or conjecture, and does not claim to comprehensively and successfully account for the one, only, and true story of Johnson's life. What he *does* do, in the best tradition of the novel—or in Johnson's preferred tradition of the novel—is take chances with form and style and invent new modes for the particular situations and persons he describes. And Johnson, as unusual as he was, certainly requires such inventiveness. A Londoner by birth, he remained in the city throughout his life with occasional, but notable, trips away: several times to Wales, where he encountered the "white goddess" who became his obsessively pursued muse; to Paris, where he met Beckett, his idol; to Hungary, where he found both much-appreciated adulation for his work and a model for his political and social ideals; and to Eastern Europe again, where his profound disenchantment found—near the end of a life cut short by suicide—confirmation. The deserving winner of the Samuel Johnson Prize for Non-Fiction, *Like a Fiery Elephant* makes sense of Johnson's life and work by keeping them as inseparable as Johnson himself, who was striking in his seriousness, did. Coe is not only writing about Johnson, but is also thoroughly inspired and influenced by him. Johnson's sad life and overlooked oeuvre (almost entirely unavailable in the U.S.) are at least partially redeemed by this biography, as Coe—who tends toward realism in his own fiction—assumes, with great success, the ambitions and risks of his subject. [Theodore Louis McDermott]

Pascale Casanova. *The World Republic of Letters.* Trans. M. B. DeBevoise. Harvard Univ. Press, 2004. 420 pp. $35.00.

Like Richard H. Brodhead's *Cultures of Letters* (1993) and Gisèle Sapiro's *La Guerre des Écrivains, 1940-1953* (1999), Pascale Casanova's *The World Republic of Letters* builds on Pierre Bourdieu's theories of literary production and reception. In its use of empirical data, Casanova's approach is much less systematic than Bourdieu's. But she extends his sociological framework to a diverse selection of cases that illustrate how "literary capital" circulates across time and around the globe. In its broadest sense, literary capital consists of "both what everyone seeks to acquire and what is universally recognized as the necessary and sufficient condition of taking part in literary competition." Central to Casanova's ideas of how literary capital circulates and acquires value is the enterprise of translation. For literature written in politically and culturally dominated languages and nations, translation "is a way of gathering literary resources, of acquiring universal texts and thereby enriching an underfunded literature—in short, a way of diverting literary assets." But for literature written in dominant languages and nations (particularly France), translation "permits the international diffusion of central literary capital." As her economic imagery suggests, Casanova tends to treat literary intentions and judgments as strategies in a competitive struggle. Consequently, she sometimes portrays literature as just another social game in which the only things that matter are seizing and maintaining dominance. But to stress her framework's positive contributions, it provides several useful theoretical tools for identifying uniquely literary forms of power. It could also aid the task of distinguishing literary judgments that acknowledge cultural differences from those that merely project ethnocentric assumptions onto other cultures. If more critics and scholars were to follow Casanova's lead and elaborate on Bourdieu's immensely rich sociological framework, they might get beyond some of the interpretive short-circuits that continue to vex socially conscious literary scholarship. [Thomas Hove]

––––––––––––––––

John Ashbery. *Selected Prose*. Ed. Eugene Ritchie. Univ. of Michigan Press, 2005. 326 pp. $29.95. Paper: $19.95

Although I admire striking passages in his poems, I'm not convinced that John Ashbery can be completely interpreted. I agree with the brilliant critic Brian McHale—see his recent study of the postmodernist poem—that Ashbery's supporters, for the most part, quote *lines* and *parts* of his poems, but do not trace *linkages* in individual works. It is relatively easy to quote lines, even stanzas, but it is almost impossible to establish a "rage for order." I have for example played with the line "on the outside looking out" many times, but I don't concretely know what it means. What is the "outside?" Does "looking out" convey a sense of paranoia? Does "outing" refer to his coded queerness? I am pleased that this marvelous volume of Ashbery's prose finally collects his invaluable criticism, highlighting his emphasis of "other traditions" (the title of his Norton Lectures). These "other traditions" give us insights into Ashbery's own techniques, and Eugene Ritchie's edition includes material that is not widely known. I can now understand Ashbery's fascination with Stein, Calvino, Jane Bowles, Borges, Roussel, Mapplethorpe. His brief reviews and essays, not easily found elsewhere, can be counted as the most playful, eccentric, insightful introductions to their work available. Consider, for example, Ashbery writing about *Stanzas in Meditation*: "In its profound originality, its original profundity, this poem that is always threatening to become a novel reminds us of the late novels of James . . ." Stein and James in their yearning to *capture thinking* use "superhuman force 'towards the condition of music.'" (But what is the meaning of the phrase "profound originality"? What is its mirror, "original profundity"? Is Ashbery writing a ghostly inversion? And does he ever deal with theme or idea? Can "reality" be coded?) There is little doubt that Ashbery is one of the most important American poets, but with this collection we see that he is also one of our most delightful critics. [Irving Malin]

––––––––––––––––

Brooke Horvath, *Understanding Nelson Algren*. Univ. of South Carolina Press, 2005. 227 pp. $34.95.

Brooke Horvath has written a useful and accessible introduction to Nelson Algren that concentrates on his fiction but also brings in his poetry, essays, and even his writing on Midwest food. Horvath argues that Algren held to a consistent purpose throughout his career, namely to bear witness to social failures and underdogs. Algren was a child of the Depression and his most famous works—*Never Come Morning*, *The Man with the Golden Arm*, and *A Walk on the Wild Side*—all form part of an extended sequence of reportage. Quite simply, Algren wanted to *reveal*, and as his career became established he developed techniques to allow his characters to speak with their own voices. Horvath shows how Algren distanced himself from the official line of Marxist fiction while participating in the John Reed club and in the Illinois Writers Project. During the 1950s Algren's career was in the doldrums and he was increasingly attacked by critics for being a literary anachronism. Despite this, Horvath shows how Algren pursued more experimental directions in his writings. Not only did he support the black humorists like Joseph Heller and Terry Southern, in *Who Lost An American?* and *Notes from a Sea Diary* he turned toward absurdist techniques. The first of these uses nonsense and non sequitur to ridicule the failure of the American Dream. *Notes* shows Algren situating himself in relation to Hemingway and also engaging with the cold war to reveal the "unfortunate consequences of America's presence abroad." It's typical of Algren's commitment to forms of reportage that his last work, *The Devil's Stocking*, should be based on the life of the heavyweight boxer Rubin "Hurricane" Carter. This was to be the last of Algren's many indictments of America. [David Seed]

Julian W. Connolly, ed. *The Cambridge Companion to Nabokov*. Cambridge Univ. Press, 2005. 258 pp. Paper: $24.99.

To read Nabokov is to be "slain / By the false azure in the windowpane": to come careening into his novels, poems, and stories on the tail of his incredible style, to realize too late that the artifice (the fairy-tale allure) has been reflected by layers of unreliable narrators, invented authors, and false clues; to glimpse (just at the thud) how much more there is behind all of it. But to be a Nabokov scholar is to fly at his work over and over again, to hit up against the complexities, to leave marks "of ashen fluff," to weaken the window in hopes that it can finally be broken, then to realize it can't be, to land on the sill instead, and to peer through the glass and marvel at what's inside the house: *The Cambridge Companion to Nabokov* is his oeuvre's floor plan. The essays collected here are grouped together into sections called "Contexts," "Works," and "Related Worlds," an organization that speaks to the volume's aim to explicate through delineation. By so doing, this book lends itself to student use, and thus to the teacher of the author's works. Alexander Dolinin's essay "Nabokov as a Russian Writer" typifies this clear-headed approach. He does not manufacture insight by overreading or overinterpretation; instead, through mind-bogglingly close readings of both the writer's work and life, he exhumes what is—once he brings it to light—clearly there. In "Nabokov and Cinema" Barbara Wyllie begins by showing the writer's real involvement with film—he was an extra in Berlin, wrote the *Lolita* screenplay himself, auditioned for parts, wrote original scenarios, sold the rights to his novels—and then uses this hard evidence to reveal the medium's effect on his prose. The breadth of these essays—some have titles as expansive as "Nabokov's Worldview"—does not negatively impact their depth. Though the *Cambridge Companion* does not always break through the density of Nabokov's art, these scholars do describe its complexity exquisitely. [Theodore Louis McDermott]

Books Received

Addonizio, Kim. *Little Beauties*. Simon & Schuster, 2005. $23.00. (NF)

Allio, Kirstin. *Garner*. Coffee House Press, 2005. Paper: $14.95. (F)

Ashenhurst, Noah. *Comfort Food*. Old Meadow, 2005. Paper: $12.95. (F)

Aslam, Nadeem. *Maps for Lost Lovers*. Knopf, 2005. $25.00. (F)

Baden, Michael, and Linda Kenney. *Remains Silent*. Knopf, 2005. $22.95. (F)

Barnes, Yolanda. *When It Burned to the Ground*. Sarabande Books, 2005. Paper: $14.95. (F)

Barone, Dennis. *God's Whisper*. Spuyten Duyvil, 2005. Paper: $10.00. (F)

Bauer, Margaret Donovan. *William Faulkner's Legacy*. Univ. Press of Florida, 2005. $59.95. (NF)

Bauman, Christian. *Voodoo Lounge*. Touchstone, 2005. Paper: $14.00. (F)

Bernard, Christopher. *A Spy in the Ruins*. Regent Press, 2005. Paper: $24.95. (F)

Beyer, Marcel. *Spies*. Trans. Breon Mitchell. Harcourt, 2005. $24.00. (F)

Block, Elizabeth. *A Gesture through Time*. Spuyten Duyvil, 2005. Paper: $14.00. (F)

Bone, Martyn. *The Postsouthern Sense of Place in Contemporary Fiction*. Louisiana State Univ. Press, 2005. $49.95. (NF)

Boyle, T. C. *Tooth and Claw*. Viking, 2005. $25.95. (F)

Brenna, Duff. *The Willow Man*. Wynkin deWorde, 2005. Paper: $16.99. (F)

Bruce, Adam. *The Voyage of a Bean*. Ara Pacis, 2005. Paper: $19.95. (F)

Burger, Mary. *Sonny*. Leon Works, 2005. Paper: $12.95. (F)

Burgin, Richard. *The Identity Club*. Ontario Review Press, 2005. $24.95. (F)

Burke, Kenneth. *Here & Elsewhere: The Collected Fiction*. Intro. Denis Donoghue. Black Sparrow, 2005. Paper: $22.00. (F)

Caldwell, Ian, and Dustin Thomason. *The Rule of Four*. Bantam Dell, 2005. Paper: $7.99. (F)

Campbell, Bebe Moore. *72 Hour Hold*. Knopf, 2005. $24.95. (F)

Capek, Karel. *The Absolute at Large*. Intro. Stephen Baxter. Univ. of Nebraska Press, 2005. Paper: $16.95. (F)

Cardinale, Valentine. *The Terranovas: A War Family.* iUniverse, 2005. Paper: $14.95. (F)

Carson, Anne. *Decreation: Poetry, Essays, Opera.* Knopf, 2005. $24.95. (P)

Castillo, Ana. *Watercolor Women / Opaque Men.* Curbstone Press, 2005. Paper: $15.00. (P)

Cates, David Allan. *X out of Wonderland.* Steerforth Press, 2005. $17.95. (F)

Chadwick, Cydney. *Cut and Run.* Texture Press, 2005. Paper: $8.00. (F)

Cherchesov, Alan. *Requiem for the Living.* Trans. Subhi Shervell. Northwestern Univ. Press, 2005. Paper: $15.95. (F)

Chiasson, Dan. *Natural History.* Knopf, 2005. $23.00. (P)

Ciuraru, Carmela, ed. *Solitude Poems .* Knopf, 2005. $12.50. (P)

Clarke, Brock. *Carrying the Torch.* Univ. of Nebraska Press, 2005. $22.95. (F)

Cleave, Chris. *Incendiary.* Knopf, 2005. $22.95. (F)

Cohen, Joshua. *The Quorum.* Twisted Spoon, 2005. Paper: $14.00. (F)

Coover, Robert. *A Child Again.* McSweeney's, 2005. $22.00. (F)

Craps, Stef. *Trauma and Ethics in the Novels of Graham Swift.* Sussex Academic Press, 2005. $65.00. (NF)

Cronin, Justin. *The Summer Guest.* Delta, 2005. Paper: $13.00. (F)

Cunningham, Brent. *Bird and Forest.* Ugly Duckling Presse, 2005. Paper: $10.00. (P)

Darnton, John. *The Darwin Conspiracy.* Knopf, 2005. $25.00. (F)

Davies, Laurence, and J. H. Stape, eds. *The Collected Letters of Joseph Conrad: Volume 7: 1920-1922.* Cambridge Univ. Press, 2004. $90.00. (NF)

De Vries, Peter. *Slouching towards Kalamazoo.* Univ. of Chicago Press, 2005. Paper: $14.00. (F)

—. *The Blood of the Lamb.* Univ. of Chicago Press, 2005. Paper: $14.00. (F)

Deborah, Noyes. *Angel and Apostle.* Unbridled Books, 2005. $23.95. (F)

Donigan, Merritt. *Possessed by Shadows.* Other Press, 2005. $22.00. (F)

Dore, Florence. *The Novel and the Obscene.* Stanford Univ. Press, 2005. $50.00. (NF)

Falco, Edward. *In the Park of Culture.* Univ. of Notre Dame Press, 2005. Paper: $15.00. (F)

Fastoff, JoAnn. *The Gordian Knot.* Vantage Press, 2005. Paper: $8.95. (F)

Ford, Ford Madox. *The Good Soldier.* Green Integer, 2005. Paper: $10.95. (F)

Fourgs, Tom. *Spookfish*. Dufour Editions/Parthian Books, 2005. Paper: $16.95. (F)

Fraser, George MacDonald. *Flashman on the March*. Knopf, 2005. $24.00. (F)

Gailly, Christian. *Red Haze*. Trans. Brian Evenson and David Beus. Univ. of Nebraska Press, 2005. Paper: $20.00. (F)

Gaines, Ernest J. *Mozart and Leadbelly*. Knopf, 2005. $22.95. (F)

Galang, M. Evelina. *One Tribe*. New Issues, 2006. $26.00. (F)

García Márquez, Gabriel. *Memories of My Melancholy Whores*. Trans. Edith Grossman. Knopf, 2005. $20.00. (F)

Gillespie, William. *The Story that Teaches You How to Write It*. Spineless Books, 2005. Paper: $10.00. (F)

—. *Letter to Lamont*. Spineless Books, 2005. Paper: $10.00. (F)

Giron, Robert L., ed. *Poetic Voices without Borders*. Gival Press, 2005. Paper: $20.00. (P)

Glover, Douglas. *Precious*. Goose Lane Editions, 2005. Paper: $14.95. (F)

Gombrowicz, Witold. *Cosmos*. Yale Univ. Press, 2005. $25.00. (F)

Gould, John. *Kilter*. Other Press, 2005. Paper: $12.95. (F)

Gracq, Julien. *The Shape of a City*. Trans. Ingeborg M. Kohn. Turtle Point Press, 2005. Paper: $16.95. (NF)

Hamburger, Aaron. *Faith for Beginners*. Random House, 2005. $23.95. (F)

Helprin, Mark. *Freddy and Fredericka*. Penguin, 2005. $27.95. (F)

Himes, Andrew, and Jan Bultmann, et al., eds. *Voices in Wartime Anthology*. Whit Press, 2005. Paper: $17.95. (NF)

Hoffman, Michael J., and Patrick D. Murphy, eds. *Essentials of the Theory of Fiction, Third Edition*. Duke Univ. Press, 2005. Paper: $27.95. (NF)

Holland, Noy. *What Begins with Bird*. FC2, 2005. Paper: $15.95. (F)

Hoover, Paul. *Fables of Representation*. Univ. of Michigan Press, 2004. Paper: $17.95. (NF)

Huysmans, J. K. *Downstream*. Trans. Robert Baldick. Turtle Point Press, 2005. Paper: $10.95. (F)

Japin, Arthur. *In Lucia's Eyes*. Knopf, 2005. $24.00. (F)

Joss, Morag. *Half Broken Things*. Delacorte Press, 2005. $22.00. (F)

Kalaidjian, Walter, ed. *The Cambridge Companion to American Modernism*. Cambridge Univ. Press, 2005. Paper: $24.99. (NF)

Kaplan-Maxfield, Thomas. *Memoirs of a Shape Shifter*. Kepler Press, 2005. $25.00. (F)

Katsuei, Yuasa. *Kannani* and *Document of Flames*. Trans., intro., and afterword Mark Driscoll. Duke Univ. Press, 2005. Paper: $19.95. (F)

Keller, Tsipi. *Jackpot*. Spuyten Duyvil, 2004. Paper: $13.00. (F)

King, Laurie R. *Locked Rooms*. Bantam Dell, 2005. $24.00. (F)

Kirwan, Valerie. *Taking a Fool to Paradise*. Indra, 2005. Paper: $17.95. (F)

Klinkenborg, Verlyn. *Timothy; or, Notes of an Abject Reptile*. Knopf, 2006. $16.95. (F)

Koch, Kenneth. *The Collected Poems*. Knopf, 2005. $40.00. (P)

—. *Collected Fiction*. Ed. Jordan Davis, Karen Koch, and Ron Padgett. Intro. Jordan Davis. Coffee House Press, 2005. Paper: $18.00. (F)

Kona, Prakash. *Pearls of an Unstrung Necklace*. Fugue State Press, 2005. Paper: $15.00. (F)

Krall, Hanna. *The Woman from Hamburg and Other True Stories*. Trans. Madeline G. Levine. Other Press, 2005. $19.00. (NF)

Krauss, Nicole. *The History of Love*. Norton, 2005. $23.95. (F)

Kreyling, Michael. *The Novels of Ross Macdonald*. Univ. of South Carolina Press, 2005. $34.95. (NF)

Lane, Patrick. *What the Stones Remember*. Trumpeter Books, 2005. $22.95. (NF)

Lewis, Jeffrey. *Meritocracy*. Other Press, 2004. $18.00. (F)

—. *The Conference of the Birds*. Other Press, 2005. $22.95. (F)

Loy, Rosetta. *The Water Door*. Trans. Gregory Conti. Other Press, 2006. Paper: $11.95. (F)

Malraux, André. *"The Kingdom of Farfelu" with "Paper Moon."* Trans. W. B. Keckler. Illus. by the author. Fugue State Press, 2005. Paper: $14.00. (F)

Margolis, Stacey. *The Public Life of Privacy in Nineteenth-Century American Literature*. Duke Univ. Press, 2005. Paper: $21.95. (NF)

Martone, Michael. *Michael Martone*. FC2, 2005. Paper: $15.95. (F)

Meno, Joe. *Bluebirds Used to Croon in the Choir*. Triquarterly, 2005. $21.95. (F)

Montero, Mayra. *Captain of the Sleepers*. Trans. Edith Grossman. Farrar, Straus & Giroux, 2005. $22.00. (F)

Montieth, Sharon, et al., eds. *Critical Perspectives on Pat Barker*. Univ. of South Carolina Press, 2005. $49.95. (NF)

Nezval, Vitezslav. *Valerie and Her Week of Wonders*. Trans. David Short. Twisted Spoon, 2005. Paper: $14.00. (F)

Niven, John. *Music from Big Pink*. Continuum, 2005. Paper: $9.95. (F)

Osgood, Lawrence. *Midnight Sun*. Goose Lane Editions, 2005. Paper: $16.95. (F)

Peterson, Jim. *Paper Crown*. Red Hen, 2005. Paper: $16.95. (F)

Phillips, Caryl. *Dancing in the Dark*. Knopf, 2005. $23.95. (F)

Podnieks, Elizabeth, and Sandra Chait, eds. *Hayford Hall: Hang-overs, Erotics, and Modernist Aesthetics*. Southern Illinois Univ. Press, 2005. $50.00. (NF)

Posnock, Ross. *The Cambridge Companion to Ralph Ellison*. Cambridge Univ. Press, 2005. Paper: $24.99. (NF)

Randolph, Ladette. *This is Not the Tropics*. Univ. of Wisconsin Press, 2005. $24.95. (F)

Reuben, Shelly. *Tabula Rasa*. Harcourt, 2005. $24.00. (F)

Roorbach, Bill. *Temple Stream*. The Dial Press, 2005. $24.00. (NF)

Rubin, Derek, ed. *Who We Are: On Being (and Not Being) a Jewish American Writer*. Schocken Books, 2005. $25.00. (NF)

Sallis, James. *The James Sallis Reader*. Point Blank, 2005. Paper: $19.95. (F)

Schickler, David. *Sweet and Vicious*. The Dial Press, 2005. Paper: $14.00. (F)

Scott, Matthew David. *Playing Mercy*. Dufour Editions/Parthian Books, 2005. Paper: $16.95. (F)

Seaman, Donna. *Writers on the Air*. Paul Dry Books, 2005. $24.95. (NF)

Shaogong, Han. *The Dictionary of Maqiao*. Trans. Julia Lovell. The Dial Press, 2005. Paper: $12.00. (F)

Shope, Nina. *Hanging: Three Novellas*. Starcherone Books, 2005. Paper: $16.00. (F)

Siegel, Lee. *Who Wrote the Book of Love?* Univ. of Chicago Press, 2005. $24.00. (F)

Sjödin, Eva. *Inner China*. Trans. Jennifer Hayashida. Litmus Press, 2005. Paper: $12.00. (F)

Smiley, Jane. *Thirteen Ways of Looking at the Novel*. Knopf, 2005. $26.95. (NF)

Stewart, Leah. *The Myth of You and Me*. Shaye Areheart, 2005. $21.95. (F)

Sukenick, Ronald. *Last Fall*. FC2, 2005. Paper: $15.95. (F)

Symington, Neville. *A Priest's Affair*. Free Association, 2005. Paper: $34.50. (F)

Thompson, Ted, and Eli Horowitz, eds. *Noisy Outlaws, Unfriendly Blobs, et al.* McSweeney's, 2005. $22.00. (F)

Torti, Sylvia. *The Scorpion's Tail*. Curbstone Press, 2005. Paper: $15.00. (F)

Vachss, Andrew. *Two Trains Running*. Pantheon Books, 2005. $25.00. (F)

Velickovic, Nenad. *Lodgers*. Northwestern Univ. Press, 2005. Paper: $16.95. (F)

Vida, Vendela, ed. *The Believer Book of Writers Talking to Writers*. Believer Books, 2005. Paper: $18.00. (NF)

Wackwitz, Stephan. *An Invisible Country*. Paul Dry Books, 2005. $24.95. (NF)

Wan, Michelle. *Deadly Slipper*. Doubleday, 2005. $23.95. (F)

Wiesel, Elie. *The Time of the Uprooted*. Trans. David Hapgood. Knopf, 2005. $25.00. (F)

Williams, Jonathan. *Jubilant Thicket*. Copper Canyon, 2005. Paper: $20.00. (P)

Wilson, D. Harlan. *Pseudo-City*. Raw Dog Screaming, 2005. Paper: $15.95. (F)

Wong, Shawn. *American Knees*. Univ. of Washington Press, 2005. Paper: $14.95. (F)

Wray, John. *Canaan's Tongue*. Knopf, 2005. $25.00. (F)

Xiaojing, Zhou, and Saina Najmi, eds. *Form and Transformation in Asian American Literature*. Univ. of Washington Press, 2005. Paper: $30.00. (NF)

Young, Kevin. *To Repel Ghosts*. Knopf, 2005. Paper: $16.95. (P)

Contributors

DAVID COZY writes regularly about books for the *Japan Times* and the *Asahi Shimbun*. In addition his work (fiction, criticism, or both) has appeared in *Harper's*, the *Threepenny Review*, *Rain Taxi*, and the *Kyoto Journal*, and he contributed the introduction to the recently published new edition of Donald Richie's *Tokyo Nights* (Printed Matter Press, 2005). A resident of Japan for more than two decades, he is an Assistant Professor at Showa Women's University in Tokyo.

DAVID GARRETT IZZO has published nine books and over forty articles of literary scholarship concerning twentieth-century British and Amercan literature, including *The Writings of Richard Stern*, the *W. H. Auden Encyclopedia*, the *Christopher Isherwood Encyclopedia*, and *Stephen Vincent Benet: His Life and Work* (co-editor with Lincoln Konkle). He has also published two novels and two plays. His historical novel, *A Change of Heart*, features Huxley as the main "character." He has a Ph. D. from Temple University and is a Professor at Fayetteville State University in North Carolina. Learn more about David and his work at www.davidgarrettizzo.com.

NEIL MURPHY has published numerous articles and book chapters on contemporary fiction and Irish literature, including work on John Banville, Aidan Higgins, Joyce, Yeats, and Beckett, postmodernism, and postcolonialism. His work has appeared in the following publications: the *Irish Review*, the *Irish University Review*, *Graph*, *Asylum Arts Review*, the *Irish Literary Supplement*, the *Literary Review*, the *Review of Contemporary Fiction*, and *Force 10*. He is the author of *Irish Fiction and Postmodern Doubt* (Edwin Mellen, 2004) and is currently working on a comprehensive study of contemporary fiction (due 2006). He is Associate Professor of English at Nanyang Technological University, Singapore.

Annual Index

References are to issue number and pages, respectively

Contributors

Books Reviewed

Reviewers' names follow in parentheses. Regular reviewers are abbreviated:
RB=Robert Buckeye; JMD=Jeremy M. Davies; JD=Joseph Dewey;
TF=Tim Feeney; TH=Thomas Hove; IM=Irving Malin;
MP=Michael Pinker; CP=Chad W. Post.

Andrukhovych, Yuri. *Perverzion*, 3: 146-147 (MP)

Antin, David. *i never knew what time it was*, 3: 140-141 (Mark Tursi)

Ashbery, John. *Selected Prose*, 3: 152 (IM)

Bachmann, Ingeborg. *Letters to Felician*, 1: 149 (RB)

Bernard, Kenneth. *The Man in the Stretcher*, 3: 147 (IM)

Bolaño, Roberto. *Distant Star*, 1: 147 (CP)

Brossard, Nicole. *Yesterday, at the Hotel Clarendon*, 3: 145 (Kate Zambreno)

Calasso, Roberto. *K.*, 2: 136-137 (TH)

Casanova, Pascale. *The World Republic of Letters*, 3: 151-152 (TH)

Cauwelaert, Didier van. *Out of my Head*, 1: 145-146 (JD)

Cendrars, Blaise. *The Astonished Man*, 2: 142-143 (Jeffrey Twitchell-Waas)

—. *Gold: The Marvelous History of General John Augustus Sutter*, 2: 140 (Jeff Bursey)

—. *Moravagine*, 1: 139-140 (Jeff Bursey)

Chevillard, Eric. *Palafox*, 3: 149 (Joanna Howard)

Coe, Jonathan. *Like a Fiery Elephant*, 3: 150-151 (Theodore Louis McDermott)

Connolly, Julian W. *The Cambridge Companion to Nabokov*, 3: 153 (Theodore Louis McDermott)

Cortázar, Julio. *The Diary of Andreas Fava*, 2: 133-134 (CP)

Daumal, René. *Mount Analogue: A Tale of Non-Euclidian and Symbolically Authentic Mountaineering Adventures*, 1: 141-142 (TF)

DePietro, Thomas. *Conversations with Don DeLillo*, 2: 144-145 (David Seed)

Déry, Tibor. *Love & Other Stories*, 3: 143-144 (MP)

Erickson, Steve. *Our Ecstatic Days*, 2: 135 (Brian Evenson)

Fattaruso, Paul. *Travel in the Mouth of the Wolf*, 1: 143-144 (Martin Riker)

Federman, Raymond. *My Body in Nine Parts*, 3: 140 (Steve Tomasula)

Genet, Jean. *The Declared Enemy: Texts and Interviews*, 1: 148-149 (Mark Spitzer)

Gombrowicz, Witold. *Bacacay*, 1: 141 (MP)

—. *A Guide to Philosophy in Six Hours and Fifteen Minutes*, 2: 143 (MP)

—. *Polish Memories*, 2: 143-144 (MP)

Hauser, Marianne. *The Collected Short Fiction*, 3: 148-149 (Brian Evenson)

CONJUNCTIONS:44

An Anatomy of Roads: The Quest Issue

Leaving home is a dangerous business. Whether it's to walk across the street or travel to another continent, one never returns the same. This issue explores in fiction and poetry the complex process of defamiliarization as the ultimate path to knowing oneself. Includes new work by John Barth, Elizabeth Hand, Jonathan Carroll, Rikki Ducornet, Susan Steinberg, Joshua Furst, Robert Antoni, Joyce Carol Oates, Forrest Gander, Jon McGregor, Robert Coover, Joanna Scott, Paul West, and many others. The issue also features a portfolio of fiction and poems by writers including William H. Gass, Elizabeth Willis, John Taggart, Martine Bellen, Rachel Blau DuPlessis, Richard Meier, and others. 404 pages.

CONJUNCTIONS
Edited by Bradford Morrow
Published by Bard College
Annandale-on-Hudson, NY 12504

To order, phone 845-758-1539,
or visit www.conjunctions.com

DELILLO FIEDLER GASS PYNCHON
University of Delaware Press
Collections on Contemporary Masters

UNDERWORDS
Perspectives on Don DeLillo's *Underworld*

Edited by Joseph Dewey, Steven G. Kellman, and Irving Malin

Essays by Jackson R. Bryer, David Cowart, Kathleen Fitzpatrick, Joanne Gass, Paul Gleason, Donald J. Greiner, Robert McMinn, Thomas Myers, Ira Nadel, Carl Ostrowski, Timothy L. Parrish, Marc Singer, and David Yetter

$39.50

LESLIE FIEDLER AND AMERICAN CULTURE

Edited by Steven G. Kellman and Irving Malin

Essays by John Barth, Robert Boyers, James M. Cox, Joseph Dewey, R.H.W. Dillard, Geoffrey Green, Irving Feldman, Leslie Fiedler, Susan Gubar, Jay L. Halio, Brooke Horvath, David Ketterer, R.W.B. Lewis, Sanford Pinsker, Harold Schechter, Daniel Schwarz, David R. Slavitt, Daniel Walden, and Mark Royden Winchell

$36.50

INTO *THE TUNNEL*
Readings of Gass's Novel

Edited by Steven G. Kellman and Irving Malin

Essays by Rebecca Goldstein, Donald J. Greiner, Brooke Horvath, Marcus Klein, Jerome Klinkowitz, Paul Maliszewski, James McCourt, Arthur Saltzman, Susan Stewart, and Heide Ziegler

$35.00

PYNCHON AND *MASON & DIXON*

Edited by Brooke Horvath and Irving Malin

Essays by Jeff Baker, Joseph Dewey, Bernard Duyfhuizen, David Foreman, Donald J. Greiner, Brian McHale, Clifford S. Mead, Arthur Saltzman, Thomas H. Schaub, David Seed, and Victor Strandberg

$39.50

ORDER FROM ASSOCIATED UNIVERSITY PRESSES
2010 Eastpark Blvd., Cranbury, New Jersey 08512
PH 609-655-4770   FAX 609-655-8366   E-mail AUP440@ aol.com

The Montage Principle
Eisenstein in New Cultural and Critical Contexts

Edited by Jean Antoine-Dunne with Paula Quigley

Amsterdam/New York, NY 2004. XVIII, 220 pp.
(Critical Studies 21)

ISBN: 90-420-0898-9   Bound € 55,-/US$ 69.-

This book of essays is quite unique in that it intervenes in a still contested area within many universities, that of the relevance of film to literature, critical theory, politics, sociology and anthropology. The essays were commissioned by Jean Antoine-Dunne whose research has explored the impact of Eisenstein's aesthetics on different areas of modernist literature and drama. The essays in this collection use Eisenstein as a point of departure into divergent fields of analysis and are concerned with the principle of montage as a transforming idea. They gather within the pages of one work contributions from Geoffrey Nowell-Smith, Richard Taylor, Paul Willemen and emerging scholars entering and altering the field of interdisciplinary scholarship, film and literature. These hitherto unpublished essays not only extend and elaborate on previous treatments of Eisenstein and montage in areas such as semiotics, film theory, and feminist film practice, but also introduce his work to areas which have not yet been considered in relation to Eisenstein and montage, such as Beckett scholarship, Caribbean aesthetics, Third Cinema, and debates around digital imagery. No other collection of essays has explored the idea of montage as a structuring cultural and critical principle and the elasticity of Eisenstein's legacy in quite this way.

USA/Canada: 906 Madison Avenue, UNION, NJ 07083, USA
Call toll-free (USA only)1-800-225-3998, Tel. 908 206 1166, Fax 908-206-0820
All other countries: Tijnmuiden 7, 1046 AK Amsterdam, The Netherlands.
Tel. ++ 31 (0)20 611 48 21, Fax ++ 31 (0)20 447 29 79
Orders-queries@rodopi.nl   www.rodopi.nl
Please note that the exchange rate is subject to fluctuations

NOON

A LITERARY ANNUAL

1369 MADISON AVENUE   PMB 298
NEW YORK   NEW YORK   10128-0711

EDITION PRICE $9 DOMESTIC $14 FOREIGN

Dalkey Archive Press announces a call
for submissions to the

DALKEY ARCHIVE
SCHOLARLY SERIES

(expanding opportunities for
specialized scholarly research)

AREAS OF INTEREST:

monographs on authors from throughout the
world in the aesthetic tradition represented
by Dalkey Archive Press's list

encyclopedic companions to contemporary
fiction from around the world

literary history and theory

cultural studies

collections of interviews

aesthetics

bibliographies of contemporary novelists

For further details related to submission, please visit
www.dalkeyarchive.com

DALKEY ARCHIVE PRESS

Dalkey Archive Press

NEW RELEASES

Things in the Night
MATI UNT

Hidden Camera
ZORAN ŽIVKOVIĆ

Trio
ROBERT PINGET

The Enamoured Knight
DOUGLAS GLOVER

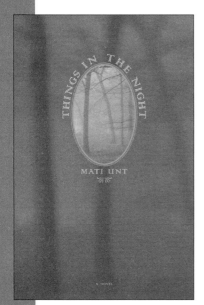

An undertaker finds an invitation to a private showing of a movie stuck in his apartment door. Upon arrival at the theater, he discovers that there's only one other person in the audience, and when the "movie" turns out to be footage of him sitting in a park, he becomes convinced that he's an unwitting participant in a sinister reality show. Certain that he's being filmed at every moment, he begins a bizarre odyssey through the dark and empty streets of his city, encountering increasingly absurd situations, and waiting for the opportunity to stage a rebellion against his hidden tormentors . . .

Hidden Camera

ZORAN ŽIVKOVIĆ
TRANSLATION BY
AIICE COPPIE-TOŠIĆ

EASTERN EUROPEAN LITERATURE SERIES
A NOVEL
$13.95 / PAPER
ISBN: 1-56478-412-6

"Winner of the 2003 World Fantasy Award . . . Zoran Živković is an immensely talented fabulist whose work is somewhat reminiscent of Italo Calvino's wry and delightfully surreal postmodern fictions."
—Paul Witcover, *Realms of Fantasy*

"Živković does a superb job of communicating the befuddlement, confusion and awe of individual characters as they wrestle with mysteries that exceed the understanding that their time, place and intellectual capacity permits."
—Stefan Dziemianowicz, *Publishers Weekly*

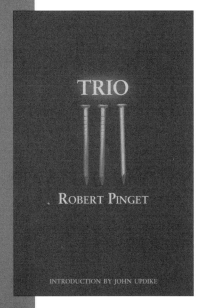

This book is filled with a great love for the art of writing and is a celebration of the act of reading. Through the prism of the renowned Russian Formalist Viktor Shklovsky, Douglas Glover provides a scrupulous reading of Cervantes's *Don Quixote*. By showing us how Cervantes constructed his novel, and how we as readers participate in his magical creation, he opens the 400-year-old Spanish masterpiece to a new generation of readers. Glover seduces us with his stunning prose, while making it possible for even the casual reader to enjoy Cervantes's genius.

The Enamoured Knight

DOUGLAS GLOVER

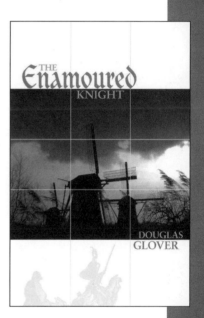

SCHOLARLY SERIES
LITERARY CRITICISM
$14.95 / PAPER
ISBN: 1-56478-404-5

"Douglas Glover's extended meditation on *Don Quixote*, *The Enamoured Knight*, is simply packed to the brim with marvelous stuff."

—Jeffrey Canton, *Quill and Quire*

"Douglas Glover is a writer of the greatest and most variegated gifts. . . . Glover is that rarest of artists, a true master in an age that needs masters desperately."

—Darin Strauss

ORDER FORM

Individuals may use this form to subscribe to the *Review of Contemporary Fiction* or to order back issues of the *Review* and Dalkey Archive titles at a discount (see below for details).

Title	ISBN	Quantity	Price

Subtotal _____

Less Discount _____
(10% for one book, 20% for two or more books)

Subtotal _____

Plus Postage _____
(domestic: $3 + $1 per book / foreign: $5 + $3 per book)

1 Year Individual Subscription to the **Review** _____
($17 domestic, $20.50 foreign)

Total _____

Mailing Address _____

_____

_____

_____

xxv/3

Credit card payment   ☐ Visa   ☐ Mastercard

Acct # _____   Exp. Date _____

Name on card _____   Phone # _____

Please make checks (in U.S. dollars only) payable to *Dalkey Archive Press*

mail or fax this form to: Dalkey Archive Press, ISU Campus Box 8905, Normal, IL 61790-8905; *fax:* 309.438.7422; *tel:* 309.438.7555